TILL DEATH
DO US PART

John Dickson Carr

with an introduction by
MARTIN EDWARDS

This edition published 2021 by
The British Library
96 Euston Road
London NW1 2DB

Cataloguing in Publication Data
A catalogue record for this book is available from the British Library

ISBN 978 0 7123 5379 3
eISBN 978 0 7123 6768 4

Front cover image © NRM/Pictorial Collection/
Science & Society Picture Library

Typeset by Tetragon, London
Printed in England by TJ Books Ltd

TILL DEATH
DO US PART

CONTENTS

INTRODUCTION

Till Death Do Us Part was first published in 1944, but the events of the story take place before the beginning of the Second World War. The memorable first chapter carries a touch of nostalgia, as well as plentiful evidence of its American author's love of England and the English way of life. Those opening pages also set the scene splendidly for one of the most tantalizing 'impossible crime' detective novels ever written by John Dickson Carr, the king of the locked room mystery.

This was the fifteenth novel to feature Dr Gideon Fell, a formidable expert on locked rooms and other impossible crimes whose physical appearance and larger than life personality were modelled on those of G. K. Chesterton, whom Carr admired enormously. However, we see events mainly through the eyes of Richard Markham. He is a playwright who has achieved success by writing psychological thrillers for the stage. We don't learn a great deal about his plays, although it must be said that the young man doesn't show especially acute psychological insight in the conduct of his private life. It is just as well that Gideon Fell is on hand to solve the baffling mystery.

When we first meet Dick Markham, he is blissfully happy. He's just become engaged to be married to the delightful, if rather mysterious, Lesley Grant. But in a crime novel, every silver lining has a cloud, and one of the star attractions at the village fete is a fortune teller. Dick is told that the fortune teller is Sir Harvey Gilman, a famous criminologist, and 'one of the greatest living authorities on crime'. Before long, Dick is shocked to learn that Lesley Grant is not the woman she appears to be. Lesley, it seems, has been associated with three poisonings; in each case the victim was the man in her life, and in each case the death occurred in a locked room. There was never any evidence to establish her guilt of murder, but the coincidence is horrifying and it seems that Lesley has found a method of committing the perfect murder.

Sir Harvey asks Dick to assist him in setting a trap for Lesley, so that he can discover the secret of her modus operandi. Dick keeps watch on a house where Sir Harvey is waiting in a locked room. When he hears a shot ring out, and sees a bullet hole in a window, he rushes in. Sir Harvey is dead. But he is not shot – he has been poisoned, in exactly the same way as Lesley's three alleged victims.

Dick faces a nightmarish dilemma. He is in love with Lesley, but he finds himself unable to fathom whether she is an innocent victim of a malevolent third party – or a sociopathic serial killer. To complicate matters even further, he also finds himself attracted to the appealing Cynthia Drew. Dick needs to answer that classic question for the protagonist of a crime novel: *who can I trust?*

By the time this book was published, John Dickson Carr (1906–77) had established an enviable reputation as an author of clever and entertaining detective fiction. Gideon Fell was his premier detective, although many fans have a soft spot for Sir Henry Merrivale, whose first recorded cases were *The Plague Court Murders* and *The White Priory Murders*, both published in 1934 under the transparent pen-name Carter Dickson.

Between them, Fell and Merrivale appeared in some of the most ingenious impossible crime mysteries ever published. Intriguingly, there is reference in *Till Death Do Us Part* to Goblin Wood – and 'The House in Goblin Wood' is Carr's finest short story, although a case for Merrivale rather than Fell. For good measure, Carr also created Colonel March of Scotland Yard, a character who appeared in short stories rather than full-length books. Like Major Price in this novel, March was modelled on Carr's friend and fellow Detection Club member, John Rhode.

In his biography of the author, *John Dickson Carr: The Man Who Explained Miracles*, Professor Douglas Greene explains that the central idea for this novel came from a radio script Carr had written for CBS, 'Will You Walk Into My Parlour?', which he rewrote for the BBC under the title 'Vampire Tower'.

Greene says that: 'At the conclusion, Carr provides a clever and, probably, practical solution to the locked-room problem. Carr himself later said that it was his favourite gimmick, "if we confine matters strictly to getting out of locked rooms rather than the general field of the impossible situation."'

In 1997 the BBC broadcast a two-part radio adaptation of the book as part of its *Gideon Fell* series starring the late Donald Sinden – these were all produced and directed by Enyd Williams and dramatized by Peter Ling.

Carr was born in Uniontown, Pennsylvania, and harboured ambitions to become a writer from his early days. After spending some time in France, he created Henri Bencolin, who appeared in short stories before Carr published his first novel, *It Walks By Night*, in 1930. The first four of the five Bencolin novels have been published as British Library Crime Classics and even though they are the work of an apprentice novelist, they are notable for their energy and imagination. Fell arrived on the scene in 1933 in *Hag's Nook*, and proceeded to become one of the most memorable sleuths of the 'Golden Age of Murder' between the two world wars. *Till Death Do Us Part* is a dazzling showcase for the great man's detective skills and a reminder of Carr's gift for constructing a fiendish mystery plot.

MARTIN EDWARDS

www.martinedwardsbooks.com

I

THINKING THE MATTER OVER AFTERWARDS, DICK MARKHAM might have seen omens or portents in the summer thunderstorm, in the fortune-teller's tent, in the shooting-range, in half a dozen other things at that bazaar.

But the fact remains that he hardly even noticed the weather. He was much too happy.

Ahead, as he and Lesley turned in at the open gates with their stone pillars topped by the heraldic design of griffin and ash-tree, stretched the grounds of Ashe Hall. The smooth lawns were gaudy with booths and striped tents. For a background they had oak-trees, and the long, low, red-brick line of the Hall.

It was a scene which, four or five years later, would come back to Dick Markham with a nostalgia like anguish. A lush, green, burning England; an England of white flannels and lazy afternoons; an England which, please God, we shall never lose for any nonsense about a better world. There it lay in opulence, a year or so before the beginning of Hitler's war, though 'opulent' was hardly a word that could be applied to the estate of George Converse, last Baron Ashe. Yet Dick Markham, a tall young man with rather too much imagination, hardly looked at it.

Lesley said, 'We're horribly late, you know,' in the breathless, half-laughing voice of a girl who does not really care.

Both of them had been walking rather fast. Both of them now stopped short.

A gust of wind, cool against that hot afternoon, raked with sudden violence across the lawns. It caught at Lesley's hat, a picture-hat with a transparent floppy brim, and made her put up her hands quickly to it. The sky had grown as dark as twilight, with smoky slow-moving clouds.

'Look here!' Dick said. 'What time is it?'

'It must be past three, anyway.'

He nodded ahead, where the shadow of the storm gave every-thing a nightmarish and unreal quality like sunlight through smoked glass. Nothing stirred on the lawns. Tents and booths, touched to uneasy life by the wind, seemed deserted.

'But... where is everybody?'

'They're probably at the cricket match, Dick. We'd better hurry. Lady Ashe and Mrs Price will be *furious*.'

'Does that matter?'

'No,' smiled Lesley. 'Of course not.'

He looked at her – laughing and breathless, with her hands at the brim of her hat. He saw the desperate seriousness of her eyes, despite the smiling mouth. All her thoughts and emotions seemed concentrated in those eyes, brown eyes, telling him what she had told him last night.

He saw the unconscious grace of the raised arms, the white frock moulded against her body by that whipping wind. She was so infernally, disturbingly attractive that even the quiver of her mouth, the turn of her eyes, were recorded in his brain as though he saw her in a thousand different pictures.

It had never occurred to Dick Markham – outwardly at least a stickler for the conventions – that at the entrance to Lord Ashe's sedate park, on the afternoon of a starched garden-party, with

Lady Ashe's phantom eye upon them, he would put his arms round Lesley Grant and kiss her without particularly caring who might be looking on.

But this is what happened, with the wind sweeping across the park and the sky darkening still more. Their conversation (let nobody mock at it) was a trifle chaotic.

'Do you love me?'

'You know I do. Do you love *me*?'

Ever since last night these same words had been repeated, over and over, with no sense of repetition. On the contrary, it seemed each time a new discovery: an increasing dazzle to the wits at the realization. Dick Markham, with some vague recollection of their whereabouts, at length disengaged his arms and swore at the universe.

'I suppose,' he said, 'we've got to go to this damned cricket match?'

Lesley hesitated. The intense concentration of emotion faded out of her eyes, and she glanced at the sky.

'It's going to pour with rain in a minute,' she answered. 'I doubt if there'll be a cricket match. And...'

'And what?'

'I wanted to see the fortune-teller,' said Lesley.

Dick could not have said why he threw back his head and roared with laughter. It was partly her naïve air, her utter seriousness; and partly that he would have roared at anything as a groping expression of how he felt.

'Mrs Price says he's awfully good,' the girl assured him quickly. 'That's why I've been so curious. She says he can tell you absolutely everything about yourself.'

'But you know that already, don't you?'

'*Couldn't* we see the fortune-teller?'

A faint stir of thunder muttered from the east. Taking Lesley's arm firmly, he led her at a rapid pace up the gravel drive towards the clutter of stalls on the lawn. No effort had been made to arrange the booths in regular or even in systematic order. From the coconut-shy to the so-called 'pond' where you fished for bottles, the proprietor of each exhibit had placed it according to his or her artistic taste. And there could be no mistaking the fortune-teller's tent.

It stood apart from the others, nearer to Ashe Hall. In shape the tent was like an overgrown telephone-box, though flaring out at the bottom and peaked at the top. Its dingy canvas had vertical stripes of white and red. Over the tent-flap hung a neat sign which read, 'THE GREAT SWAMI, PALMIST AND CRYSTAL-GAZER: SEES ALL, KNOWS ALL', together with a big cardboard chart of a human hand pierced by explanatory arrows.

The sky had now grown so dark that Dick could discern a light inside the fortune-teller's lair, which must have been hot to suffo-cation all afternoon. A heavier gust of wind ran among the tents, thrumming and rattling at canvas, and making the tents sway up like half-inflated balloons. The sign of the human hand was agitated, grotesquely as though it were beckoning to them or waving them away. And a voice said:

'Hoy!'

Major Horace Price, behind the 'counter' of the miniature shooting-gallery, had made a trumpet of his hands and was address-ing them in a parade-ground voice. Most of the other stalls were deserted, their proprietors having evidently gone off to the cricket match. Major Price doughtily remained. Catching their attention, he ducked under the counter and hurried towards them.

'I imagine – he's heard?' asked Lesley.

'I expect everybody's heard,' said Dick conscious at once of acute embarrassment and bursting pride. 'You don't mind?'

'Mind!' cried Lesley. '*Mind?*'

'My dear chap!' said the major, clutching his tweed cap more firmly to his head and skidding a little on the smooth grass. 'My dear girl! I've been looking everywhere for you all afternoon! So has my wife! Is this true?'

Dick tried to look casual, though he could manage to look no more casual than a wind-whipped tent.

'Is what true, major?'

'This marriage!' emphasized Major Price, in almost a tone of agony. He pointed at them. '*Are* you going to get married?'

'Yes, It's true enough.'

'My dear chap!' said the major.

He lowered his voice to a solemnity more suited to a funeral than to a wedding. Major Price had, on great occasions, a sentimentality which could be acutely embarrassing. He reached out and wrung the hand of each in turn.

'I'm delighted!' he declared, with an honest sympathy which warmed Dick Markham's heart. 'It couldn't be more suitable! Couldn't! I think so, and so does my wife. When's it to be?'

'We haven't quite decided yet,' said Dick. 'Sorry to be so late for the garden-party. But we were…'

'Occupied!' said the major. 'Occupied! I know! Say nothing more about it!'

Though not strictly entitled to be called major, since he had never been a Regular Army man and only gained this rank in the last war, the term so suited Horace Price that he was addressed by no other.

Actually he was a solicitor, and a shrewd one. The village of Six Ashes, to say nothing of half the countryside round, came to snarl itself in litigations at his office in the High Street. But his bearing, his thick-set figure, his cropped sandy moustache, speckled round-jowled face and light blue eye, no less than a knowledge exhaustive and sometimes exhausting about all things military or sporting, made him Major Price even to magistrates.

He stood beaming on them now, teetering back and forth on his heels, and rubbing his hands together.

'We must celebrate this, you know,' he announced. 'Everybody'll want to congratulate you. My wife, and Lady Ashe, and Mrs Middlesworth, and everybody! In the meantime...'

'In the meantime,' suggested Lesley, 'hadn't we better get to shelter?'

Major Price blinked at her.

'Shelter?'

A discarded paper bag, blown on that vast wind, sailed past overhead. The oak-trees round Ashe Hall were distorted, and the flapping of loose canvas now resembled a hurricane of cracking flags.

'The storm's going to break,' said Dick. 'I hope these tents are pegged down securely. They'll be all over the next county if they're not.'

'Oh, they'll be all right,' the major assured him. 'And the storm doesn't matter now. This show's nearly over.'

'Has business been good at your stall?'

'Business,' said the major, 'has been excellent.' Impressed enthusiasm lightened his pale-blue yes. 'Some of these people, you know, turned out to be devilish good shots. Cynthia Drew, for instance –'

Major Price stopped abruptly. His colour came up abruptly too, as though he had made a diplomatic error. Dick hoped with a sort of weary anger that they weren't going to start throwing Cynthia Drew in his teeth again.

'Lesley,' he said loudly, 'is very anxious to see this famous fortune-teller. That is, if he's still at his post. And, if you'll excuse us, I think we'd better hurry along.'

'Oh, no, you don't!' said the major with decision.

'Don't what?'

Major Price reached out and took Lesley firmly by the wrist.

'See the fortune-teller, by all means. He's still there. But first of all,' grinned the major, 'you're going to patronize *my* show.'

'Guns?' cried Lesley.

'Absolutely!' said the major.

'No! Please! I'd rather not!'

Dick turned round. The urgency of Lesley's voice surprised him. But Major Price, with a massive and smothering benevolence, paid no attention.

As a drop of rain stung Dick's forehead, the major impelled both of them towards the miniature shooting-range. This was a narrow shed with wooden walls and a canvas roof, backed by a black-painted sheet of steel. Half a dozen small cardboard targets, run on pulleys so that they could be drawn back to the counter after you fired, were suspended against this back wall.

Ducking under the counter, Major Price touched a switch. A small electric light, on an ingenious arrangement of dry-cell batteries, glowed out over each target. On the counter lay a large collection of light rifles, chiefly .2's, which the major had been borrowing all over Six Ashes.

'You're first, young lady!' he said, and pointed sternly to a well-filled money bowl on the table. 'Six shots for half a crown. I know it's an outrageous price, but this is a charity do. Try it!'

'Honestly,' said Lesley, 'I'd rather not!'

'Nonsense!' said the major, picking up a small rifle and running his hand lovingly along the top. 'Now here's a neat little model: Winchester 61 hammerless. Very suitable for polishing off your husband after marriage.' He chuckled uproariously. 'Try it!'

Dick, who had put half a crown into the money bowl and was turning to urge her as well, stopped short.

Lesley Grant's eyes were shining with an expression he could not quite read: except that there was pleading in it, and fear too. She had removed her picture hat; her rich brown hair, worn in a long bob that curled outwards at the shoulders, was a little more ruffled by the wind. She had never been prettier than at that moment of intensity. She looked about eighteen years old, in contrast to the twenty-eight she admitted.

'I know it's silly,' she said breathlessly. Her slim fingers crushed the picture hat. 'But I'm frightened of guns. Anything to do with death, or the thought of death...!'

Major Price's sandy eyebrows went up.

'Damme, young woman,' he expostulated, 'we're not really asking you to kill anybody. Just take the rifle and blaze away at one of those targets. Try it!'

'Look here,' said Dick, 'if she'd rather not do it...'

Evidently with the idea of being a sport, Lesley fastened her teeth in her lower lip and took the rifle from Major Price. First she tried holding it at arm's length, and saw that this would not do. She looked round, hesitating; then she put her cheek to the stock and fired blindly.

The lash of the rifle-shot, less a report than a spitting noise, was drowned out by thunder. No bullet-pock appeared on the target. And the thunder seemed to complete Lesley's demoralization. She put down the rifle quietly enough on the counter. But Dick saw with sudden consternation that her body was trembling, and that she was almost crying.

'I'm sorry,' she said. 'I can't do it.'

'Of all the clumsy oxen in the world,' snapped Dick Markham, 'I must be the worst! I didn't realize…'

He touched her shoulders. The sense of her nearness was so strong and disturbing that he would have put his arms round her again if it had not been for the presence of Major Price. Lesley was now trying to laugh, and nearly succeeding.

'It's quite all right,' she assured him with sincerity. 'I know I oughtn't to be so foolish. It's just that –!' She made a fierce gesture, finding no words. Then she took up her picture hat from the counter. '*Couldn't* we go and see the fortune-teller now?'

'Of course. I'll go with you.'

'He won't admit more than one at a time,' said Lesley. 'They never will. You stay here and finish the round. But – you won't go away?'

'My going away,' Dick said grimly, 'is just about the unlikeliest thing you can think of.'

They looked at each other for a moment before she left him. How badly Dick Markham had got it may be deduced from the fact that, though she was merely going to a tent some dozen yards away, it had all the effect of a separation. For upsetting Lesley in this matter of the rifle, he now stood and swore at himself with such comprehensiveness that even Major Price, listening in guilty silence, seemed disturbed.

The major cleared his throat.

'Women!' he said, shaking his head with gloomy profundity.

'Yes. But, hang it all, I ought to have known better!'

'Women!' repeated the major. He handed the rifle to Dick, who took it automatically. Then he spoke rather enviously. 'You're a lucky young fellow, my lad.'

'My God, don't I know it?'

'That girl,' observed the major, 'is a kind of witch. She comes here six months ago. She turns the heads of half the males in this vicinity. Money, too. And –' Here he hesitated. 'I say!'

'Yes, Major Price?'

'Have you seen Cynthia Drew to-day?'

Dick glanced at him sharply. The major, who would not meet his eye, was looking very hard at the line of rifles on the counter.

'Look here,' said Dick. 'There never has been anything between Cynthia and me. I want you to understand that.'

'I know it, my dear fellow!' said the other hastily, though with every appearance of casualness. 'I'm perfectly sure of it! All the same, in a way, the women...'

'What women?'

'My wife. Lady Ashe. Mrs Middlesworth. Mrs Earnshaw.'

Again Dick glanced at his companion's elaborate unconcern. Major Price was leaning one elbow on the counter, a thick-set silhouette against the little lights over the targets. Again wind whooped among the tents, scattering dust and lifting canvas; but neither of them noticed it.

'A minute ago,' Dick pointed out, 'you were saying they wanted to congratulate us. You intimated they were practically roaring round the country in search of us, just to pour out congratulations.'

'Exactly, my dear chap! That's quite true!'

'Well?'

'But they do feel – mind, I only wanted to warn you! – they do feel, in a way, that poor old Cynthia…'

'"Poor old Cynthia?"'

'In a way. Yes.'

Motioning Major Price to one side, Dick raised the rifle to his shoulder and fired. The lash of the shot was like a comment, while he noted in an absent-minded way that he had scored a hit on the middle target a little off bull's-eye. Both he and the major spoke in that guarded, conspiratorial tone which men employ to discuss dangerous domestic matters.

But he was conscious of tugging forces, the closing net of the spoken word, moving behind this tiny life at Six Ashes.

'For over two years,' he said bitterly, 'this whole village has been trying to get Cynthia and me together, whether we like it or not.'

'I understand, my dear chap. I quite understand!'

Dick fired again.

'There's nothing to it, I tell you! I've never paid any attentions, any serious attentions, to Cynthia. And Cynthia knows that. She can't have misinterpreted it, whatever the others have done.'

'My dear chap,' said the major, regarding him shrewdly, 'you can never pay *any* attentions to a gal without her wondering whether that might not be behind it. Not that I don't understand your point of view, mind!'

Dick fired again.

'And, as for getting married just to please the community, I don't see that. I'm in love with Lesley. I've been in love with her ever since she came here. That's all there is to it. Though what she can possibly see in *me*...'

Major Price chuckled.

'Oh well!', he said deprecatingly, looking Dick up and down, and dismissing this with a wave of his hand. 'After all, you're our local celebrity.'

Dick grunted.

'Or I should say,' amended the major, 'that you're now one of our two local celebrities. Has anybody told you about the fortune-teller?'

'No. Who is the fortune-teller? I mean, it can't be anyone from hereabouts, or everybody would know him and know the whole thing was a fake. But they all seem to think he's outstandingly good. Who is the fortune-teller?'

There was an open box of cartridges on the counter. Major Price picked up a handful idly, letting them run through his fingers back into the box. He hesitated, as though amused at a memory.

'Remind me,' he said, 'to tell you of a devilish good joke I played on Earnshaw this afternoon. Earnshaw –'

'Hang it, major, don't evade! Who *is* the fortune-teller?'

Major Price glanced round cautiously.

'I'll tell you,' he confided, 'if you don't let it get any farther for the moment, because he wants it kept quiet. He's probably one of the greatest living authorities on crime.'

2

'A UTHORITY ON CRIME?' REPEATED DICK.

'Yes. Sir Harvey Gilman.'

'You don't mean the Home Office Pathologist?'

'That's the chap,' agreed Major Price complacently.

As startled as he was impressed, Dick swung round to stare at the red-and-white striped tent, beside whose door the ghostly cardboard hand writhed and beckoned in the wind.

And he saw a weird shadow-play.

It was now so tumultuously dark that he could barely make out the sign which read, 'THE GREAT SWAMI, PALMIST AND CRYSTAL-GAZER: SEES ALL, KNOWS ALL', adorning this gaudy structure. But there *was* a light inside, an overhead light. Against the darkness it threw on the tent-wall discernible shadows of the two persons inside.

They were smudgy shadows, wavering as the tent belled uneasily. Nevertheless Dick could make out the silhouette of a woman at one side; and on the other side, with some sort of table between, a squat shadow with a curiously bulbous head, which seemed to be waving its hands.

'Sir Harvey Gilman!' Dick muttered.

'Sitting in there,' explained the major, 'with a turban round his head, telling people all about themselves. He's been the hit of the show all day.'

'Does he know anything about palmistry or crystal-gazing?'

Major Price spoke dryly.

'No, my lad. But he knows a lot about human nature. That's the whole secret of fortune-telling, anyway.'

'But what's Sir Harvey Gilman doing *here?*'

'He's taken Pope's cottage for the summer. You know – in Gallows Lane, not very far from your place.' Again the major chuckled. 'The Chief Constable introduced him to me, and I got an inspiration.'

'Inspiration?'

'That's right. I thought it'd be an excellent idea if we asked him to play fortune-teller, and not reveal his identity until later. What's more, I think the old boy's enjoying himself.'

'What's he like, actually?'

'Little dry old chap, with a glittering eye. But, as I say, I think he's enjoying himself no end. The Ashes know about it – he nearly made Lady Ashe faint, last night – and Dr Middlesworth and one or two others.'

Here Major Price broke off, with another parade-ground hail past Dick's ear. For one of the persons he had just mentioned was hurrying up through the clutter of tents towards Ashe Hall.

Dr Hugh Middlesworth, bare-headed and with a bag of golf-clubs slung over his shoulder, moved at long strides to get ahead of the rain. He had been in charge of the golf hazard at the garden-party: that is, you tried various short shots from an improvised tee, and received nominal prizes in relation to the fewest strokes it took to reach the cup. He shook his head violently at Major Price's hail; but the major became so insistent that he reluctantly came over to the shooting-gallery.

Hugh Middlesworth was both a good doctor and a very popular man.

The reasons for his popularity might be difficult to determine. He was not a talkative person. He was also the mildest-mannered of men, having a devoted if sharp-tongued wife and a rather large family.

Lean and fortyish, his thin-spun brown hair going thin on top, Dr Middlesworth wore as a rule a vaguely harassed look. There were lines round his eyes and his mouth, with its narrow brown line of moustache. There were hollows in his cheek-bones and temples. But he had, in place of conversation, an understanding smile which suddenly lighted up his whole face. It was unconscious; it was his only bed-side mannerism; yet it worked wonders.

Tramping over towards them now, slinging the golf-bag from one shoulder to the other, he surveyed Major Price in astonishment.

'Aren't you at the cricket match?' he demanded.

'No,' said the major, both question and answer being a little super-fluous. 'I thought I'd hang on here, and – well! keep an eye on the fortune-teller. I've just been telling Dick about Sir Harvey Gilman.'

'Oh,' said Dr Middlesworth.

He opened his mouth as though to add something, but changed his mind and closed it again.

'As a matter of fact,' pursued the major, 'Lesley Grant is in there having her fortune told now. If he tells her she's met a fair man and will go on a journey, that's absolutely right.' He pointed to Dick. 'Those two *are* going to make a match of it, you know.'

Dr Middlesworth did not comment. He merely smiled and extended his hand, with a grip of strong capable fingers. But Dick knew it was sincere.

'I'd heard something about it,' he confessed. 'From my wife.' His vaguely harassed look returned, and he hesitated. 'As for Sir Harvey…'

'In this lad's profession,' continued the major, tapping Dick impressively on the shoulder, 'he ought to be invaluable. Eh?'

'Invaluable,' Dick said with some fervour, 'isn't the word for it. That man has given expert evidence in every murder case, celebrated or obscure, for the past thirty years. A friend of mine used to live near him in Bayswater; and said he'd come home, as often as not, with somebody's insides in an open glass jar. Ralph says the old boy's a walking encyclopedia about murders, if you can only persuade him to talk. And...'

This was the point at which all three of them jumped.

It was partly the brief glare of lightning, illuminating the whole grounds with a deathly pallor, and followed by a shock of thunder striking close. Lightning picked out every detail as though in the flash of a photograph.

It caught, in the background, the dull red-brick shape of Ashe Hall, with thin chimneys and mullioned windows now moonlit: venerable and yet shabby, like their owner. It caught the writhe of seething trees. It caught the thin careworn face of Dr Middlesworth, and the fat comfortable countenance of Major Price, now turned towards the fortune-teller's tent. When darkness came again, with the crash of thunder dying to a rattle, it directed their attention towards another thing.

There was something wrong inside the fortune-teller's tent.

The shadow of Lesley Grant had jumped to its feet. The shadow of the man was also standing, pointing a finger at her across the table. And the weirdness of that shadow-play, wavering on a lighted wall, could not disguise its urgency.

'Here!' cried Dick Markham, hardly knowing what he protested at.

Yet the agitation of those figures he could feel as clearly as though they were there. The shadow of Lesley Grant turned round, and Lesley herself bolted out of the tent.

Aimlessly, still carrying the rifle under his arm, Dick ran towards her. He saw her stop short – a white figure in the gloom – and she seemed to be bracing herself.

'Lesley! What's wrong?'

'Wrong?' echoed Lesley. Her voice was cool and gentle, hardly raised above its usual key.

'What was he saying to you?'

Dick felt rather than saw the brown eyes, with their strongly luminous whites and very thin eyebrows, searching his face.

'He wasn't saying anything to me!' Lesley protested. 'I didn't think he was very good, really. Just the usual thing about a happy life; and a little illness, but nothing serious; and a letter arriving with some pleasant news.'

'Then why were you so frightened?'

'I wasn't frightened!'

'I'm sorry, darling. But I saw your shadow on the wall of the tent.' More and more oppressively disturbed, Dick came to a decision. Hardly realizing what he was doing, he thrust the rifle into Lesley's hands. 'Here, hold this for a minute!'

'Dick! *Where are you going?*'

'I want to see this bloke myself.'

'But you mustn't!'

'Why not?'

The rain answered for her. Two or three large drops spattered down, and then ran across the lawn as though the hissing of all these trees were gathering together to let the skies open like a tank.

Glancing round, Dick could see that the hitherto almost deserted lawn was now being invaded by people hurrying back from the cricket match at the other side of the grounds. Major Price was hastily gathering up an armful of rifles. Beckoning to him, and pointing at Lesley, Dick touched her arm.

'Go on up to the house,' he said. 'I'll not be long.' Then he pushed open the tent-flap and ducked inside.

A voice, pitched in a sing-song deliberately guttural and assumed, struck at him sharply from the close, stuffy confines of the tent.

'I regret!' it said. 'You find me fatigued. That was the last sitting. I can oblige no more ladies or gentlemen to-day.'

'That's all right, Sir Harvey,' said Dick. 'I didn't come to get my fortune told.'

Then they looked at each other. Dick Markham could not understand why his own voice stuck in his throat.

In an enclosure barely six feet square, a shaded electric light hung from the roof. It shone down across a gleaming crystal ball, against the plum-coloured velvet cover of the little table, and added a hypnosis to this stuffy place.

Behind the table sat the fortune-teller, a lean dry shortish man of fifty-odd, in a white linen suit and with a coloured turban wound round his head. Out of the turban peered an intellectual face, a sharp-nosed face, with a straight mouth, a bump of a chin, and an ugly worried forehead. His rather arresting eyes were pitted with wrinkles at the outer corners.

'So you know me,' he said in his normal voice – a dry voice, like a schoolmaster's. He cleared his throat, and coughed several times to find the right level.

'That's right, sir.'

'Then what *do* you want, young man?'

Rain-drops struck the roof of the tent with a drum-like noise.

'I want to know,' returned Dick, 'what you were saying to Miss Grant.'

'Miss who?'

'Miss Grant. The young lady who was just in here. My *fiancée*.'

'*Fiancée*, eh?'

The wrinkled eyelids moved briefly. Major Price had said that Sir Harvey Gilman was enjoying himself at his job. It would require a sardonic humour, Dick reflected, to sit here all day in the airless heat, speaking with a fake accent and enjoying the dissection of those who sat opposite him. But there was no hint of any enjoyment now.

'Tell me, Mr...?'

'My name is Markham. Richard Markham.'

'Markham.' The Great Swami's eyes seemed to turn inwards. 'Markham. Don't I periodically see, in London, plays written by a certain Richard Markham? Plays of a sort that are called, I believe,' he hesitated, 'psychological thrillers?'

'That's right, sir.'

'Analysing, if I recall correctly, the minds and motives of those who commit crimes. You write them?'

'I do the best I can with the material,' said Dick, suddenly feeling on the defensive before that eye.

Yes, he thought, the old boy *was* pleased. Sir Harvey uttered a sound which might have been laughter if he had opened his mouth a little more. Yet the ugly forehead remained.

'No doubt, Mr Markham. This lady's name, you said, was...?'

'Grant. Lesley Grant.' He uttered the words just as the storm broke and the rain tore down. It struck the roof of the tent with such a hollow, heavy drumming that Dick had to raise his voice above it. 'What's all this mystery?'

'Tell me, Mr Markham. Has she lived here in Six Ashes for very long?'

'No. Only about six months. Why?'

'How long have you been engaged to her? Believe me, I have a reason for asking that.'

'We only got engaged last night. But –'

'Only last night,' repeated the other without inflexion. The hanging lamp in the tent swung a little, sending smooth bright reflexions slipping across that crystal ball. The drumming drive of rain deepened to a roar, making canvas walls vibrate. Behind the crystal ball, regarding his visitor with those curious eyes, Sir Harvey Gilman upturned the palm of his hand and knocked with the finger-joints, lightly and leisurely, on the velvet-covered table.

'One other thing, young man,' he remarked in an interested way. 'Where do you get the material for your plays?'

At any other time Dick would have been only too glad to tell him. He would have been flattered, even tongue-tied. He realized that he was probably offending the sharp-nosed old pathologist, even making an enemy of him. But he had reached a point of desperation.

'For God's sake, man, what is it?'

'I have been wondering how to break it to you,' said Sir Harvey, showing for the first time a gleam of humanity. He looked up. 'Do you know who this so-called "Lesley Grant" really is?'

'Who she really is?'

'I suppose,' said Sir Harvey, 'I had better tell you.' Drawing a deep breath, he got up from his chair behind the table. And it was at this point that Dick heard the crack of the rifle-shot.

After that, the world dissolved in nightmare.

Though the noise was not loud, Dick's thoughts were so entwined already with rifles and shooting-ranges that he had almost a pre-vision of it.

He saw the small bullet-hole jump up black in the side wall of the tent, now growing greyish where the wet crawled down. He saw Sir Harvey flung forward as by the blow of a fist – striking just beside and under the left shoulder-blade. He saw, in one momentary flash, the inscrutability of the pathologist's face cracked open by a look of sheer terror.

Table and man pitched forward almost into Dick's arms. But there was not even time to stretch out a hand before the whole clutter landed round him. Sir Harvey's own hand was twitching convulsively; he dragged the table-cover with him; and the crystal ball dropped with a thud on flat-trodden grass. Then, as Dick saw the ghost of a blood-stain take form and deepen on the side of the white linen suit, he heard a clear voice raised outside.

'Major Price, I couldn't *help* it!'

It was Lesley's voice.

'I'm terribly sorry, but I couldn't help it! Dick shouldn't have given me this rifle to hold! Somebody touched my arm, and my hand was on the trigger, and the rifle seemed to fire itself by accident!' The voice came from a little distance away, of anguished sweetness and sincerity against the tumult of rain. 'I – I do hope I haven't hit anything!'

3

AT HALF-PAST NINE THAT NIGHT, WHEN JUNE TWILIGHT WAS deepening outside the windows, Dick Markham paced endlessly up and down the study of his cottage just outside Six Ashes.

'If I could stop thinking,' he told himself, 'I should be all right. But I can't stop thinking.

'The fact remains that Sir Harvey Gilman's shadow was clearly outlined against the wall of that tent, a perfect target if anybody *had* wanted to shoot at it.

'But what you're thinking is impossible!

'This whole affair,' he further told himself, 'will prove to have a perfectly simple explanation if you don't get into a fever about it. The main thing is to get rid of these cobwebs of suspicion, these ugly clinging strands that wind into the brain and nerves until you feel the spider stir at the end of every one of them. You're in love with Lesley. Anything else is of no consideration whatever.

'Liar!'

'Major Price believes this shooting was an accident. So does Dr Middlesworth. So does Earnshaw, the bank manager, who turned up so unexpectedly after Sir Harvey Gilman tumbled over with a bullet in him. You alone…'

Dick stopped his pacing to look slowly round the study where he had done so much work, good and bad.

There were the fat-bowled lamps on the table, throwing golden light across its comfortable untidiness, and reflected back from the little line of diamond-paned windows. There was the dark brick fire-place with its white overmantel. The walls were hung with framed theatrical photographs, and garish playbills – from the Comedy Theatre, the Apollo Theatre, the St Martin's Theatre – announcing plays by Richard Markham.

Poisoner's Mistake was proclaimed from one wall, *Panic in the Family* from another. Each an attempt to get inside the criminal's mind: to see life through his eyes, to feel with his feelings. They occupied such wall-space as was not taken up by stuffed shelves of books dealing with morbid and criminal psychology.

There was the desk with its typewriter, cover now on. There was the revolving bookcase of reference-works. There were the overstuffed chairs, and the standing ashtrays. There were the bright chintz curtains, and the bright rag rugs underfoot. It was Dick Markham's ivory tower, as remote from the great world as this village of Six Ashes itself.

Even the name of the lane in which he lived...

He lit another cigarette, inhaling very deeply in a curious per-verse effort to make his own head swim. He was taking still another deep draw when the telephone rang.

Dick snatched up the receiver with such haste that he almost knocked the phone off the desk.

'Hello,' said the guarded voice of Dr Middlesworth.

Clearing his throat, Dick put the cigarette down on the edge of the desk so as to grip the phone with both hands.

'How's Sir Harvey? Is he alive?'

There was a slight pause.

'Oh, yes. He's alive.'

'Is he going to – be all right?'

'Oh, yes. He'll live.'

A dizzy wave of relief, as though loosening something in his chest, brought the sweat to Dick's forehead. He picked up the cigarette, mechanically took two puffs at it, and then flung it at the fireplace.

'The fact is,' pursued Dr Middlesworth, 'he wants to see you. Could you come over here to his cottage now? It's only a few hundred yards away, and I thought perhaps…?'

Dick stared at the phone.

'Is he allowed to see anybody?'

'Yes. Can you come straight away?'

'I'll come,' said Dick, 'just as soon as I've phoned Lesley and told her it's all right. She's been ringing here all evening, and she's nearly frantic.'

'I know. She's been phoning here too. But' – there was more than a shade of hesitation in the doctor's manner – 'he says he'd rather you didn't.'

'Didn't what?'

'Didn't phone Lesley. Not just yet. He'll explain what he means. In the meantime' – again the doctor hesitated – 'don't let anybody come with you, and don't tell anybody what I've just said. Do you promise that?'

'All right, all right!'

'On your word of honour, do you promise?'

'Yes.'

Slowly, staring at the phone as though he hoped it might give back a secret, Dick replaced the receiver. His eyes wandered towards the diamond-paned windows. The storm had cleared away long ago: a fine night of stars showed outside, and there was a drowsy scent of wet grass and flowers to soothe bedevilled wits.

Then he swung round, with an animal-like sense of another presence, and saw Cynthia Drew looking at him from the doorway of the study.

'Hello, Dick,' smiled Cynthia.

Dick Markham had sworn to himself, had sworn a mighty oath, that he wouldn't feel uncomfortable the next time he saw this girl; that he wouldn't avoid her eye; that he wouldn't experience this exasperating sense of having done something low. But he did.

'I knocked at the front door,' she explained, 'and couldn't seem to make anyone hear. And the door was open, so I came in. You don't mind?'

'No, of course not!'

Cynthia avoided his eye too. Conversation seemed to drop away, a dried-up gulf between them, until she decided to speak her mind.

Cynthia was one of those healthy, straightforward girls who laugh a good deal and yet sometimes seem more complex than their flightier sisters. There could be no denying her prettiness: fair hair, blue eyes, with a fine complexion and fine teeth. She stood twisting the knob of the study door, and then – *click!* – you saw her make up her mind.

It was no better for guessing not only what she would say, but exactly how she would say it. Cynthia looked straight at him. She drew a deep breath, her figure being set off by a pinkish-coloured jumper and a brown skirt above tan stockings and shoes. She walked forward, with a sort of calculated impulsiveness, and extended her hand.

'I've heard about you and Lesley, Dick. I'm glad, and I hope you'll both be terribly happy.'

At the same time her eyes were saying:

'I didn't think you could do this. It doesn't really matter, of course; and you see what a good sport I'm being about it; but I hope you realize you *are* rather low?'

(Oh, hell!)

'Thanks, Cynthia,' he answered aloud. 'We're rather happy about it ourselves.'

Cynthia began to laugh; and immediately, as though conscious of the impropriety, checked herself.

'What I really came about,' she went on, her colour going up in spite of herself, 'is this dreadful business about Sir Harvey Gilman.'

'Yes.'

'It *is* Sir Harvey Gilman, isn't it?' She nodded towards the windows, and continued to speak rapidly. If Cynthia had not been such a solid girl, you would have said that there was about her a flounce and brightness. 'I mean, the man who moved into Colonel Pope's old cottage a few days ago, and kept so mysteriously in the background so he could play fortune-teller. It *is* Sir Harvey Gilman?'

'Yes. That's right.'

'Dick, what happened this afternoon?'

'Weren't you there?'

'No. But they say he's dying.'

On the point of speaking, Dick checked himself.

'They say there was an accident,' Cynthia continued. 'And Sir Harvey was shot near the heart. And Major Price and Dr Middlesworth picked him up and got him into a car and drove him down here. Poor Dick!'

'Why are you pitying *me?*'

Cynthia pressed her hands together.

'Lesley's a dear girl' – she spoke with such obvious and earnest sincerity that he could not doubt her – 'but you shouldn't have given her that rifle. Really you shouldn't! She doesn't know how to deal with practical things. Major Price says Sir Harvey's in a coma and dying. Have you heard anything more from the doctor?'

'Well – no.'

'Everybody is dreadfully upset. Mrs Middlesworth says it only goes to show we shouldn't have had a shooting-range. Mrs Price took her up rather sharply, especially as the major was in charge of it. But it does seem a pity: the padre says we collected well over a hundred pounds from the whole bazaar. And people are starting the most absurd rumours.'

Cynthia was standing by the typewriter-desk, picking up scattered books only to put them down again, and talking breathlessly. She meant so well, Dick thought; she was so infernally straightforward and friendly and likeable. Yet one problem, the problem of Sir Harvey Gilman, scratched at his nerves as Cynthia's voice was beginning to scratch.

'Look here, Cynthia. I'm sorry, but I've got to go out.'

'Nobody has seen Lord Ashe to ask him what *he* thinks. But then we so seldom do see him, do we? By the way, why does Lord Ashe always look so oddly at poor Lesley, on the few occasions when he *has* seen her? Lady Ashe…' Cynthia broke off, waking up. 'What did you say, Dick?'

'I've got to go out now.'

'To see Lesley? Of course!'

'No. To see what's happening down at the other cottage. The doctor wants to speak to me.'

Cynthia was instantly helpful. 'I'll go with you, Dick. Anything at all I can do to help –'

'*I tell you, Cynthia. I've got to go alone!*'

It was as though he had hit her in the face.

A complete swine, now. Well, let it go.

After a brief silence Cynthia laughed: the same deprecating laugh, slurring things over, he had heard her give on a tennis-court when somebody lost his temper and flung down a racket with intent to break it. She regarded him soberly, the blue eyes concerned.

'You're so temperamental, Dick,' she said fondly.

'I'm not temperamental, curse it! It's only...'

'All writers are, I suppose. One expects it.' She dismissed the idiosyncrasy as a matter she did not understand.

'But – funny, isn't it? – one doesn't associate it with a person like you. I mean, an outdoor person, and a fine cricketer, and all that. I mean – oh, dear! There I go again! I must be pushing off.' She looked at him steadily. With colour under the blue eyes, her placid face became almost beautiful.

'But you can count on me, old boy,' she added.

Then she was gone.

It was too late to apologize now. The villain of the piece waited until she had time to get well away towards the village. Then he left the house himself.

In front of his cottage a broad country lane ran east and west, curving among trees and open fields. On one side of the lane ran the low stone wall which bounded the park of Ashe Hall; on the opposite side, set something over a hundred yards apart, were three cottages.

The first was Dick Markham's. The second stood untenanted. The third, farthest east, had been rented furnished by their enigmatic newcomer. They were intriguing to visitors, these cottages in Gallows Lane. Each stood well back from the road, and made up in picturesqueness for its shilling-in-the-slot electric meter and lack of main drainage.

As Dick emerged into the lane, he could faintly hear the church clock to the west striking ten. The lane swam in dusky light, though it seemed less dark than the print of bright stars overhead, which you saw as though from a well. Night-scents and night-noises took on a peculiar distinctness here. By the time Dick reached the last cottage, he was running blindly.

Dark.

Or almost dark.

Across the road from the Pope cottage, a thick coppice of birch-trees pressed up close inside the boundary wall of the park. Close beside the cottage itself, bounding the lane for some distance eastward, stretched a fruit-orchard. It was a dusky place even by day, damp and wasp-haunted. By night Dick could see nothing of the cottage except chinks of light showing through imperfectly drawn curtains on two windows facing the road.

He must have been heard or seen stumbling across the front garden. Dr Middlesworth opened the front door and admitted him into a modern-looking hall.

'Listen,' the doctor began without preamble. He spoke in his customary mild tone, but he meant it. 'I can't go on with this pretence. It's not fair asking me to.'

'What pretence? How badly is the old boy hurt?'

'That's just the point. He's not hurt at all.'

Dick closed the front door with a soft bang, and whirled round.

'He fainted from shock,' Dr Middlesworth went on to explain, 'so of course everybody thought he was dying or dead. I couldn't be sure myself until I'd got him here and used the probe. But, unless you get a direct head or heart wound, a bullet from a .22 target-rifle isn't usually very dangerous.'

A faint twinkle of amusement showed in the mild eyes under the lined forehead. Dr Middlesworth put up a hand and rubbed his forehead.

'When I extracted the bullet, he woke up and yelled bloody murder. That rather surprised Major Price. The major insisted on tagging along, though I tried to keep him away.'

'Well?'

'All Sir Harvey's got is a flesh-wound. He didn't even lose much blood. His back will be sore for a few days; but, barring that, he's as fit as he ever was.'

Dick took some moments to assimilate this.

'Do you know,' he said, 'that Lesley Grant's nearly out of her mind? She thinks she's killed him?'

All the amusement died out of Middlesworth's face.

'Yes. I know.'

'Then what's the big idea?'

'When Major Price left here,' replied the doctor, evading a direct answer, 'Sir Harvey made him promise not to say anything. Sir Harvey intimated it would be best to circulate a report that he was in a coma and couldn't last long. Knowing the major, I rather doubt whether the secret will be kept for any length of time.'

Some emotion had startled Hugh Middlesworth almost to volubility.

'Anyway,' he complained, '*I* can't keep it. I warned him of that. It's unprofessional. It's unethical. Besides…'

Again, as once before that day, the doctor opened his mouth to say or suggest something, and thought better of it.

'But I keep asking you, Doctor! *Why?*'

'He wouldn't tell the major. He wouldn't tell me. Maybe he'll tell you. Come along.'

Abruptly Middlesworth stretched out his hand and turned the knob of a door on the left-hand side of the hall, motioning Dick to precede him. It opened into a sitting-room, large though rather low of ceiling, with two front windows facing the lane. In the exact centre of the room was a big writing-table, lighted by a hanging lamp just over it. And, in an arm-chair beside this table, his back out from it so as not to touch the back of the chair, sat the fortune-teller now divested of his raiment.

Sir Harvey Gilman's face was so grim that it swallowed up other impressions. Dick noticed that he wore pyjamas and a dressing-gown. His head, shorn of the turban, was now revealed as bald, above the sceptical eyes and sharp-pointed nose and hard sardonic mouth. He looked Dick up and down.

'Annoyed, Mr Markham?'

Dick made no reply.

'I rather imagine,' said Sir Harvey, 'that *I'm* the one to be annoyed.' He arched his back, winced, and shut his lips hard before opening them to continue.

'I've proposed a little experiment. The doctor there doesn't seem to approve. But I imagine you'll approve, when you hear my reasons. No, Doctor, you may remain in the room.'

There was a half-smoked cigar on the edge of an ashtray on the writing-table. Sir Harvey picked it up.

'Understand me!' he pursued. 'I don't give a rap for abstract justice. I should not go a step out of my way to inform against anybody. But I am intellectually curious. I should like, before I die, to know the answer to one of the few problems that ever defeated my friend Gideon Fell.

'If you agree to help me, we may be able to set a trap. If not –' He waved the cigar, put it into his mouth, and found it dead. There was more than a little vindictiveness in his manner. 'Now about this woman, the so-called "Lesley Grant".'

Dick found his voice.

'Let's have it, sir. What were you starting to tell me before this thing happened?'

'About this woman,' pursued the other in his leisurely way. 'You're in love with her, I suppose? Or think you are?'

'I know I am.'

'That's rather unfortunate,' said Sir Harvey dryly. 'Still, it *has* happened before.' He turned his head round to the desk-calendar on the writing-table, which registered the date as Thursday, June tenth. 'Tell me. Has she by any chance invited you to dinner at her house, one day this week or next, as a sort of celebration?'

'As a matter of fact, she has. To-morrow night. But –'

Sir Harvey looked startled.

'To-morrow night, eh?'

What rose most clearly in Dick's mind was the image of Lesley herself, against the background of her house on the other side of Six Ashes. Lesley, with her good temper. Lesley, with her impracticality. Lesley, with her fastidiousness. Lesley, who hated ostentation in any form, and never wore lipstick or jewellery or conspicuous clothes. Yet these retiring qualities were caught together by an intensity of nature which, when she fell in love, seemed to make her utterly reckless in anything she said or did.

All this flashed through his mind as her face rose in front of him, moulded into an image of passion and gentleness that obsessed his mind. Inexplicably, he found himself shouting.

'I can't stand any more of this!' he said. 'What *is* all this nonsense? What accusation are you making? Are you trying to tell me her name isn't Lesley Grant at all?'

'I am,' answered Sir Harvey. He lifted his eyes. 'Her real name is Jordan. She's a poisoner.'

4

For a space while you might have counted ten, nobody spoke. When Dick did reply, it was as though the meaning of the words had failed to register with him. He spoke without anger, even with a certain casualness.

'That's absurd.'

'Why is it absurd?'

'*That* little girl?'

'That little girl, as you call her, is forty-one years old.'

There was a chair at Dick's elbow. He sat down in the chair. Colonel Pope, the owner of this cottage, had turned the sitting-room into a place of shabby and slippered comfort. Pipe-smoke had tinged grey the white-plaster walls, and seasoned the oak beams. Round the walls ran a single line of military prints from the early and middle nineteenth century, their colours of battle and uniform softened by time yet still vivid. Dick looked at these pictures, and the colours grew blurred.

'You don't believe me,' said Sir Harvey calmly. 'I didn't expect you to. But I've phoned London. There'll be a man down from Scotland Yard to-morrow who knows her well. There'll also be photographs and fingerprints.'

'Wait a minute! Please!'

'Yes, young fellow?'

'What, according to you, is Lesley supposed to have done?'

'She poisoned three men. Two of them were her husbands; that's where she gets her money. The third...'

'*What* husbands?'

'Does it shock your romantic soul?' inquired Sir Harvey. 'Her first husband was an American corporation lawyer named Burton Foster. Her second was a Liverpool cotton-broker called Davies; I forget his first name. Both were wealthy men. But the third victim, as I was saying…'

Dick Markham pressed his hands to his temples.

'*God!*' he said. And out of that monosyllable suddenly burst all the incredulousness, all the protest, all the dazed bewilderment which welled up inside him. He wanted not to have heard; he wanted to blot the last thirty seconds out of his life.

Sir Harvey had the grace to look a little fussed, and to turn his eye away.

'I'm sorry, young fellow' – he flung his dead cigar into the ashtray – 'but there it is.' Then he eyed Dick keenly. 'And if you're thinking…'

'Go on! What was I thinking?'

The other's mouth grew still more sardonic.

'You write psychological tosh about the minds of murderers. I enjoy the stuff; I don't mind admitting it. And among my colleagues I am supposed to have rather a peculiar sense of humour. If you think I am inventing things and playing an elaborate joke on you, by way of poetic justice, get the idea out of your head. My purpose, believe me, is not a joke.'

And, as Dick found out only too soon, it wasn't.

'This woman,' said Sir Harvey clearly, 'is a thoroughgoing bad hat. The sooner you get used to that idea the sooner you'll get over it. And the safer you'll be.'

'Safer?'

'That's what I said.' The ugly stamp appeared again on Sir Harvey's forehead. He twisted his body in the chair, to get a more comfortable position; then, stung with pain, he subsided angrily.

'But that's the trouble,' he went on. 'In my estimation, this woman isn't even particularly clever. Yet she goes on, and on, and on, and gets away with it! She's devised a method of murder that beats Gideon Fell as much as it beats me.'

This was the first time that the flat word 'murder' had been applied to Lesley. It opened new chasms and new doors into evil rooms. Dick was still groping blindly.

'Stop a bit!' he insisted. 'A minute ago you said something about fingerprints. You mean she's been on trial?'

'No. The fingerprints were obtained unofficially. She's never been on trial.'

'Oh? Then how do you know she's guilty?'

Exasperation sharpened the other's countenance.

'*Won't* you believe me, Mr Markham, until our friend arrives from Scotland Yard?'

'I didn't say that. I ask why you state it as a fact. If Lesley was guilty, why didn't the police arrest her?'

'Because they couldn't prove it. Three occasions, mind you! And still they couldn't prove it.'

Once more the Home Office pathologist thoughtlessly tried to move his position. Once more pain burnt him. But he was absorbed now. He hardly noticed it. His fingers lifted up and down on the padded arms of the chair. His monkey-bright eyes, fixed on Dick Markham, held so richly sardonic an expression that it might have been one of admiration.

'The police,' he went on, 'will supply exact dates and details. I can only tell you what I know from personal observation. Kindly don't interrupt me more than is necessary.'

'Well?'

'I first met this lady thirteen years ago. Our so-called Government had not yet awarded me a knighthood. I was not yet Chief Pathologist to the Home Office. I often served in the capacity of police-surgeon as well as pathologist. One morning in winter – the police, I repeat, can supply dates – we learned that an American named Foster had been found dead in his dressing-room, adjoining the bedroom, of his home in Hyde Park Gardens. I went out there with Chief Inspector Hadley, now Superintendent Hadley.

'It seemed to us a clear case of suicide. The deceased's wife had been away from home for the night. The deceased was found half-sitting, half-lying on a sofa beside a little table in the dressing-room. The cause of death was hydrocyanic acid, injected into the left forearm by means of a hypodermic syringe found on the floor beside him.'

Sir Harvey paused.

A rather cruel smile pinched in the wrinkled flesh round his mouth.

'Your studies, Mr Markham' – he spread out his fingers '– your studies, I say, will have taught you about hydrocyanic, or prussic, acid. Swallowed, it is agonizing but rapid. Injected into the bloodstream, it is agonizing but even more rapid.

'In Foster's case, suicide seemed plain. No man in his senses allows a murderer to inject him, neatly in a vein, with a hypodermic smelling of bitter almonds from ten feet away. The windows of the dressing-room were locked on the inside. The door was not only bolted on the inside, but had an immensely heavy chest of drawers drawn across it. The servants had great difficulty in breaking in.

'We reassured the stricken widow, who had just returned home in prostration and floods of tears. Her grief, delicate creature as she was, became quite touching.'

Dick Markham tried to hold hard to reason.

'And this widow,' he said, 'was –?'

'It was the woman who called herself Lesley Grant. Yes.'

Again there was a silence.

'We now come to one of those coincidences mistakenly supposed to be more common in fiction than in real life. Five years later, some time in the spring, I happened to be in Liverpool, giving testimony at the Assizes. Hadley was also there, on a completely different matter. We ran into each other at the sessions-house, where we met the local Superintendent of Police. In passing the time of day, the Superintendent said...'

Here Sir Harvey cast up his eyes.

'He said, "Rather queer suicide out Prince's Park way. Man killed himself with prussic acid in a hypodermic. Elderly chap, but plenty of money; good health; no troubles. Still, there's no doubt about it. The inquest's just over now." He nodded along the hall. And we saw somebody in black coming along that dirty hall, amid a group of sympathizers. I'm pretty tough, young man. I'm not easily impressed. But I've never forgotten the look on Hadley's face when he turned round and said, "By God, it's the same woman".'

The words were bald enough. Yet they had an intolerable vividness.

Quietly, as Sir Harvey Gilman musingly ceased to speak, Dr Middlesworth crossed the room, circled round the big writing-table, and sat down in a creaky basket-chair near the windows.

Dick started a little. He had completely forgotten the doctor. Even now Middlesworth did not comment or obtrude into the conversation. He merely crossed his long legs, propping a bony elbow on the arm of the chair and his chin in his hand, and stared with thoughtful eyes at the tan-shaded lamp over the writing-table.

'You're telling me,' snarled Dick Markham, 'or trying to tell me, it was Lesley again? *My* Lesley?'

'Your Lesley. Yes. Slightly second-hand.'

Dick started to get up from his chair, but sat down again.

His host had no notion of being offensive. You could guess that he was merely trying, like a surgeon, to cut out of Dick Markham's body, with a sharp knife, what he considered a malignant growth.

'Then,' he added, 'the police *did* start an investigation.'

'With what result?'

'With the same result as before.'

'They proved she couldn't have done it?'

'Excuse me. They proved that they couldn't prove it. As in Foster's case, the wife had been away from home that night…'

'Alibi?'

'No provable alibi, no. But it wasn't necessary.'

'Go on, Sir Harvey.'

'Mr Davies, the Liverpool broker,' continued the other, 'had been found lying across the desk in his so-called "den". And once more the room was locked up on the inside.'

Dick pressed a hand across his forehead.

'Securely?' he demanded.

'The windows were not only locked, but had wooden-barred shutters as well. The door had two bolts – new, tight-fitting bolts which couldn't be tampered with – one at the top, and one at the bottom. It was a big, florid, old-fashioned house; that room could be sealed up inside like a fortress. Nor was that all.

'Davies, they showed, had begun life as a dispensing chemist. He was well acquainted with the odour of prussic acid. He couldn't have injected the stuff into his own arm by accident, or by somebody's telling him it was a harmless concoction. If this wasn't suicide, it was murder. Yet there had been no struggle and no drugging. Davies was a gross old man, but he was still a big man: he wouldn't have submitted tamely to a needle redolent of hydrocyanic acid. And the room remained locked up on the inside.'

Sir Harvey pursed up his lips, cocking his head on one side the better to admire this.

'The very simplicity of the thing, gentlemen, drove the police mad. They felt certain; yet they couldn't prove.'

'What,' asked Dick, fighting black things in his own mind, 'what did Les… I mean, what did the wife say to this?'

'She denied it was murder, of course.'

'Yes; but what did she *say?*'

'She was simply wide-eyed and horrified. She said she couldn't understand it. She admitted she was the girl who had married Burton Foster, but said the whole thing was a dreadful coincidence or mistake. What could the police answer to that?'

'Did they do anything else?'

'Investigated her, naturally. What little could be found out.'

'Well?'

'They tried to get her on *any* charge,' said Sir Harvey. 'And they couldn't. No poison could be traced to her. She'd married Davies under a false name; but that's not illegal unless there's a question of bigamy or fraud. There was no such question. Full-stop.'

'And then?'

The pathologist lifted his shoulders, and winced again. His wound, or the emotion caused by it, had begun to madden him.

'The final step in her progress I can tell you very briefly. *I* didn't see it happen. Neither did Hadley. The pretty widow, now with quite a sizeable fortune, simply disappeared. I more or less forgot her. It was three years ago that a friend of mine living in Paris, to whom I'd once told the lady's story as a classic example, sent me a cutting from a French newspaper.

'The press-cutting reported an unfortunate suicide in the Avenue George V. The victim was M. Martin Belford, a young Englishman, who had a flat there. It appeared that he had just become engaged to be married to a certain Mademoiselle Lesley Somebody – the name escapes me now – whose house was in the Avenue Foch.

'Four days later he dined with this lady at her home, as a sort of celebration of the engagement. He left the house at eleven o'clock that night, apparently in the best of health and spirits. He went home. Next morning he was found dead in his bedroom. Do I need to tell you under what circumstances?'

'The same?'

'Exactly the same. Room locked up, in the comprehensive French style. Intravenous poisoning by hydrocyanic acid.'

'And then?'

Sir Harvey stared at the past.

'I sent the cutting to Hadley, who got in touch with the French police. Even those realists wouldn't hear of anything but suicide. The newspaper reporters, who are allowed a broader style than they are here, spoke in tones of tragedy and sadness about mademoiselle. *"Cette belle anglaise, très chic, très distinguée."* They suggested that there had been a lovers' tiff, which mademoiselle didn't like to admit; and in a fit of despair the man had gone home and killed himself.'

In the creaky basket-chair across the room, Dr Middlesworth took out a pipe and blew down the stem.

It gave him something to do; it eased, Dick knew, his acute discomfort. And it was the doctor's presence, representing Six Ashes and normality, which made the whole affair so grotesque. The faces of Mrs Middlesworth, of Mrs Price, of Lady Ashe, of Cynthia Drew, floated in front of his mind.

'Look here,' Dick burst out. 'This whole thing is impossible.'

'Of course,' agreed Sir Harvey. 'But it happened.'

'I mean, they must have been suicides after all!'

'Perhaps they were.' The other's tone remained polite. 'Or perhaps not. But, come, now, Mr Markham! Let's face it! Whatever your interpretation of the facts, don't you find this situation just a *little* suspicious? Just a *little* unsavoury?' Dick was silent for a moment.

'Don't you, Mr Markham?'

'All right. I do. But I don't agree that the circumstances are always the same. This man in Paris… what was his name?'

'Belford?'

'Belford, yes. You say she didn't marry him?'

'Always thinking of the personal, eh?' inquired Sir Harvey, eyeing him with a sort of clinical interest and pleasure. 'Not thinking of death or poison at all. Merely thinking of this woman in some other man's arms.'

This was so true that it made Dick Markham rage. But he tried to put a dignified face on it.

'She didn't marry the fellow,' he persisted. 'Did she stand to gain anything by his death?'

'No. Not a penny.'

'Then where's your motive?'

'Damn it all, man!' said Sir Harvey. 'Don't you see that by this time the girl can't help herself?'

With considerable awkwardness, holding himself gingerly, he put his hands on the arms of the chair and propelled himself to his feet. Dr Middlesworth started to rise in protest, but their host waved him away. He took a few little steps up and down the shabby carpet.

'*You* know that, young man. Or at least you profess to know it. The poisoner never does stop. The poisoner can't stop. It becomes a psychic disease, the source of a perverted thrill stronger – more violently exciting! – than any in psychology. Poison! The power over life and death! Are you aware of that, or aren't you?'

'Yes. I'm aware of it.'

'Good! Then consider *my* side of it.'

He reached round to touch his back, gingerly.

'I come down here for a summer holiday. I'm tired. I need a rest. I ask them as a great favour if they won't keep my identity a secret, because every fool wants to jaw to me about criminal trials I'm already sick of.'

'Lesley –!' Dick was beginning.

'Don't interrupt me. They say they'll consider keeping it a secret, if I consent to playing fortune-teller at their bazaar, Very well. I didn't mind that. In fact, I rather liked it. It was an opportunity to read human nature and surprise fools.'

He pointed his finger, compelling silence.

'But what happens? Into my tent walks a murderess whom I haven't seen since that Liverpool affair. And not looking a day older, mind you, than when I first saw her! I improve the opportunity (as who wouldn't?) to put the fear of God into her.

'Whereupon, as quick as winking, she tries to kill me with a rifle. This wasn't her usual suicide-in-the-locked-room technique. A bullet-hole in the wall doesn't give you any such opportunity. No; the lady lost her head. And why? I was beginning to see it even before she fired at my shadow. Because she's arranging a little poisoning-party for someone else. In other words' – he nodded at Dick – '*you*.'

Again there was a silence.

'Now don't tell me it hadn't occurred to you!' said Sir Harvey, with broad scepticism and a fishy shake of his head. 'Don't say the idea never even crossed your mind!'

'Oh, no. It's crossed my mind all right.'

'Do you believe the story I've been telling you?'

'I believe the story, yes. But if there's been some mistake… if it isn't Lesley at all…!'

'Would you credit the evidence of fingerprints?'

'Yes. I'd be bound to.'

'But, even granting that, you still don't believe she would try to poison you?'

'No, I don't.'

'Why not? Do you think she would make an exception in your case?'

No reply.

'Do you think she's really fallen in love at long last?'

No reply.

'Even supposing she has, do you still want to marry her?'

Dick got up from his chair. He wanted to lash out with his fist at the air; to shut away from his ears the voice that was crowding him into a corner, making him face facts, cutting away each alternative as he seized at it.

'You can adopt,' pursued the other, 'one of two courses. The first, I see, has already suggested itself to you. You want to have this thing out with her, don't you?'

'Naturally!'

'Very well. There's a telephone out in the hall. Ring her up, ask her if it's true, and pray she'll deny it. Of course she *will* deny it. Your common sense, if you have any left, must tell you that. Which leaves you exactly where you were in the first place.'

'What's the other course?'

Sir Harvey Gilman paused in his tentative pacing behind the easy-chair. His scrawny neck seemed to emerge, like a turtle's, from the collar of the ancient dressing-gown and pyjamas. He tapped his forefinger on the back of the chair.

'You can set a trap,' he answered simply. '*You* can discover for yourself what sort of person she is. And *I* can discover just how the devil she manages to commit these murders.'

5

DICK SAT DOWN AGAIN. HE HAD MORE THAN A VAGUE IDEA of the trend this conversation was taking now.

'What sort of trap?' he demanded.

'To-morrow night,' said Sir Harvey, 'you are having dinner with the lady at her house. Is that correct?'

'Yes.'

'As a sort of celebration of your engagement? Just as Martin Belford had dinner with her a few hours before he died?'

A sensation of physical coldness crept into Dick's stomach. It was not fear: fear was too absurd an emotion to consider in relation to Lesley. But it wouldn't go away.

'Look here, sir! You don't think *I'm* going to go home afterwards, and lock myself up in a room, and be found dead next morning of prussic-acid poisoning?'

'Yes, young man. I do.'

'You expect me to kill myself?'

'That, at least, will be the effect.'

'But why? Because of something that will be said or done or suggested at this dinner?'

'Very probably. Yes.'

'*What*, for instance?'

'I don't know,' returned Sir Harvey, spreading out his hands. 'That's why I want to be there and see for myself.'

He was silent for a moment, pondering courses.

'Please observe,' he went on, 'that for the first time we're in a position to see for ourselves. Deductions will get us nowhere; Gideon Fell found that out; we must use our eyes. And there's just one other thing we can use our eyes on. Now tell me something you must have discovered about "Lesley Grant".' Again Sir Harvey pointed his finger. 'She doesn't like jewellery, does she?'

Dick reflected.

'Yes, that's true.'

'And doesn't own any? And, furthermore, never keeps large sums of money in the house?'

'No. Never.'

'We now come to something which didn't emerge fully until the death of the third victim. When she married Foster, the American lawyer, somebody installed in their bedroom a small but very efficient wall-safe. When she married Davies, the Liverpool broker, a wall-safe was installed in their house too. In each case she explained it was her husband's idea, to use for business papers. There seemed nothing suspicious about that.

'*But*,' added Sir Harvey with extraordinary intensity, 'when she was living alone, on her own, in the Avenue Foch in Paris, a similar type of safe turned up there too.'

'Meaning what?'

'She doesn't own jewellery. She doesn't keep money in the house. Then what does she want with a burglar-proof little safe? What does she keep in this safe, which is never examined until *after* the murder?'

Cloudy guesses, all unformed but all unpleasant, drifted through Dick Markham's mind.

'What do you suggest, sir?'

He tried to keep his face straight, he tried to avoid Sir Harvey's very sharp eye. Yet, as usual, this dry old devil fastened on his thoughts rather than his spoken words.

'There's a safe like that in her house now, young man. Isn't there?'

'Yes, there is. I happen to know, because the maid commented on it.' Dick hesitated. 'Lesley only laughed, and said that was where she kept her diary.'

He paused, his mind stumbling over what seemed the ugliest implication of them all.

'Her diary,' he repeated. 'But that's –!'

'Will you please face the fact,' said Sir Harvey, 'that this girl isn't normal? That the poisoner has got to confide in someone or something, and that it usually is a diary? All the same, I should expect to find something besides that. No poison, you recall, was ever traced to her. Not even a hypodermic syringe. It may be that. Or it may be…'

'Well?'

'Something even more unpleasant,' replied Sir Harvey, and his mouth had an odd expression as he stared into vacancy. 'Yes. Something even more unpleasant. Gideon Fell once said –'

There was an interruption.

'I heard at the pub to-day,' suddenly observed Dr Middlesworth, taking the still-empty pipe out of his mouth, 'that Dr Fell is spending the summer at Hastings. He's got a cottage there.'

It was as though a piece of furniture had spoken. Sir Harvey, ruffled, glanced round in some irritation. Middlesworth, continuing to draw at the empty pipe, kept meditative eyes fixed on the lamp.

'Gideon Fell near here?' said Sir Harvey, with a mood changing to one of lively satisfaction. 'Then we must have him in. Because Hadley consulted him after the Davies case, and these locked rooms utterly beat him. Whereas we, you see, shall proceed to unlock the room...'

'With my help?' Dick asked bitterly.

'Yes. With your help.'

'And what if I won't do it?'

'I think you'll do it. Miss Lesley Grant, so-called, thinks I'm in a coma and dying. So *I* can't have betrayed her. Don't you begin to follow the scheme?'

'Oh, yes. I follow it.'

'She's being a fool, of course. But she *must* play with this bright shiny wonderful toy called murder by poison. It's got her. She's obsessed. That's why she took the risk of shooting at me, and trusting to innocent eyes and general gullibility to have it called an accident. All her preparations are made for somebody's death. And she *won't* be cheated of the thrill.'

Sir Harvey tapped one finger on the edge of the writing-table.

'You, Mr Markham, will go to this dinner. You will do whatever she tells you, and accept whatever she tells you. I shall be in the next room, listening. With your assistance, we shall find out what she keeps in this famous hiding-place. And, when we do discover how a not-very clever lady has managed to beat the police of two nations...'

'*Excuse me,*' interrupted Dr Middlesworth again.

Both the others jumped a little.

But Dr Middlesworth remained casual. Getting up from the basket-chair, he walked to the nearer of the two windows.

Both were curtained in some heavy rough flowered material, now faded as well as darkened with age and tobacco-smoke. The curtains had not been quite drawn together on either window, and the nearer window was wide open. Middlesworth threw the curtains apart, so that lamplight streamed out into the front garden. Putting his head out of the window, he glanced left and right. Then he lowered the window, and stared at it for a moment – a long moment – before closing the curtains.

'Well?' demanded Sir Harvey. 'What is it?'

'Nothing,' said the doctor, and returned to his chair.

Sir Harvey studied him. 'You, Doctor,' he observed dryly, 'haven't said a great deal so far.'

'No,' agreed Middlesworth.

'What do *you* think about the whole thing?'

'Well!' said the doctor, in acute discomfort. He looked at the pipe, at his time-worn shoes, and then across at Dick. 'This thing is rotten for you. You hate thrashing it out in front of me, in front of an outsider, and I don't blame you.'

'That's all right,' said Dick. He liked the doctor, and he felt a certain reliance on that mild, intelligent judgement. 'What do you say?'

'Frankly, I don't know what to say. You can't go on with a murderess, Dick. That's only common sense. But...'

Middlesworth hesitated and tried a new tack.

'This trap of Sir Harvey's may be worth trying. I think it is. Though the girl must be really insane if she tries any funny business against you only forty-eight hours after this business with the rifle. What's more, it's going to queer the whole pitch if any news leaks out that Sir Harvey isn't badly hurt. Major Price already knows, for instance.'

Brooding, Middlesworth chewed at the stem of the pipe. Then he rose at Dick with a kind of gentle roar of reassurance.

'This whole thing may be a mistake, even though Sir Harvey and all the police in Christendom swear it isn't. There's just that possibility. But the point is, Dick… confound it, one way or the other, you've got to *know*.'

'Yes. I see that.'

Dick leaned back in the chair. He felt bruised and deflated; but he was not feeling the worst yet, for the shock had not passed off. This placid sitting-room, with its military prints and its dark oak beams and its Benares brass ornaments on the mantelpiece, seemed as unreal as the history of Lesley. He pressed his hands over his eyes, wondering how the world would look in proper focus. Sir Harvey eyed him paternally.

'Then shall we say – to-morrow evening?'

'All right. I suppose so.'

'You shall have your final instructions,' their host said with meaning, 'to-morrow morning. I have your word, I hope, that you will drop no word or hint of this to our nimble friend?'

'But suppose she *is* guilty?' said Dick, suddenly taking his hands away from his eyes and almost shouting out the words. 'Suppose by any chance she is guilty, and this trick of yours proves it. What happens then?'

'Frankly, I don't much care.'

'They're not going to arrest her. I warn you of that, even if I have to perjure myself.'

Sir Harvey raised one eyebrow. 'You would prefer to see her continue her merry course of poisoning?'

'I don't give a damn *what* she's done!'

'Suppose we leave that,' suggested the pathologist, 'until you see how you feel after the experiment? Believe me, you may have a considerable revulsion of feeling by this time to-morrow night. You may find yourself not quite as infatuated as you thought. Have I your word not to upset the apple-cart by saying anything to our friend?'

'Yes. I'll do it. In the meantime…'

'In the meantime,' interposed Dr Middlesworth, 'you're going home, and try to get some sleep. You,' he turned to Sir Harvey, 'are going to lie down. You tell me you've got some luminal with you; and you can take a quarter-grain if that back starts to hurt. I'll look in in the morning to change the dressing. For the moment, will you please sit down?'

Sir Harvey obeyed, lowering himself gingerly into the easy-chair. He also looked a little exhausted, and wiped the sleeve of his dressing-gown across his forehead.

'I shall not sleep,' he complained. 'Whatever I take, I shall not sleep. To find out the game at last… to discover how she can poison husbands and lovers, but nobody else…!'

Dick Markham, who had got up heavily and was turning towards the door, swung round again.

'Nobody else?' he repeated. 'What exactly do you mean by that?'

'My dear fellow! Why do you think *you* were chosen?'

'I still don't understand.'

'Please note,' retorted Sir Harvey, 'that each victim was a man in love with or at least violently infatuated with her. Blind. Uncritical. Unreasoning. I'm theorizing now, I confess. But you surely don't think the choice was accident or coincidence? The victim *had* to be in that state of mind.'

'Why so?'

'To do what she asked him. Naturally.'

'Half a moment,' protested a harassed Dr Middlesworth. He had picked up his hat and medicine-case from a side table, and was trying to shove Dick out through the door into the hall; but even he turned round now.

'Let's be sensible about this, Sir Harvey,' he suggested. 'You can't be thinking this girl would say, "Look, here's a hypodermic full of prussic acid. Go home and inject it into your arm, will you, just to oblige me"?'

'Not quite as crudely as that, no.'

'Then *how?*'

'We propose to find out. But if we have any clue to these sealed-room affairs, my guess is that there's the clue. It would work with an addle-headed man in a duped and bedazed state of mind. It would not work for a second with anybody else.'

'It wouldn't work, for instance, with you or me?'

'Hardly,' replied their host with dry ponderousness. 'Good night, gentlemen. Many thanks!'

And they saw him smile, his eyes now less hypnotic as at a task well accomplished, when they went out into the hall.

Some distance away over the fields to the west, the church clock at Six Ashes was striking eleven. Its notes brushed across the veil of stillness, a tangible stillness, when Dick and Dr Middlesworth left the house. Heavy constraint held them both dumb. Going ahead with an electric torch, Middlesworth indicated his car in the lane.

'Climb in,' he said. 'I'll drop you off at your place.'

The same rigidity of silence obsessed them, their eyes straight ahead on the windscreen, during that very brief ride. The wheels of the car jolted in an uneven lane; Middlesworth kept on revving the motor with unnecessary violence, and he drew up outside Dick's cottage with a squeal of brakes. While the engine breathed with a carbonized rattle, Middlesworth glanced sideways and spoke above it.

'All right?'

'Quite all right,' said Dick, opening the car-door.

'You're in for a bad night. Like a sleeping-tablet?'

'No, thanks. I've got plenty of whisky.'

'Don't get drunk.' Middlesworth's hands tightened on the steering-wheel. 'For God's sake don't get drunk.' He hesitated. 'Look here. About Lesley. I was just thinking –'

'Good night, Doctor.'

'Good night, old man.'

The car slid into gear and moved away westwards. While its tail-light disappeared between a curve of the hedgerow on one side, and the low stone boundary wall of Ashe Hall park on the other, Dick Markham stood by the gate in the fence round his own front garden. He stood there motionless for several minutes. A sheer blackness of spirits, a blackness like an extinguisher-cap, descended on him as the noise of that motor-car faded away.

Sir Harvey Gilman, he thought, had read his mind with profound clearness.

As a first consideration, he wasn't thinking about murder at all. He wasn't thinking about the men Lesley was supposed to have killed. He was thinking about the men she professed to have loved before they died.

Scattered words and phrases, sometimes whole sentences, returned to him and jostled through his head with audible vividness, as though he could hear them all at the same time.

'That little girl, as you call her, is forty-one years old.' 'Prostration and floods of tears.' 'Slightly second-hand.' 'A gross old man.' 'Their bedroom.' 'A dreadful coincidence or mistake.' 'Don't you find this situation just a *little* suspicious? Just a *little* unsavoury?'

Infantile. No doubt! Puerile. No doubt!

He tried to tell himself so. But this is how a person in love really does feel; and he loved Lesley, and therefore he raged. If those words have been deliberately chosen, each as a tiny knife to nick against the same nerve, they could not have had more of an effect.

He found himself trying to create mental pictures of these men. Burton Foster, the American lawyer, he pictured as a swaggering good-natured sort of chap with a suspicious manner which could be the more easily hoodwinked. It was not difficult to imagine Mr Davies, the 'gross old man', against the background of his 'big, florid, old-fashioned house.'

Martin Belford, the last of the three, remained more shadowy yet for some reason less disliked. Young, it appeared. Probably careless and genial. Belford didn't seem to matter so much.

If you regarded it with half an eye of reason, to stand here disliking dead men, torturing yourself with the images of persons you had never met and now never could meet, was the height of absurdity. What should matter, what did matter, what had seemed to matter most in every criminal record, was the blatant fact of a hypodermic full of poison.

'She can't help herself.' 'A psychic disease.' 'This girl isn't normal.' 'She won't be cheated of the thrill.' These were the words which should have come back to him first; and, with them, a vision of a stealthy flushed face beside a wall-safe.

Facts? Oh, yes.

He had mouthed a lot of fine words about a mistake. But in his heart of hearts Dick Markham didn't believe in a mistake. Scotland Yard didn't make mistakes like that. And yet, even so, it was the first set of Sir Harvey's phrases rather then the second which returned to jar and pierce and inflame him. If only she hadn't told him all those lies about her past life...

But she hadn't told him any lies. She hadn't told him anything at all.

Oh, Christ, why was everything so complicated!

Dick struck his hand on the top of the gate-post. The lights of his cottage were shining up there behind him, making the dew gleam on the grass under the windows, and illuminating the crazy-paved path to the front door. Even as he started to walk towards it, he was conscious of a sense of loneliness – intense, unpleasant loneliness – as though something had been cut away from him. It startled him, because he had thought he liked loneliness. And now he was afraid of it. The cottage seemed a hollow shell, booming as he closed the front door behind him. He walked down the passage to the study, opened the door, and stopped short.

On the sofa in the study sat Lesley.

6

S HE HAD BEEN ABSENTMINDEDLY TURNING OVER THE PAGES OF a magazine, and looked up quickly as the door opened.

A fat-bowled lamp on the table behind the sofa brought out the smoothness of Lesley's clear skin as she raised her eyes. It shone on the soft brown hair, curling outwards at the shoulders. She had changed her white frock for one of dark green, with winking buttons. '*Cette belle anglaise, très chic, très distinguée.*' Not a line showed in the smooth flesh of the neck. Her wide-open, innocent brown eyes looked frightened.

Neither of them spoke for a moment. Perhaps Lesley noticed the expression on his face.

She threw aside the magazine, got up, and ran towards him.

He kissed her – after a fashion.

'Dick,' Lesley said quietly. 'What's wrong?'

'Wrong?'

She stood back at arm's length to study him. The candid eyes went over his face searchingly.

'You've – gone away,' she said, and shook him by the arms. 'You're not there any longer. What is it?' Then, quickly: 'Is it this fortune-teller? Sir – Sir Harvey Gilman? How is he?'

'He's as well as can be expected.'

'That means he's going to die, doesn't it?' asked Lesley. Enlightenment seemed to come to her. 'Dick, listen! Is that why you're looking and acting like this?' Then she regarded him with horror. 'You don't think I did that *deliberately*, do you?'

'No, of course not!'

('So help me,' he swore to himself, 'I will not drop a single hint! No incautious word, no blurted question that would give the show away!' The whole thing was full of pitfalls. His own voice sounded hollow and hypocritical and false, at least to his own ears. Patting her arm, he raised his eyes to the wall beside the fireplace; and the first thing he saw was the yellow broadsheet of one of his own plays, called *Poisoner's Mistake*.)

'Do you?' persisted Lesley.

'My dear girl! Shoot at him deliberately? You'd never even met the old boy before, had you?'

'Never!' A film of tears came over her eyes. 'I – I didn't so much as hear his name, until afterwards. Somebody told me.'

He attempted a laugh.

'Then there's nothing to worry about, surely? Just forget it. By the way, what *had* he been saying to you?'

Dick hadn't meant to ask this. He had sworn an oath to himself; he could have yelled with exasperation when the words slipped out. Some uncontrollable impulse pushed him and seized him and swept him along in spite of himself.

'But I told you!' replied Lesley. 'The usual thing about a happy life, and a little illness, and a letter arriving with some pleasant news – You do believe me?'

'Of course.'

She moved back towards the sofa, and he followed. He would have liked to sit opposite her, to study her under the light, to get away from the disturbing nearness of her physical presence. But her eyes expected him to sit down beside her, and he did so.

Lesley stared at the carpet. Her hair fell a little forward, hiding the line of her cheek.

'If he does die, Dick, what will they do to me?'

'Nothing at all. It was an accident.'

'I mean… will the police come and see me, or anything like that?'

The room was absolutely silent.

Dick stretched out his hand for the cigarette-box on the table behind the sofa. A pulse shook in his arm, and he wondered if he could keep the hand from shaking. They seemed poised in an unreal void, of books and pictures and lamplight.

'There'll have to be an inquest, I'm afraid.'

'You mean it'll be in the papers? Shall I have to give my name?'

'It's only a formality, Lesley – And why not?'

'No reason! Only…' She peered round at him; evidently frightened, yet with a smile of wry wistfulness. 'Only, you see, all I know about such things is what you've taught me.'

'What *I've* taught you?'

She nodded towards the ranks of books, riddled with their curious criminal histories like worms in apples, and at the garish pictures and playbills which had seemed such excellent fun when you dealt with crime on paper.

'You're awfully interested in such things.' She smiled. 'I hate death, but I think I'm interested too. It is fascinating, in a way. Hundreds of people, all with funny thoughts locked up inside them…' Then Lesley said a surprising thing. 'I want to be respectable!' she cried out suddenly. 'I do so want to be respectable!'

He essayed a light tone.

'And can't you manage to be respectable?'

'Darling, please don't joke! And then I get involved in this dreadful mess, through no fault of my own.' Again she turned round, with such a yearning of appeal that it destroyed his power to reason. 'But it won't spoil *our* celebration, will it?'

'You mean – to-morrow night?'

'Yes. Our dinner together.'

'Nothing could keep me away. Will there be any other guests?' She stared at him.

'You don't *want* any other guests, do you? – Dick, what's wrong? Why are you going away from me? In another minute, you know, I shall be getting funny ideas myself.'

'There's nothing wrong! I only…'

'I want everything to be perfect for us! Everything! And especially (am I being sentimental?) I want everything to be perfect to-morrow. Because I've got something to tell you. And I've got something to show you.'

'Oh? What have you got to tell me?'

He had taken a cigarette from the box and lighted it. And as he asked this question, the knocker out on the front door began to rap sharply. Lesley uttered an exclamation and sat back.

Dick hardly knew whether to be glad or sorry for the interruption. Probably glad, since the emotional temperature was going up again and for the life of him he could not look away from Lesley's eyes. He could relax, for a moment at least, the fever of concentration on giving nothing away. So he hurried out to the front door, opened it, and blinked in surprise at the visitor who was shifting from one foot to the other on the doormat.

'Er – good evening,' said the visitor. 'Sorry to trouble you at this time of night.'

'Not at all, sir. Come in.'

Down by the gate stood a dilapidated Ford, its engine throbbing. The visitor made a sign with his hand to someone inside the Ford, who switched off the motor. Then he entered with an air of some diffidence.

George Converse, Baron Ashe, was the only peer of the realm in Dick's acquaintance. Having frequently met such persons in fiction, however – where they are always haughtily aristocratic, or languidly epigrammatic, or dodderingly futile – Dick found Lord Ashe something of a surprise.

He was a middle-sized wiry man in his early sixties, with iron-grey hair and a pinkish complexion, but a scholarly preoccupied face. You seldom saw him. He was supposed to be compiling an interminable history of his family. His clothes had always a vaguely shabby look, not surprising when you considered his taxes and his chronic state of being hard up. But he could be good company when he chose, or when he did not seem to run down like a clock.

And, as he followed Dick down the passage, Dick was thinking of certain words which Cynthia Drew had used in that very cottage earlier this evening. 'Why does Lord Ashe always look so oddly at poor Lesley, on the few occasions when he *has* seen her?'

For Lord Ashe stopped abruptly on the threshold of the study, and he was looking oddly at Lesley now.

Lesley jumped to her feet.

'H'm, yes,' muttered the visitor. 'Yes, yes, yes!' Then he roused himself, with a courteous bow and smile. 'Miss Grant, isn't it? I – er – thought…' Evidently at a loss, he turned to Dick. 'My dear boy, there's the very devil to pay.'

'About what?' cried Lesley.

'It's perfectly all right, Miss Grant!' Lord Ashe assured her soothingly. 'On my word of honour, there is nothing to worry about. But I *am* rather glad to find you. I – er – didn't expect to find you here.'

'I – I only dropped in!'

'Yes, yes. Of course.' Again he turned to Dick. 'I've just been down to –' He nodded towards the other cottage. 'I thought it was my duty to go.' Lord Ashe did not seem to relish this duty. 'But the place is all dark, and nobody answered when I knocked.'

'That's all right. Sir Harvey's settled in for the night.'

Lord Ashe looked surprised.

'But isn't the doctor there? Or a trained nurse?'

'No. Dr Middlesworth didn't think it was necessary.'

'But, my dear boy! Is that wise? Still, I suppose Middlesworth knows his business. How is the patient? I – er – I suppose everybody's been bothering you with that question all evening, but I felt I ought to come in and ask.'

'The patient,' said Dick, 'is as well as can be expected. What's this about there being the devil to pay?'

'Somebody's stolen a rifle,' answered Lord Ashe.

There was a silence.

An evil silence, suggesting a design completed. Taking a spectacle-case from the pocket of his loose tweed coat, Lord Ashe extracted a rimless pince-nez and fitted the pince-nez into place on his nose.

'Please tell me, Miss – er – Grant. After the regrettable accident this afternoon, when the rifle went off by accident, do you happen to remember what you did with that rifle?'

Lesley regarded him wide-eyed.

'I gave it back to Major Price. Anyone can tell you that.'

'Yes. Exactly. So everyone agrees. But you don't by any chance recall what happened to the rifle *after* you gave it to Major Price?'

Lesley shook her head and shivered.

'Major Price,' she replied, 'was collecting up the guns when the storm broke. He had them all in a line on the counter of the shooting-range. After that ghastly thing happened, I – I just threw the rifle at him. I think he put it with the others on the counter. But I'm not sure. I was horribly upset. I asked Dick here to take me home.'

'H'm, yes. Do you happen to remember, my boy?'

Dick tried to focus his mind on that scene of rain and confusion and blowing tents, which seemed so long ago as to be part of another age.

'Yes, that's what happened,' he agreed. 'When Sir Harvey collapsed, I stuck my head out of the tent and called to Major Price and Dr Middlesworth.'

'And then?'

'Bill Earnshaw – that's the bank-manager, you know,' Dick explained, with a hazy notion that Lord Ashe lived so remote from village-life as not to recognize this name – 'Bill Earnshaw had just come up. Major Price asked Bill to mind the rifles while the major and Dr Middlesworth carried Sir Harvey to the doctor's car. That's all I can tell you.'

'Exactly,' said Lord Ashe.

'Then what's wrong, sir?'

'Major Price, you see, says that nobody abstracted a rifle while *he* was there. Mr Earnshaw declares that nobody abstracted a rifle while *he* was there. Yet the rifle is gone.'

Lesley hesitated. 'It wasn't the same rifle as I...?'

'Yes.'

On the third finger of Lord Ashe's left hand was a small seal ring, dullish and unobtrusive. Dick noticed it as the other lifted a hand to his pince-nez. So did Lesley, who seemed to have grown more flustered than ever since their visitor's entrance. Lord Ashe now played his celebrated trick of running down and trailing off like a gramophone.

'Er – I daresay it's of no importance,' he said at length. The needle had caught its groove; the record revolved again. 'But Major Price and Mr Earnshaw were rather heated about it. I believe the major played some stupid joke on Mr Earnshaw at the shooting-range this afternoon, and suspected Mr Earnshaw of trying – as they say – to get level.

'But it's extraordinary. Most extraordinary! Especially when you consider all the rumours that are going about.'

'What rumours?' asked Lesley. She clenched her hands. 'Please tell me! Are they saying things about me?'

'My dear young lady! Good heavens! No! But I have even heard, for instance, that Sir Harvey Gilman is not seriously hurt. Let us hope so. My grand-uncle Stephen, in the South African War, received a very dangerous bullet-wound and yet survived. He was alive then, of course. That is to say, the incident occurred during his lifetime. My dear boy, I shall not intrude on you any longer. Er – have you transportation, Miss Grant?'

'Transportation?'

'To go home,' explained Lord Ashe.

'No. I – I walked.'

'Then may I offer you a lift? I have the Ford outside, and Perkins is a careful driver.'

'Thank you, Lord Ashe. I suppose I'd better go.'

Her eyes begged Dick Markham to suggest an excuse for her to stay and talk a little longer. There was almost a hysteria in her manner, silently asking for that word. And he would not give the word.

If she stayed for five minutes longer, he knew, he would blurt out the whole story. Under the sanity and placidness of Lord Ashe's presence, values were shifting and sinking back to normal. For a second he had forgotten, or nearly forgotten, the situation as it existed. Then, with a shock, it was back again. He realized very clearly that he loved Lesley, and would continue to love her. He was fed up; he couldn't stand any more.

So they left him, and it tore at his heart to watch Lesley's face. They were no sooner outside than he wanted to call out, 'Come back! This isn't true! Let me tell you about it!'

But the Ford moved away.

His cigarette had gone out. He threw it away into the damp grass of the front garden, standing at the door under the high incurious stars. Then he turned back into the cottage.

He went into the little dining-room, from which he fetched a glass, a syphon, and a bottle of whisky. He took these into the study, and put them down on the typewriter-desk. But his head swam inexplicably. He was tired, dizzily tired, so that it seemed an exertion out of all proportion to remove a metal bottle-cap or press the handle of a soda-syphon.

So he went over and lay down on his back on the sofa.

'I'll just close my eyes for a moment,' he said. 'The lights being on will keep me awake. Anyway, I don't want to sleep. I'll just close my eyes for a moment. Then I'll get up and pour myself a drink.'

The calm lamplight lay on his eyes. The diamond-paned windows, looking out over the side-garden to the east, had been set open like little doors; their catches rattled to a night-wind that made a frothing of leaves outside. Presently the distant church-clock struck midnight, but he did not hear it.

If anybody had peered in through the window – and it is now certain that, in the thin dwindling hours, a certain face did peer in – this person would have seen a light-haired young man, with a strong jaw but far too much imaginative development in the forehead, lying on a rucked-up sofa in grey flannels and an untidy sports-coat, and muttering white-faced in his sleep.

His dreams were horrible. He does not now remember what they were: perhaps because of the sequel. To Dick Markham those hours, when he did not 'go' to sleep but was knocked out by it, remain only as a blank black severance from the real world until something pierced through it. Something clamoured and called with an intensity of shrillness...

Dick started to half-wakefulness, rolled, and saved himself from tumbling off to the floor.

He had it now.

The telephone was ringing.

Dazed-eyed, cramped about the back and waist, he struggled to sit upright. His first thought was that he had wormed out of a very unpleasant dream, something about Lesley Grant poisoning husbands; but, thank God, that was all over now. His next thought was surprise to find himself here on the sofa; and the lights burning; and the eastern windows tinged a pinkish-blue colour – ethereal, making the glass luminous – from the rising sun.

All this time the telephone kept ringing. He got up, on cramped leg-muscles, and stumbled across to the typewriter-desk. Though he was still only half awake when he picked up the receiver, the whispering voice which breathed out of the phone recalled him with its urgency.

'Colonel Pope's cottage,' said that thin voice. 'Come at once. If you don't come at once, you'll be too late.'

The line went dead.

And Dick Markham remembered everything.

7

'WHO'S SPEAKING?' HE SAID. 'WHO'S...?'

But there was no response. It had been a mere whisper of a voice, unidentifiable.

Putting down the receiver, Dick pressed his hands against his eyes and shook his head violently to clear it. The ghostly light outside the windows, its bluish tinge fading, washed this room with indeterminate colour. His wrist-watch had stopped, but the time must be past five o'clock.

There was not even time to think, now. He hurried out of the cottage, feeling grimy and unshaven as he emerged into the hush and dimness of morning, and ran eastwards along the lane as hard as he could run.

All sounds acquired a new sharpness in this dead world. The twitter of a bird, a rustle in the grass, the thud of his own running footfalls in a dirt lane, rose as clearly to the ear as the clean freshness of dew rose to the nostrils. He had passed the untenanted house, and was just within sight of Sir Harvey Gilman's cottage beyond, when he saw that something was happening there.

A light went on in the sitting-room.

Ahead of him it was still dusky. On his left, parallel with the lane, began the thick coppice of birches which pressed up along the stone boundary wall. On his right, some hundred odd yards ahead, stood the cottage. There was no obstruction in front of it: he could dimly see the whitewashed stone, and the black beams, and the low-pitched shingled roof, set back from the road in its front garden.

But beside and beyond it, also eastwards and parallel with the lane, stretched the thick orchard of fruit-trees which formed a kind of tunnel with the birch-copse opposite. That tunnel was the narrow lane. Through it poured narrowly the pinkish light, now tinged with watery yellow, of the rising sun.

It penetrated only there, leaving the sides of the road in shadow. Glints of it were caught and held in thick foliage. But it paled the glow of thin electric light which had been switched on inside two windows – ground-floor windows, now uncurtained – of Sir Harvey Gilman's cottage.

The sitting-room, not a doubt of it.

The sitting-room, where he had been talking to the old boy last night, with its windows facing the lane.

Dick Markham stopped short, his heart thudding and the queasiness of an empty stomach taking hold at early morning.

He did not quite know he was running so hard, or what he expected to find. Apparently Sir Harvey was up early, since he had already drawn back the curtains and switched on the light. Dick walked forward slowly in that eerie dusk, facing the tunnel of sunlight which fell at his feet, and repeated to himself that he did not know. But, when he was less than thirty yards from the cottage, at last he knew.

A slight rasping noise, as of metal against stone, made him turn his eyes to the left, along the boundary wall of Ashe Hall Park.

Somebody, hidden from sight behind that low stone wall, was running out a rifle. Somebody was steadying the barrel of the rifle on top of the wall; somebody was aiming, with carefully drawn sights, at one of the lighted windows in the cottage opposite.

'Hoy!' yelled Dick Markham.

But it went unheard when somebody fired a shot.

The report of the rifle cracked out with inhuman loudness, sending birds whirring up from the trees. Dick's long eyesight caught the star of the bullet-hole in window-glass. Then the rifle vanished. Somebody was running, thrashing, perhaps even laughing, in the birch-coppice among the dense twilight trees. Echoes settled back to disturbed chirpings; the marksman had gone.

For perhaps ten seconds Dick stood there motionless.

He did not run now, since he believed with horrible certainty that he knew what had happened. To chase any marksman in that dense coppice – even if you wanted to chase the marksman – would be hopeless.

The edge of the sun showed itself, a tip of fiery white-gold behind the dark screen of trees, with only the little lane between. The light shone straight along that lane into Dick's eyes. Some third person, who must also have heard the shot, appeared in the lane from the easterly direction.

Though the sunlight was still not bright, that figure remained for a few moments a silhouette, hurrying towards Dick.

'What is it? Who's there?' the figure called.

He recognized the voice of Cynthia Drew, and he ran forward even as she ran to meet him. They met just outside the front garden of Sir Harvey's cottage. Cynthia, wearing the same pinkish-coloured jumper and brown skirt she had worn the night before, stopped short and stared at him in astonishment.

'Dick! *What is it?*'

'It's trouble, I'm afraid.'

'But what on earth are you doing here?'

'If it comes to that, Cynthia, what are *you* doing here?'

She made a gesture. 'I couldn't sleep. I went for a walk.' Cynthia, slim yet very sturdy, should have been the last girl in the world to be called fanciful or imaginative. But she saw his expression, and her hands moved up and pressed against her breast. The sun behind her turned the edges of her hair to clear gold. 'Dick! Was what we heard...?'

'Yes. I think so.'

Until this moment, until he had come fully in front of the cottage, he would not turn fully round to the right and look at it. But he did so now, seeing what he expected to see.

Set some thirty feet back from the road in an unkempt front garden, the cottage had a longish frontage. But it was a little low doll's house of a place, with little dormer windows projecting from the slope of the dark-shingled roof to form an upper floor. Its white-washed stone front and crooked black beams lay shadowed by the fruit-orchard eastwards. On the ground floor, the two illuminated windows – just to the left of the front door – showed what was inside.

Last night, Dick remembered, Sir Harvey Gilman had been sitting in an easy-chair beside the big writing-table in the middle of the room. Now the easy-chair had been moved round to face the table, as though someone were sitting there to write. Someone *was* sitting there; even the dwarfed view through the window showed it to be Sir Harvey; but he was not writing.

The hanging lamp in its tan-coloured shade shed light down across the pathologist's bald head. His chin was sunk forward on his chest. His arms lay quietly along the arms of the chair. You might have thought him dozing, a figure of peace, if you had not noticed the light on the whitish-edged, clean-drilled bullet-hole through window-glass – and seen that this bullet-hole was just in line with the bald skull.

Dick felt a physical sickness rising in his throat. But he conquered this. Cynthia, very steady and composed, followed the direction of his glance; her teeth fastened in her lower lip.

'That's the second time,' Dick said. 'Yesterday I saw the bullet-hole jump up in the wall of the tent. To-day I saw it jump up in the window. But it doesn't get any easier. I think... Just a minute!'

He swung round to look at the stone boundary wall, opposite those windows, with the screen of birch-trees rising dark above it. In three strides he crossed the strip of coarse grass separating the wall from the lane, and peered into the semi-gloom beyond the wall. Something had been thrown down under the trees there, left behind when the marksman fled.

Vaulting over the wall, completely disregarding any question of fingerprints, Dick picked up this object. It was a .22 calibre slide-action repeating rifle: a Winchester 61. He could not doubt it was the same one he expected to find.

After Lesley Grant had given back this rifle to Major Price yesterday afternoon, the rifle had been stolen from the shooting-gallery. That was what Lord Ashe had said.

'Don't!' cried Cynthia Drew.

'Don't what?'

'Don't look like that!'

But Dick's expression was not consternation. It was one of crazy triumph. For, whoever might have stolen that rifle, it could not possibly have been Lesley Grant.

He, Dick Markham, had been with her all the time after the 'accident'; he had taken her home; he had remained with her for several hours. And she had not taken the rifle. Not only was he prepared to swear to this: he knew it to be the simple truth.

Dropping the rifle on the ground again, Dick vaulted back over the wall. Lesley, at least, couldn't have done *this*. He hardly saw or heard Cynthia, who was saying something he did not afterwards remember. Instead he set off at a run towards Sir Harvey's cottage.

No fence enclosed the front garden. Unkempt grass dragged at your shoes like wires as you crossed it. It was going to be a hot day, too; the earth breathed up moist warmth, dissolving dew-cobwebs; a wasp circled up out of the fruit-orchard; the front of the cottage itself exhaled an odour of old wood and stone. Dick approached the window with the bullet-hole – it was the right-hand one as you faced the house – and flattened his face against the grimy glass.

Then, cupping his hands round his eyes, he stared again.

Under dusty lamplight, contrasting with broadening day, the figure of the little pathologist sat motionless in front of the big table. You saw his face in profile, its chin-muscles sagging and the eyes partly open. That he was looking at a dead man Dick Markham did not doubt. But there was something wrong here, something very wrong…

'Dick,' breathed Cynthia's voice at his elbow. *'That bullet didn't hit him.'*

It was true.

In the back wall of the room, facing them as they looked through the window, was the brick fireplace with its overmantel ornaments of Benares brass. Above this hung a big coloured print depicting some phase of the battle of Waterloo. The rifle-bullet had drilled through the window, passed close to the top of Sir Harvey's head, and shattered the lower edge of the picture – which now hung askew – before burying itself in the wall. But it had not touched him.

There had been urgency in Cynthia's voice, and bewilderment, and something like relief. Dick turned to stare at her.

'Then what the devil's the matter with the fellow?'

'I don't know.'

'Sir Harvey!' yelled Dick, putting his mouth close against the window. 'Sir Harvey Gilman!'

There was no reply.

Dick glanced from one window to the other. He inspected the first, then the second. Since the cottage was built rather low against the ground, the lower sills of the windows were not much above the level of his waist. They were ordinary sash-windows, fastening with metal catches on the inside. By putting one knee on the outer sill, and hauling himself up with a hand on the frame at each side, Dick was able to see through the glass that both windows were locked on the inside.

A very ugly notion began to creep through his mind now.

'Wait here a minute,' he said to Cynthia.

Hurrying to the front door, he found it unlocked and only partly on the latch above two stone steps. He threw it open, and found himself in the small modern-looking hall he remembered from last night.

On his left, he also remembered, was the door leading into the sitting-room. If he opened this door now, it would bring him into the sitting-room at a point behind the back of the motionless figure seated at the table. But he was not able to open this door, though he wrenched with violent hands at the knob. It was fastened on the inside.

He tore out into the front garden again, where Cynthia was still staring through the window.

'You know,' she declared, 'there's something awfully queer about him. His face seems a funny colour. Bluish? Or is that the effect of the light? And there's something about his mouth: is it froth? And… Dick! what on earth are you doing?'

With a hazy idea that the bullet-hole might be required as evidence, Dick did not touch that right-hand window. Instead he went to the other window. From the unkempt grass of the garden he picked up half a brick, and flung it at the window with a crash that brought glass rattling down in shards.

From that stuffy room, very distinct in morning air, stirred a breath which drifted out of the window with a small but perceptible odour of bitter almonds. It came at their faces in a wave. Cynthia, beside him, put a hand on his arm.

'It – it smells like finger-nail varnish,' she said. 'What is it?'

'Prussic acid.'

Reaching inside the shattered window, Dick put up his hand, unlocked the catch of the window, and pushed it up. Then he hauled himself up across the sill and dropped into the room amid crunching glass.

The bitter-almonds odour was more distinct now. It required some effort to go close and touch that body, but Dick did it. The man he knew as Sir Harvey Gilman had been dead for only a few minutes, since the body was still almost at blood-heat. It was still dressed in pyjamas and dressing-gown; the velours-covered easy-chair supported it upright except for the lolling head, and gave an appearance of ease to the arms along the arms of the chair. But the cyanosis and froth of prussic-acid poisoning, the half-open eye, showed, with hideous plainness when you went closer.

Dick glanced across at the door leading to the hall.

Frantically he went over and inspected it. The key was turned in the lock, and a small tight-fitting bolt was solidly pushed fast on the inside.

Of the two windows which constituted the only other entrance, one window now had its lower glass shattered, and the other bore a bullet-stamp a few inches below the joining of the sashes. But there could be no doubt – Dick himself could swear, however much the police might disbelieve him – that both windows had been locked on the inside too.

'So,' Dick remarked aloud, 'he said it couldn't possibly happen to *him?*'

It was only then that he noticed something else.

The light of the hanging lamp caught a faint gleam near the floor beside the easy-chair: a smallish hypodermic syringe, with slender glass barrel and nickelled plunger. It had dropped beside the chair, sticking point upwards in the carpet, as though it had fallen there from the dead man's relaxing fingers. It set the seal of finality on this wicked scene, while the odour of hydrocyanic acid seemed to grow even more overpowering in a stuffy room, and daylight broadened fully outside the windows.

Another suicide.

8

D ICK WAS STILL STANDING BY THE DOOR, TRYING TO ARRANGE
thoughts that would not cohere, when he heard a scrap-
ing noise at the window. Cynthia with supple agility had swung
herself through, and landed on her feet lightly, like a cat, amid
broken glass.

Her face was composed but concerned – concerned, you would
have said, more for Dick Markham than for the shrivelled figure
in the chair.

'This is dreadful!' she said, and then, as though conscious of
the weakness of these words, added, 'Simply dreadful!' in a flat
positive tone before going on: 'You said prussic acid, Dick. Prussic
acid's a poison, isn't it?'

'Yes. Very much so.'

Cynthia cast a glance of repulsion at the chair.

'But what on earth happened to the poor man?'

'Come here,' requested Dick. 'Er – are you all right?'

'Oh, dear, yes. Perfectly all right.' It would take more than this
to upset Cynthia. She went on with vehemence: 'But it *is* horrible
and ghastly and everything else! You mean someone gave him
some poison?'

'No. Look here!'

As she circled round the writing-table, he pointed to the hypodermic needle stuck point upright in the floor. Then – which
required more steeling of the nerves – he leaned across the body

and lifted the left arm from the elbow. Its loose dressing-gown and pyjama sleeves fell away, exposing a thin hickory-like arm streaked with blue congested veins. The injection with the hypodermic had been clumsily made: you could see the tiny fleck of dried blood against the forearm.

'Dick! Wait! Ought you to be doing that?'

'Doing what?'

'Breaking windows, and touching things, and all the rest of it? In those books you've loaned me... heaven knows some of them are difficult to understand; nasty people!... but they always say you must leave everything as it is. Isn't that right?'

'Oh, yes,' he said grimly. 'I'm going to catch the devil for doing this. But we've got to *know!*'

The blue eyes studied him.

'Dick Markham, you look absolutely frightful. Didn't you go to bed at all last night?'

'Never mind that now!'

'But I do mind it. You never get any proper rest, especially when you're working. And there's something on your mind that's worrying you. I could tell that last night.'

'Cynthia, will you *please* look at this?'

'I am looking at it,' answered Cynthia, though she looked away instead, and clenched her hands.

'This is suicide,' he explained, impressing it on her by fashioning the words with careful violence. 'He took a hypodermic full of hydrocyanic acid – there it is! – and injected it into his left arm. You yourself can testify,' he swept his arm round, 'that this room is locked up on the inside? So that proves (don't you see) that nobody tried to kill him?'

'But, Dick! Somebody did try to kill him! Somebody shot at him with a rifle!'

'The bullet didn't hit him, did it?'

'No,' returned Cynthia, 'but that jolly well wasn't for want of trying!' Her breast rose and fell. She added: 'Is it about Lesley?'

Dick swung round.

'Is what about Lesley?'

'This thing that's worrying you,' said Cynthia with simple feminine directness.

'Why should you think it's about Lesley?'

'What else could it be?' inquired Cynthia. She did not stop to explain the logic of this remark, but went on: 'That horrid little man,' and she pointed to the figure in the chair, 'has been upsetting everything and everybody at Six Ashes. First there was the accident with the rifle yesterday afternoon. Of course it *was* an accident' – briefly, the blue eyes seemed to ponder – 'but it does seem queer that somebody deliberately tried to shoot him this morning. And, on top of that, you say he poisoned himself with what's-its-name acid!'

'There's your evidence, Cynthia.'

She spoke abruptly. 'Dick, it just isn't good enough.'

'How do you mean, isn't good enough?'

'I don't know! That's just the point. But – did you hear about the row between Major Price and Mr Earnshaw, late last night? Over somebody stealing the rifle?'

'Yes. Lord Ashe told me.'

Again Cynthia pointed to the figure in the chair.

'Dick, what did he tell you about Lesley?'

'Nothing! Why in God's name do you think he said anything about Lesley?'

'He was reading things in the crystal about everybody else. I bet he read something about Lesley, and that's what's worrying you.'

Hitherto Dick had always considered Cynthia as a good fellow but not exactly as a model of intelligence. To avert this danger-point now, he laughed until it seemed to him that the military prints round the walls rattled in their frames.

'If there is anything,' insisted Cynthia, with a sort of coaxing motherliness, 'tell me. Do tell me!'

'Look here! You don't think Lesley had anything to do with this?'

'But why ever should I think that?' asked Cynthia, with her eye on a corner of the carpet. Faint colour tinged her face. 'Only... it's all so *queer*! Hadn't we better report this to the police? Or do something about it?'

'Yes. I suppose so. What time is it?'

Cynthia consulted a wrist-watch.

'Twenty minutes past five. Why?'

Dick walked round to the front of the desk. The motionless figure, one eye partly open, surveyed him with so sardonically lifelike an expression that this dead man might have been laughing in hell.

'I've got to phone Bert Miller, of course.'

Miller was the local constable, and it should take him no great time to get here. Though Gallows Lane technically ended in open fields a few hundred yards eastwards – a gallows *had* stood there in the eighteenth century; Dick's stomach turned over at the thought – still there was a path over the fields to Goblin Wood. Bert Miller lived near there.

'But the person I must get on to,' he insisted, 'is Dr Middlesworth.'

'Why Dr Middlesworth?'

'Because he's heard about the other cases! And we've got to decide –'

'What other cases, Dick?'

As near a slip, as near a betrayal, as made no difference! Dick pulled himself together.

'I mean, criminal cases in general!'

'But you said this wasn't a criminal case,' pointed out Cynthia, who was watching him fixedly and seemed to be breathing faster. 'You said he killed himself. Why do you say something different now?'

That he did not answer this question was due less to being concerned than to the fact that his attention was caught by something else, which added a touch of the grotesque to the dead man's expression. Again he went forward to inspect the body, this time from the opposite side.

On the carpet at the side of the chair, this time as though fallen from the victim's left hand, lay a spilled box of drawing-pins.

A little cardboard box, with drawing-pins or thumbtacks spilled on the carpet. Hypodermic syringe near the right hand, drawing-pins near the left. It made the wits whirl even more, with its neat arrangement. Dick picked up one of the drawing-pins, pressing its sharp point against his thumb and noting in an idle sort of way that it would have made much the same sort of puncture in a human arm as (say) a clumsily administered hypodermic...

'Dick!' cried Cynthia.

He scrambled hastily up off his knees.

'Telephone,' he said, to forestall the torrent of questions he saw in her eyes. 'Excuse me.'

The telephone, he remembered, was out in the hall. He unlocked and unbolted the door, observing both the weight of the lock and the small tight-fitting closeness of the bolt.

Talking to Middlesworth, he thought, was going to be infernally difficult with Cynthia in the next room. The ringing-tone buzzed interminably, before it was answered by the unmistakable bedside voice of a woman just roused from sleep.

'Sorry to trouble you at this hour, Mrs Middlesworth! But –'

'The doctor's not in,' said the voice, controlling itself. 'He's up at the Hall.'

'At the Hall?'

'At Ashe Hall. One of the maids was taken badly in the night, and Lady Ashe was worried. Isn't that Mr Markham speaking?'

'Yes, Mrs Middlesworth.'

'Can I take a message, Mr Markham? Are you ill?'

'No, no! Nothing like that! But it's rather urgent.'

'Indeed. I am sorry he's not here,' murmured the voice, with restrained suspicious pleasantness. A G.P.'s wife learns how to manage this. 'If it's urgent you could ring him there. Or walk across the park and see him. Good-bye.'

Walk across the park and see him.

That would be better yet, Dick decided. If he cut through the coppice and up over South Field, he could reach Ashe Hall in two minutes. He hurried back to the sitting-room, where he found Cynthia biting uncertainly at her pink under-lip. He took her hands, though she seemed reluctant to extend them, and pressed them firmly.

'Listen, Cynthia. I've got to go up to the Hall; Middlesworth is there now. I don't mean to be gone longer than ten minutes. In the meantime, will you ring Bert Miller and then stand guard? Just tell Bert that Sir Harvey Gilman has committed suicide, and that he needn't hurry in getting here.'

'But –!'

'The old boy did commit suicide, you know.'

'Are you going to trust me, Dick? Tell me about it later, I mean?'

'Yes, Cynthia. I will.'

It was good to have somebody he could trust, to have Cynthia's straightforwardness and practicality in the mists of nightmare. He pressed her hands again, though she would not look at him. Afterwards – when he left the house – crossed the lane, made his way through the dark birch-coppice and up over the green slope of South Field to Ashe Hall – the image of a very different girl went with him.

Let's face the ugly fact, now. If Lesley *had* done this…

'But surely,' argued his common sense, 'Lesley wouldn't have killed Sir Harvey Gilman just to keep him from betraying her identity to the people of Six Ashes?'

'Why not?' inquired a horned and devilish doubt.

'Because,' said common sense, 'it will only bring in the police, and betray her identity in any case.'

'Not necessarily,' returned the doubt, 'if it is handled by the local authorities and treated as a featureless suicide.'

'But Sir Harvey Gilman is a well-known figure,' common sense insisted. 'This will be in the papers. It will probably meet the attention of someone at Scotland Yard.'

The doubt took on a kind of evil laughter.

'You yourself,' it said, 'are a rather well-known young playwright. Your suicide would be in the papers. Yet Sir Harvey himself never doubted that this angel-faced lady might well be arranging to poison *you!*'

Here the doubt fastened deeply: it took on claws, tight-holding, as it grew in Dick Markham's imagination.

'Sir Harvey,' it said, 'obviously hated Lesley Grant. He was pursuing her if any man ever pursued her. He nearly betrayed her yesterday afternoon, when she did try to shoot him. Her attitude towards him would hardly have been one of sweetness and light. If a poisoner's character does hide in that pretty body, she would have been just in the mood to strike back at him – with an undetectable method of poisoning.'

But that was where you came up with a bump against the final bewilderment. Sir Harvey Gilman certainly hadn't killed himself; and, the one man of all men to be on his guard, he couldn't have been gulled by any trick into injecting a hypodermic into his own arm. This you could swear to. Yet, on the other hand, it was absolutely impossible for anybody to have murdered him.

Dick walked blindly up the slopes of South Field.

Ahead of him now he could see the south wing of Ashe Hall, its ancient bricks showing dark in the polished morning air. Though no smoke went up yet from its kitchen chimneys, all the visible doors stood wide open.

And the first person Dick saw was Lord Ashe, coming round the side of the house – in his usual corduroys and ancient coat, wearing gardening gloves and with a pair of rose-tree shears in his right hand. He stopped short as he caught sight of Dick, waiting for him to come up.

'Er – good morning,' said Lord Ashe in a puzzled tone.

'Good morning, sir. *You're* up early.'

'I'm always up at this time,' said Lord Ashe.

Dick's gaze strayed along the south wing of the Hall.

'Don't you ever lock any doors or windows here, sir?'

Lord Ashe laughed.

'My dear boy,' he answered, making a slight gesture with the shears and pressing the pince-nez more firmly on his nose, 'there's nothing to steal. The pictures are all copies. My elder brother Frank presented the family jewels to a celebrated – er – lady of easy virtue years ago. There's the plate, of course, what there is left of it; but you'd want a lorry to take that away.'

Here he pondered, setting his pince-nez more firmly and looking curiously at his companion.

'If you'll excuse my mentioning it, Mr Markham, *you* have rather a wild and tousled look. Is anything wrong?'

Dick let him have it straight. He wanted the reaction of this solid man, with his soft voice and his ruddy complexion and his iron-grey hair, to a situation that would presently have Six Ashes by the ears.

'Sir Harvey Gilman has committed suicide.'

Lord Ashe stared back at him.

'Good God!'

'Exactly!'

'But this' – Lord Ashe looked round for a place to put down the shears, and, finding none, kept them in his hands, '– this is fantastic!'

'I know.'

'Come to think of it,' muttered Lord Ashe, 'I did fancy I heard a shot in the middle of the night. Or was it later? Was it –?' He stared at memory.

'Sir Harvey didn't shoot himself. He took a hypodermic, apparently containing prussic acid, and injected it into his arm. Cynthia Drew and I found him not half an hour ago.'

'Prussic acid,' repeated Lord Ashe. 'We used to use a derivative of that for fruit-tree spray. I dare say Sir Harvey would have access to some. But why, my dear boy? *Why?*'

'We don't know.'

'He seemed in the best of health and spirits, except for that unfortunate acci –' Lord Ashe rubbed his forehead with the hand that held the shears, endangering pince-nez and eyes. 'Could he have been depressed, or anything of that sort? I've seldom seen a man with more – what shall I say? – zest for life. He reminded me of a chap who was once here selling Bibles. And… er… may I ask why you come *here?*'

'I've got to see Dr Middlesworth. His wife said he was at the Hall.'

'Oh. Yes. Middlesworth was here. Cicely, that's one of the maids, had a bad turn in the night. Appendicitis. Middlesworth found it wasn't necessary to operate. He thinks he can do what they call "freeze it". But he's not here now. He left some time ago. Said he had to run over to Hastings.'

It was Dick's turn to stare.

'To Hastings? At half-past five in the morning? Why?'

Lord Ashe looked puzzled.

'I can't say, my dear fellow. Middlesworth was rather mysterious about it.'

The sweet-scented grass, the glare of green lawns in broadening sunlight, caused a feeling of light-headedness. Dick was badly prepared for the next bombshell. Suddenly, with an odd sensation of imminent danger, he found Lord Ashe studying him with an intent expression, a close long look, which had in it a knife-edge of shrewdness before the other's face smoothed itself out.

'What's this I hear,' Lord Ashe asked in his soft voice, 'about Lesley Grant being a murderess?'

9

MISS LESLEY GRANT – TO GIVE HER THAT NAME – AWOKE AT a quarter past eight in the morning.

Her house, the old Farnham house towards the southern end of the High Street at Six Ashes, faced east towards the front grounds of Ashe Hall. It was pleasant and tree-shaded, with a deep front garden. From the upstairs bedroom windows you could look diagonally left across the High Street towards the heraldic griffin and ash-tree carved on the stone pillars of the entrance-gates. And brilliant sunshine was pouring through these windows when Lesley awoke.

For a moment she lay as still as death, staring at the ceiling with wide-open eyes.

A clock ticked on the bedside table, the only noise there. Lesley's eyes moved sideways, apparently noting the time, before quickly resuming their stare at the ceiling.

She did not look as though she had slept well; or, in fact, slept very long. There were faint shadows under the naïve-looking brown eyes, the brown hair seemed tumbled on the pillow, and there was a curious expression round her mouth. Her bare arms, outside the coverlet, were stretched out straight on either side. For minutes she lay motionless, listening to the tick of the clock, while her eyes now roved.

It was a comfortable room, she saw, furnished with the same shrinking fastidiousness of good taste. It contained only one picture: a framed black-and-white drawing, of somewhat grotesque design, hanging between the two front windows. When her gaze encountered this, Lesley's teeth fastened in her lower lip.

'It's *silly!*' she said aloud.

Anybody who saw her then – fortunately or unfortunately, nobody did see her – would have been a little disquieted by the stealth of her movements. Slipping out of bed, in a white silk nightgown trimmed with lace, she ran across to the picture and lifted it down from the wall.

Underneath showed the front of a small circular wall-safe, dull steel, of a pattern imported from the United States. It had no key: it opened with a letter-lock whose combination was known only to its manufacturers and to the so-called Lesley Grant.

Lesley's breathing grew shallower; her breast hardly seemed to rise and fall under the silk nightgown. She touched the dial of the safe, and had given its knob two partial turns when a heavy tread on the staircase outside in the passage, with the rattle of crockery on a tray, warned her that Mrs Rackley was on the way with morning tea.

She replaced the picture and flew back to bed. She was sitting up in bed, the pillows propped behind her – shaking back her hair, with scarcely a heightened colour or quicker breathing – when Mrs Rackley opened the bedroom door.

'Awake, miss?' inquired Mrs Rackley, with her usual formula. 'Lovely morning! Here's a nice cup of tea.'

Mrs Rackley, as a sort of maid-cook-housekeeper, was invaluable to any woman who did not mind her smothering protectiveness. After glancing round the room, noting with approval its tidiness and its open windows, she creaked across to asthmatic accompaniments and set the tea-tray in Lesley's lap. Afterwards she stood back, her hands on her hips, and surveyed her charge.

'You don't,' stated Mrs Rackley, 'look well.'

'I'm perfectly all right, Mrs Rackley!'

'You don't,' Mrs Rackley repeated more firmly, 'look well.' Her voice grew coaxing. 'Why not have a nice lie-up and let me bring you breakfast in bed?'

'No, no! I'm getting up in a minute!'

'It's no trouble,' insinuated the tempter.

'But I don't *want* breakfast in bed, Mrs Rackley.'

Mrs Rackley pursed her lips and apparently took the darkest possible view of this. Shaking her head, she glanced round the room again. Her eye halted at a chair over whose back lay, neatly folded, a black skirt and white knitted jumper, with slip, stockings, and a suspender-belt on the seat of the chair.

'Now, then!' said Mrs Rackley, in a voice rather suggestive of a Metropolitan police-constable. She added in a more casual tone: 'Was you out last night, miss?'

Lesley, who had poured out the tea and was raising the cup to her lips, looked up quickly.

'Out?' she echoed.

'Was you out,' explained Mrs Rackley, 'after 'is Lordship drove you home from Mr Markham's last night?'

'Good heavens, no!'

'When you come home from Mr Markham's,' stated Mrs Rackley, 'you was wearing the dark green frock. I distinctly remember thinking how well you looked in it. And now –'

She pointed to the back of the chair, indicating the black skirt and the white jumper. Her voice grew reproachful.

'You're delicate, miss. As delicate as my youngest ever was. You hadn't ought to do them sorts of thing.'

'*What* sort of thing?'

'Going out,' said Mrs Rackley, vaguely but stubbornly.

'But I didn't go out!' protested Lesley. Her elbow jerked so that she almost upset the tea-cup. An odd expression flashed through her eyes and was gone, but it sent the colour up in her cheeks. 'I didn't go out, do you hear? If anybody says I did, it's a wicked lie!'

Mrs Rackley was taken aback. That she did not reply, however, was due to the fact that she noticed something even more compelling. Mrs Rackley was now peering out of the window with such curiosity that Lesley crawled out of bed, setting down the tea-tray with a thump, and ran to join her.

Out by the front gate, some distance away, Major Horace Price was standing in the strong sunshine and talking to Mr William Earnshaw the bank-manager.

Major Price's bulky thick-set form contrasted with the erect trimness of the bank-manager. Earnshaw had removed his hat, showing a head of jet-black hair, very carefully brushed and parted, which gleamed under the sun. Though they were too far away for the watchers to hear anything, bad feeling certainly existed between these two. Both had drawn themselves up; you imagined that the major's colour was a little higher. But this was not what attracted the attention of the watchers.

Along the High Street, from the southerly direction where Gallows Lane turned at right angles, came the local police-constable on his bicycle.

But Bert Miller was pedalling at a speed he had seldom in his life achieved before. Both the major and Earnshaw whirled round to look. When Major Price hailed him, he pulled up so abruptly as almost to land in the ditch.

Then ensued an evil little pantomime, with the constable speaking very fast. It seemed to impress his listeners a good deal. Once Major Price turned round to look at Lesley's house. You could see his speckled face, the round large face with its jowls under the soft hat he wore during legal-business days, and his mouth partly open.

The conference broke up. And Major Price, as though coming to a decision, opened the front gate and came up the path towards the house.

'In your nightgown, too!' Mrs Rackley was insisting. 'He'll see you! Go back to bed, miss. And – and I'll draw your bath.'

'Never mind my bath now,' said Lesley, as Mrs Rackley evidently expected. Lesley's voice was not altogether steady. 'Go down and find out what's happened. Tell Major Price I'll be downstairs in half a minute.'

It was, as a matter of fact, less than ten minutes before she ran downstairs: fully dressed in a costume which was neither of the disputed ones of last night. There was no sign of Mrs Rackley, who had evidently been dismissed with some sharp words from the major. She found Major Price standing in the lower hall, turning his hat round in his hands. He cleared his throat.

'My dear girl,' the major began, 'I've just been talking to Bert Miller.'

'Yes, I know. Well?'

'I'm afraid, my dear girl, I've got some rather serious news. Sir Harvey Gilman is dead.'

It was a big cool hall, dusky despite its fanlight. At the back of it a grandfather clock ticked with a noise like a metronome.

'I didn't do it deliberately,' cried Lesley. 'I didn't shoot him deliberately! It was an accident yesterday! I swear it was!'

'S – h! My dear girl! Please!'

'I'm s-sorry! But –'

'And it isn't a question of his being shot,' continued Major Price, moving a thick neck inside his soft collar. 'It seems the poor old chap poisoned himself last night. But... can we go somewhere and talk?'

Wordlessly Lesley indicated a door, which led them into a long cool sitting-room with green-painted walls and a fireplace of rough cobble-stones. Lesley, who seemed too stunned to speak, allowed Major Price to lead her to a chair. He sat down opposite her, putting his hat carefully on the floor and spreading out his fingers on one thick knee before bending forward with a sort of confidential heartiness.

Major Price lowered his voice.

'Now you're not to be alarmed,' he assured her soothingly. 'But, as your legal adviser – and I hope you still do consider me as your legal adviser –'

'Naturally!'

'Good girl!' He leaned across to pat her arm. 'As your legal adviser, there are one or two small points, nothing important,' his gesture dismissed them, 'I think we ought to clear up. Eh?'

'Poisoned himself, you said?' repeated Lesley. Shaking her head violently, she seemed to be fighting a cloud in her mind; and tears rose in a thin film to her eyes. 'I simply don't understand! Why ever should the poor man have done that?'

'Well,' admitted the major, 'it's one of the small but rather sticky points connected with this whole affair. His body was found very early this morning by Dick Markham.'

Lesley sat up straight.

'By Dick?'

'Yes. So Miller says. It appears somebody rang Dick up on the telephone…'

'Who rang him up?'

'He can't tell. Just a kind of "whispering voice", apparently. It intimated, as far as I can gather from Miller' – Major Price frowned – 'that something pretty rough might happen unless he cut along to Pope's old cottage straight away.'

'Yes?'

'Down he went in a hurry,' continued the major. 'Just after he'd come in sight of the cottage, somebody turned on the light in the sitting-room.'

Major Price paused for a moment, obviously envisaging this. His sandy eyebrows drew together, and the breath whistled thinly in his nostrils.

'Very shortly after *that*, somebody stuck a rifle over the park boundary-wall and fired through the sitting-room window. No, wait! It's not what you're thinking! Dick ran to the place in a hurry, and Cynthia Drew with him…'

'Cynthia Drew? What was she doing there with him?'

Major Price dismissed this.

'Out for an early walk, or something of that sort. Anyway, they rushed up to the cottage, only to find that the bullet hadn't hit Sir Harvey after all. They discovered the chap in a chair in front of the writing-table. He'd locked himself in, it seems, and taken prussic acid with a hypodermic injection.

'Damned queer show,' added the major, shaking his head dubiously. 'Damned queer show altogether. Because, d'ye see, somebody fired that bullet at him at just about the same time – more or less the same time, certainly – when he was injecting the poison into his own arm!'

There was a long silence.

Lesley did not comment. She started to say something, but merely made instead a gesture of hopelessness and nerve-strung bewilderment.

As for Major Price, he was clearly ill at ease. He cleared his throat. He eyed the bowl of red roses on the centre-table, the roses which added a splash of colour to this sombre, tasteful room with its grand piano and its old silver. He looked up and down. Finally he plunged into it.

'Now look here, my dear. I don't want you to misunderstand me. But –'

'But what?'

'As a matter of fact,' said the major, 'I'd intended having a little talk with you to-day, anyway. You've been good enough to let me handle your financial affairs since you came here. You don't understand such things. That's very proper; not fitting you should.' He nodded approvingly. 'But, now you're going to get married –'

Lesley looked even more hopelessly confused.

'What on earth are you talking about?'

'Well!' said the old-fashioned Major Price. 'Your husband will expect an accounting, won't he? Expect me to turn things over to him? Natural! Only business!'

'Good heavens, no!' exclaimed Lesley. 'Dick's almost as bad as I am about business. He lets his literary agent handle all that; he never knows how much money he *is* making.'

The major was fidgeting.

'But in any case,' he said, still evading the real point, 'in any case, I want you to look at all these things as an outsider might look at them. For instance... have you got any living relatives?'

Lesley sat up.

'Why do you ask that?' she demanded.

'I know so little about you, you see. And, since I want to help you in any way I can –'

'Please, Major Price! I'd much rather you stopped beating about the bush! Won't you explain just what you're getting at?'

'Well!' said the major, dropping his hands on his knees. 'I want you to tell me just exactly what the "fortune-teller" *did* say to you yesterday afternoon.'

And now the room was so quiet that you could distinctly hear the metronome-ticking of the grandfather clock outside in the hall.

'Now look here,' urged the major, forestalling her. 'Don't say it was the usual thing you get from fortune-tellers. It wasn't. Hang it, my dear, I was *there*. I saw you.

'I want you to look at these things as an outsider might look at them. My wife, for instance. Or – or anyone. The fortune-teller says something that badly upsets you. Dick Markham dashes in to find out what it is. A rifle goes off – by accident, of course! – and the old chap's knocked over. Fortunately, he isn't badly hurt...'

'Isn't badly hurt?' cried Lesley.

'Well... no.' The major looked discomfited.

Again Lesley's eyes roved round the room in that curiously stealthy way. She appeared to be sorting thoughts as swiftly as a conjurer handling cards. Her lips were half parted; there was a fixed, wondering expression on her face.

'Dick knew that?' she cried. 'Dick knew that? And didn't tell me?'

The major shook his head.

'Oh, no. The boy didn't know.'

'Are you sure of that?'

'Middlesworth and I, if you remember, carried Sir Harvey home. The old chap swore us to secrecy about his only getting a flesh-wound. He said it would be in the interests of justice. And the Home Office pathologist... hang it, my dear girl, what could I do? I can't say what they may have told Dick Markham afterwards, but he certainly didn't know about Sir Harvey being all right at the time *I* left.

'But just look at what happens. The old chap has a great secret which seems to concern you. Right! Somebody pinches a rifle, the very same rifle, and shoots at him through the window. At the same time he's apparently poisoned himself. Tut, tut, now! Come!'

Lesley moistened her lips.

'You said "apparently". Is there any doubt?'

'In my own mind, absolutely none!' The Major chuckled a little, raising sandy eyebrows over guileless light-blue eyes. 'And you couldn't very well have got in and out of a locked-up room, now could you?' Then he lowered his voice. 'But if you have got anything to tell me, don't you think you'd better tell me now?'

Lesley's fingers fastened on the arms of the chair, as though she would raise herself towards him from sheer fervour of earnestness.

'I haven't got anything to tell you. *Please* believe that!'

'Not even what the fortune-teller said? Eh?'

'Major Price, I never saw the man before in all my life!'

'And that's all you have to tell me?'

'It's all I *can* tell you!'

'Well...' muttered her visitor.

Drawing a deep breath, he blinked round him. He picked up his hat. He seemed to meditate, as he got up, making some remark about the weather. In the midst of a strained uncomfortable silence Lesley followed him out into the hall.

'I shall be at my office,' said Major Price, 'if you want me.'

When he had gone Lesley stood for a time in the middle of the hall, her arms crossed on her breast and the fingers of each hand tightly pressing the opposite shoulder. It was a dumb-show of perplexity and even agony.

'No!' she said aloud. 'No, no, no!'

The ticking of the big clock seemed to creep into her mind. She noticed the time, which was a few minutes to nine o'clock. The smell of frying bacon, heartening enough at most times, drifted through faintly from the kitchen. Mrs Rackley, crammed with questions, could not be far off.

Lesley hurried upstairs. She went blindly into her own bedroom, closed the door behind her, twisted the key in the lock, and rested her hot face against the door panel until – with a back-flash of something half seen but not registering – she whirled round.

The black-and-white drawing was no longer hanging before that wall-safe. The drawing rested face-downwards on the floor.

In front of the safe, her fingers on the combination-knob of the dial, stood Cynthia Drew.

For a space while you might have counted ten, the two girls stood and looked at each other. Summer, with its heavy scents and murmurs, washed in through the open windows and breathed across them in moving sunlight. The solid girl with the yellow hair and blue eyes, the more fragile girl with the brown hair and brown eyes, regarded each other with a sudden heightening of emotion which was very near hysteria.

Cynthia's voice struck against the rigidity of silence.

'I want to know what's in this safe,' she said. 'And I mean to find out before I leave here, or I think I'll kill you.'

A T ABOUT THE SAME TIME THAT MORNING – NINE O'CLOCK – Dick Markham sat alone on the top of the two stone steps leading to the front door of Sir Harvey Gilman's cottage.

'Well,' he was thinking, 'that's that!'

The real trouble would now have to be faced. He remembered his interview with Lord Ashe. He remembered the arrival of the local constable – who, having been up until three in the morning because of a drunken man causing trouble at Newton Farm, showed annoyance at being dragged out – and the endless time of questioning while Bert Miller wrote down everything in longhand.

He remembered a hasty breakfast, taken off the kitchen-table at his own cottage, with Cynthia Drew sitting across from him and begging him to tell her what was on his mind.

He remembered, as the hours crawled on, Bert Miller's getting through on the phone to the police-superintendent at Hawkstone; and Bert's departure to fetch a car which should meet at Loitring Halt a Scotland Yard official who was coming down from London by rail.

Superintendent Hadley was coming.

That tore it.

Dick hadn't told Cynthia anything, in spite of her persistent questions and reminders of his promise. He couldn't face telling her about Lesley.

Even Lord Ashe, it developed, knew nothing definite. After the noble lord's bombshell with those words, 'What's this I hear about Lesley Grant being a murderess?' it turned out that this had reference merely to certain innuendoes dropped by village-ladies. 'That accident with the rifle: wasn't it *rather* curious?'

Gossip, gossip, gossip! You couldn't trace it or pin it down. It gathered and darkened, assuming a hostile tinge towards Lesley ever since news of his engagement to her had got out. And yet, on the other hand, there was more to Lord Ashe's remark than this. Dick could have sworn that Lord Ashe was definitely trying to tell him something, trying to convey something, trying to hint at something.

But what?

And so here he sat, on the front doorstep of the cottage, with even Cynthia departed on some mysterious errand of her own. Here he sat on guard over a dead body, until Bert Miller should return.

He hadn't told Cynthia anything about the facts in the life of Lesley Grant. But would it have mattered a damn if he had?

No, it would not.

It would not have mattered if he broadcast it to the whole village. Superintendent Hadley would be here soon, and the story would come out in all its unpleasant detail. Gossip should chew on a lasting mouthful; gossip should have enough at last. In the meantime...

'Hello there!' called a voice from the lane.

It was very warm now. A wasp droned from the direction of the fruit-orchard. Bill Earnshaw, his footsteps swishing in the grass, cut across the garden towards the cottage.

'I shall be late at the bank,' Earnshaw said. 'But I thought I'd better turn back here and...' His voice trailed away in a kind of inflectionary shrug. He stared at the house. 'Bad business, isn't it?'

Dick agreed that it was.

'Where,' he asked, 'did you hear about it?'

Earnshaw nodded back over his shoulder.

'I was standing outside Lesley's house, having a word with that – that ass Horace Price.' His forehead darkened, for this was not bank-managerial language. 'Bert Miller came past on his bike, and told us all about it. See here!'

Earnshaw hesitated. His was a well-tailored, erect figure which just escaped being dapper. His sallow face, not unhandsome, showed a man in the middle forties but looking younger. His collar was starched, and he fanned himself with an Anthony Eden hat. His black, shining hair had a knife-like white parting; his cheek gleamed from close-shaving.

A great social enthusiast was Earnshaw. He laughed a good deal, and prided himself on his sense of humour. He was a good business-man, a keen bridge and squash player, a Territorial officer with some pretensions to excellence in pistol and rifle shooting, though his behaviour as a rule remained humorous and retiring. But you could easily guess his approach to this.

'I was just thinking, Dick,' he said. 'This rifle…'

'Damn the rifle!' Dick burst out, with such unnecessary violence that Earnshaw looked at him in surprise. It was sheer nerves. 'I mean,' Dick corrected himself, 'that the fellow wasn't shot. He was…'

'I know, I know. But look here.' Earnshaw's dark eyes travelled along the front of the cottage. His lips outlined a soundless whistling. 'Hasn't it occurred to you – I may be wrong, of course – that whoever *did* fire the rifle is the most important figure in the whole business?'

Dick blinked at him.

'No, it certainly hadn't occurred to me. How so?'

'Well, suppose there's something queer about this thing? Suppose they suspect Sir Harvey didn't commit suicide after all?'

'He did commit suicide! Look at the evidence! Don't you believe that?'

'Frankly, old man,' smiled Earnshaw, and continued to fan himself idly with his hat, 'so many peculiar things have been happening that I don't know what to believe.' (The whole voice of Six Ashes was in that.) 'By the way,' Earnshaw added, with his eyes on the ground, 'I haven't yet congratulated you on your engagement to Lesley. Good luck and long life!'

'Thanks.'

Something had got into Dick's chest, and was hurting like hell. He felt it as a physical pain, at which you tried not to cry out. Earnshaw seemed slightly embarrassed.

'But – er – about what I was telling you!'

'Yes?'

Earnshaw nodded towards the sitting-room windows. 'Mind if I take a look in there?'

'Not at all. I'm not the police.'

Walking on tiptoe evidently with some vague idea of respect for the dead, Earnshaw approached the right-hand window and peered in. Shading his eyes with his hat, he studied the exhibit. Then he turned round with a mouth of genteel distaste but a frowning certainty of suspicions confirmed.

'A would-be murderer,' he argued, pointing to the boundary wall across the lane, 'is hiding behind that wall to take a pot-shot. Somebody turns on a light in this sitting-room. All right! Then the whole point is that *the person with the rifle could see who was in this room.*'

Earnshaw paused.

Dick Markham got slowly to his feet.

'This person,' continued Earnshaw, 'is a witness. On the one hand he can say, "Yes; Sir Harvey was alone. I couldn't know he was giving himself a dose of prussic acid, so I whanged away with a bullet." On the other hand this witness can say, "Sir Harvey wasn't alone; there was somebody with him." In either case, it would settle the matter. Don't you agree?'

There are certain things so obvious that the mind does not immediately grasp them. Dick nodded, in a rage at not having seen this for himself.

Earnshaw's innate caution manifested itself.

'Mind, I don't say this *is* so.' He laughed awkwardly. 'And I'm not setting up in business as a detective, thanks. All I say is that's what I should do if I were this detective Miller says is coming down from London. Ask the witness to come forward…'

'But the witness wouldn't come forward! He'd be accused of attempted murder if he did.'

'Couldn't the police promise him immunity?'

'And compound a felony?'

Earnshaw put on his Anthony Eden hat, adjusting it not rakishly but with a certain cavalier slant. He dusted his hands together.

'I don't understand these legal terms,' he declared, and muscles worked along his lean jaws. 'You must ask,' slight hesitation, 'Major Price about that. It's none of my business, anyway.' Then he looked squarely at Dick, with bright dark determined eyes. 'But I *have* got a special interest in that rifle, if it's the one everybody seems to think it is. Where's the rifle now?'

'In the sitting-room. Miller had a look at it.'

'May I see it?'

'Certainly. Any special reason for asking?'

'In the first place,' returned Earnshaw, 'it's my rifle. You remember, Price went round borrowing guns from everybody for his shooting-gallery?'

'Yes.'

'In the second place, having a certain standing in this community –' Earnshaw gave his amiable diplomatic laugh, not very convincingly. 'Never mind. Let's go in.'

The echo of that laugh, which you heard so often from the manager's office of the City and Provincial Bank at Six Ashes, became even less convincing when they entered the sitting-room.

The hanging lamp over the writing-table had long ago been switched off, so that the dead man sat amid shadow and dazzle from the sun. Though Earnshaw was nerving himself to a polite indifference, he could not help a wince of some emotion when he skirted gingerly round the table and caught sight of the dead man's sardonic half-open eye. He turned round with some quickness, eager to get away from it, when Dick produced the rifle.

'Don't be afraid to handle it, Bill. I've already messed up any possible finger-prints. Is it your gun?'

'Yes, it is,' answered Earnshaw. 'Now look here!'

'Wait a minute,' Dick urged wearily. 'If you're going to ask me who stole the rifle yesterday afternoon, I've already told Lord Ashe that I don't know!'

'But –'

'All I can be certain of,' Dick said with conviction, 'is that neither Price nor Middlesworth took it, because I remember watching them carry Sir Harvey away. Lesley or I certainly didn't; we were together. And there was nobody else there, until you arrived and said you'd take charge of the guns.'

Though Earnshaw kept on smiling, the expression round his eyes and mouth did not indicate amusement.

'If anybody took that rifle, it was Price himself.'

'Damn it, Bill, he didn't! You can't stick a rifle in your pocket or shove it under your coat.'

'That's exactly what I mean, old man. Nobody came near while *I* was in charge. *I* didn't do it, though Price pretends to think I did. Lift my own gun? It's absurd. I ask you! And I hope you don't suggest it was done by witchcraft?'

Dick was on the point of replying that it wouldn't surprise him. But he was sick of rifles, sick to death of everything in the anticipation of waiting for the arrival of Superintendent David Hadley. So he only muttered something conciliatory, propping the rifle back up against the wall by the fireplace.

Earnshaw laughed, to show no ill-feeling.

'I hope you're not thinking I'm making a mountain out of a molehill,' he suggested. 'But, if you'll excuse my mentioning it, I've got a certain standing to maintain. And this thing is going to have repercussions.'

'How?'

Earnshaw grew very quiet.

'That fellow never killed himself, Dick. You must guess it as well as I do.'

'Can you suggest how anybody could have killed him?'

'No. But it's a detective-yarn come to life. Corpse found in a locked and bolted room. On one side of him' – Earnshaw nodded – 'a hypodermic needle. On the other side' – Earnshaw nodded again – 'a box of drawing-pins.' He grew thoughtful. 'Of course, there's no special mystery about the drawing-pins. I mean, about their being here. You'll probably find boxes of them all over the house. You didn't live here in Colonel Pope's time, did you?'

'No.'

'Colonel Pope,' said Earnshaw, 'used to use them for the wasps.'

Dick felt that that he could not have heard properly.

'He used drawing-pins for the wasps?'

'Waspy place,' explained Earnshaw, nodding in the direction of the fruit-orchard. 'Colonel Pope said he couldn't keep the windows open in summer without being devilled half to death.'

'Well? What about it?'

'Somebody mentioned an American thing called "screens". We don't have 'em in England, but we ought to have. You know: wire-mesh things with sliding wooden frames. You prop 'em in the windows to keep out insects. Colonel Pope couldn't get any, but it gave him an idea. He used to take pieces of cloth netting, gauzy stuff, and fasten 'em round the edges of the window-frames with a lot of drawing-pins. He did that solemnly every day.'

Earnshaw pointed to the writing-table.

'You'll undoubtedly find more of the things in the drawer there,' he went on. 'But what they mean lying beside a dead man's hand…'

Dick restrained an impulse to answer that the points of those drawing-pins would make just the same sort of puncture as a clumsily administered hypodermic. But this was only a meaningless fancy, of no value. An odour of prussic acid, still exhaling from the dead man's pores, tinged the thickening heat of the sitting-room. It was affecting Earnshaw too.

'Let's get out of here,' he said curtly.

They were in the garden again when Earnshaw added:

'Seen Lesley this morning?'

'Not yet.' ('Here we go again,' Dick thought desperately; 'by God and His earth and altars, here we go again!') 'Why do you ask, Bill?'

'No reason at all. I mean,' laughed Earnshaw, 'she'll be glad to hear *she* didn't –' This time his nod indicated the sitting-room. 'Incidentally, Dick, I don't want you to think I pay any attention to gossip. No fear!'

'No, of course not!'

'But I can't help feeling, sometimes, that there is a bit of a mystery about Lesley.'

'What sort of mystery?'

'I remember,' Earnshaw said reflectively, 'the first time I ever saw her to speak to her. She's one of our clients, you know.'

'So are most of the rest of us. What's so very sinister about that?'

Earnshaw paid no attention to the question.

'What I am telling you is no secret, of course. She'd come to Six Ashes about a fortnight before and taken the Farnham house. She came to my office and asked whether I'd mind transferring her account from our Basinghall Street branch in London to the branch here. I said, naturally, that I'd be only too pleased.' Earnshaw looked complacent. 'Then she said, "Do you have safe-deposit boxes here?"'

Again Earnshaw laughed. Dick Markham took out a packet of cigarettes and offered one to Earnshaw, who shook his head.

'I said no, if she meant the sort of thing we have at the bigger branches in London. But, I said, we always accommodated customers by keeping valuables for them in a sealed box in our strong-room. She gave me an oddish look, and said she hadn't anything valuable; but there were one or two things that would be better off in a safe place.'

'Well?'

'Then she said, "Do you have to know what's in the box I give you?" I said, on the contrary, that we prefer *not* to know. The receipt we give is always marked, "contents unknown". Then, old man, I'm afraid I made a diplomatic howler. I said – meaning it as a joke – "Of course, if I became suspicious, it would be my duty to investigate." She never mentioned the matter again.'

'Contents unknown.'

Dick lit a cigarette and watched the smoke curl up. He could picture that little office in the High Street: Earnshaw behind the desk, with his finger-tips together and his sleek head bent forward. And the eternal, torturing riddle of what was not valuable, yet had to be kept secret from all eyes; the riddle of Lesley herself; seemed to reach its final point.

'Hullo!' muttered Earnshaw.

The clanking noise of a motor-car, approaching eastwards along the lane, was followed by the appearance of Dr Middlesworth's dusty Hillman. It drew up outside the cottage. Middlesworth, a pipe in his mouth, climbed out from under the wheel and opened the back door of the car.

'Good Lord!' exclaimed Earnshaw. 'Isn't that…?'

From the back of the car, like a very large genie out of a very small bottle, there slowly emerged an immensely tall and immensely stout figure wearing a box-pleated cape and a clerical shovel-hat. It was a complicated business in which this figure clutched the hat to its head, kept firm a pair of eyeglasses on a broad black ribbon, manoeuvred itself with many wheezes through the restrictions of the door, and at the same time supported itself by leaning forward on a crutch-handled cane.

Then the figure upreared in the road, its cape and eyeglass-ribbon flying, to take a broad survey of the cottage. The face with its several chins and bandit's moustache was pinker from exertion. But its war-cry remained, making every chin quiver, when the stout gentleman cleared his throat.

'Yes,' said Dick, who had seen the Gargantuan presence many times in illustrated papers. 'That's Gideon Fell.'

And now he remembered the meaning of the reference to Hastings.

Middlesworth had said last night – during one of those odd little spurts of speech which punctuated Middlesworth's thoughtful silence – that Dr Fell was spending the summer at Hastings not far away. Middlesworth had driven over to fetch Dr Fell at a crazily early hour. Why?

It didn't matter. Dr Fell knew just as much about this business as Superintendent Hadley. Lesley's story would be out now; and in front of Bill Earnshaw. He was feeling even sicker when he saw Middlesworth exchange a word with Dr Fell, after which the Gargantuan doctor lumbered forward towards the cottage.

Dr Fell, in fact, seemed possessed of a subdued and savage wrath. He cut at the grass with his crutch-handled stick. Immense, like a sailing galleon in his cape, he towered a good head over any man there. He stopped in front of Dick Markham, wheezing heavily, and regarded Dick with an extraordinary air of concern.

Again he cleared his throat.

'Sir,' intoned Dr Fell, removing his shovel-hat, with old-fashioned stateliness, 'am I addressing Mr Richard Markham?'

'Yes.'

'Sir,' said Dr Fell, 'we have come to bring you good news.'

In the ensuing silence, while he continued to blink at Dick with an air of concern, you could hear a dog barking from very far away.

'Good news?' Dick repeated.

'Despite the fact,' pursued Dr Fell, replacing his hat and peering round at Middlesworth, 'despite the fact that on our way here we met a certain Major... Major –?'

'Price,' supplied Middlesworth.

'A certain Major Price, yes, who told us of this morning's occurrences and somewhat abated our triumph, I still think you will find it good news.'

Dick stared from Dr Fell to Middlesworth. Middlesworth, with his lined forehead and his thinning brown hair, remained as usual non-committal; but the expression of his eyes, even of the deep lines round his mouth, conveyed a puzzling reassurance.

'We can settle it, anyway,' said Middlesworth, taking the pipe from his mouth and knocking it out against his heel. He went to the sitting-room window and tapped its glass. 'Dr Fell,' he added, *who is that dead man?'*

Growling from deep in his throat, Dr Fell lumbered forward and approached the window as closely as the mountainous ridges of his waistcoat would allow. He adjusted his eyeglasses, bending forward as though for intense concentration. But it was no more than a few seconds before he swung round again.

'Sir,' replied Dr Fell, with the same air of subdued wrath, 'I have not the slightest idea who he is. But he is not Sir Harvey Gilman.'

TOO MANY SHOCKS, NUMBING THE EMOTIONS, PRODUCE A kind of torpor in which it is easy to pretend calmness.

'What's the joke?' asked Dick Markham.

He became conscious of three faces looking at him: of Earnshaw open-mouthed, of Middlesworth bitterly wry, of Dr Fell in such a genuine glory of rage that his upthrust under-lip seemed to meet the bandit's moustache.

'There's no joke,' answered Middlesworth.

Then Dick shouted: '*Not Sir Harvey Gilman?*'

'He's an impostor,' Middlesworth said simply. 'I couldn't tell you last night what I suspected, because I didn't want to raise false hopes. But...' Middlesworth woke up: 'Excuse me, Bill,' he said to Earnshaw, 'but won't you be needed at the bank?'

No hint could have been plainer and yet, in Middlesworth's mild voice, containing less offence. It says much too for Earnshaw's urbanity, or his good nature, or both, that the bank-manager merely nodded.

'Yes,' he agreed, 'I'm late already. I shall have to excuse myself, I'm afraid. See you later.'

And he turned round and marched off like a man in a trance, though he must have been boiling with curiosity.

Middlesworth waited until the straight back, the Anthony Eden hat, the trim dark-blue suit had got some distance away.

'Tell him, Dr Fell,' Middlesworth suggested.

Dr Fell wheeled round, a mighty galleon, to face Dick.

'Sir,' he intoned, setting his eyeglasses more firmly, 'you have been made the victim, I can't say why, of as cruel and brutal a hoax as comes within my experience. I wish to reassure you about this Miss... Miss...?'

'Lesley Grant,' supplied Middlesworth.

'Oh, ah. Yes.' Dr Fell's face was fiery; his cheeks puffed out. 'Miss Grant is not a poisoner. She is not, so far as I am aware, a criminal of any kind. I will itemize exactly what I mean.'

He checked off the points on his fingers.

'She never married, or murdered, or in fact had any concern with an American lawyer called Burton Foster, for the excellent reason that no such person ever existed –'

'*What?*'

Dr Fell waved him to silence.

'She is guiltless of poisoning the elderly Mr Davies of Liverpool in a locked room or anywhere else, because Mr Davies never existed either. She never invited Mr Martin Belford of Paris, to an engagement-celebration dinner at her house, and then sent him home to die, because *he* is a figment of the imagination too. In short, sir: the whole story against Miss Grant is nothing but a pack of lies from start to finish.'

If pain can be felt in a detached way, that was how Dick Markham felt the bite that seared between the first two fingers of his right hand. He woke up partly to the fact that his cigarette had burnt down against them. He stared at the cigarette, and then threw it away.

'Steady, now!' came Middlesworth's voice out of the mist.

And it was Middlesworth's homely, heartening grin which broke the spell.

'Then,' said Dick, 'who in God's name is he? I mean, who was he?'

Words alone could not express what poured through his mind. Dick Markham fell back on pantomime, like a child. He pointed to the sitting-room window, to the evil exhibits and the leering corpse beyond.

'As to who he is,' replied Dr Fell, 'I can only repeat that I don't know. *I* never saw him before, in spite of the fact that he seems to have claimed acquaintance with me. But he was, I suspect, a good deal of a genius.'

'And why,' yelled Dick, 'did he tell that pack of lies? *Why?* What was his purpose?'

Dr Fell scowled.

'I refuse to imagine, you know, that the whole thing was an elaborate joke.'

'It wasn't a joke,' Middlesworth agreed dryly. 'You should have watched his face last night.'

Again Dr Fell turned to Dick, with a sort of massive and cross-eyed benevolence which had in it a note of apology.

'You see, my lad, that story of his was in its own way a minor work of art. It was directed solely and simply at *you*: at every chink in your armour, every receptive part of your mental make-up.'

(True! True! True!)

'Each word was designed to get its own particular response from you. On to this young lady he grafted a psychological character in which you could believe, an irony that would strike you as right, a situation which your own imagination would compel you to accept. It was the perfect picture of – ahem – a dramatist hoist with his own petard. But I'm rather surprised...'

Dr Fell's big voice trailed off, and he frowned. Dick, to whom certain small indications were now coming back, looked at Middlesworth.

'I'd rather like to shake your hand, Doctor,' he said.

'That's all right,' said Middlesworth, embarrassed.

'*You* thought he was a wrong 'un from the start?'

'We-el,' said Middlesworth, 'not exactly that.'

'But your behaviour last night…'

'I shouldn't have gone so far as to say I thought he was a wrong 'un, no. But I haven't been altogether happy about it. When Major Price first introduced him to me, and said Sir Harvey made us all promise to keep his real identity a secret for a while –'

'I'll bet he made you promise,' observed Dr Fell grimly. 'By thunder, but wouldn't "Sir Harvey" make you promise!'

'I was interested,' said Middlesworth. 'I asked him about one of his famous cases. He answered me, all right. But he made some grandiose reference to the two chambers of the heart. That brought me up a bit. Because any medical student knows the heart has four chambers. And then those stories he told last night.'

Dick spoke with a vilely bitter taste in his mouth.

'Did he catch me,' Dick asked, 'with some wild absurdity in a crime story?'

Middlesworth reflected.

'Not absurd, no. Nothing impossible. Just unlikely. Such as a pathologist being called on to act as police-surgeon in the London area. Or, in the Liverpool story, holding the inquest at St George's Hall when the crime took place in a suburb like Prince's Park. I'm only a G.P.,' explained Middlesworth apologetically, 'but – hang it all!'

He put his empty pipe into his mouth and drew at it.

'Anyway,' Middlesworth added, hunching up his shoulders, 'I thought it might be a good idea to get in touch with Dr Fell.' His mild eye twinkled towards Dick. 'Feeling better, old son?'

Better?

How to explain that he hadn't got rid of the nightmare even yet? And that the hypnotic eye of the alleged Sir Harvey Gilman – a much-too-hypnotic eye, he now realized – still bored into his mind? Over the fields now, reminding him, drifted the sound of the church clock striking ten in the morning.

'It's just exactly twelve hours,' answered Dick, 'since I got pitched into this nightmare. It seems like twelve days or twelve years. I've got to get used to the idea that Lesley isn't a murderess, and that these "murdered men" never existed. There never was any prussic-acid poisoning! There never was any locked room!'

Dr Fell coughed.

'I beg your pardon,' he observed, with polished courtesy. 'But there is very much a prussic-acid poisoning. And there is very much a locked room. Kindly glance into the sitting-room and see.'

The church clock ended its striking.

And the three of them looked at one another wildly.

'Dr Fell,' said Dick, 'what does the whole mess mean?'

A long sniff rumbled in Dr Fell's nose. He took a few lumbering steps up and down the garden, cutting at the grass with his crutch-handled stick. He seemed in his own mind to be addressing a ghostly parliament; you saw the gestures even if the words were inaudible. When he did in fact turn to address his two companions, he reared back his head so that the eyeglasses should remain firmly on his nose.

'Why, sir,' he replied, shaking the crutch-handled stick in the air, 'the main outline of the affair would appear to be before us. This impostor's story was not true. But somebody *made* it come true.'

'Meaning?'

Again Dr Fell paced.

'We shall not be in any firm position,' he went on, 'until we learn who the impostor is, and what his game was, and why he spun this appalling yarn merely to... do what? Merely, as I understand it, to be present in the house while Mr Markham has dinner with Miss Grant! Is that correct?'

Both Dick and Middlesworth nodded.

Dr Fell blinked at the latter.

'But one suggestion you made, when we heard of this morning's work from a certain Major Price,' he resumed, 'does seem to me to be whang in the bull's-eye. Oh, ah. Yes. Whatever explanation we put on the situation, the centre of the whole plot is still Miss Lesley Grant.'

Dick spoke sharply.

'How do you work that out?'

A radiant beam appeared in Dr Fell's eye, illuminating his pink face like the glow of a vast furnace, and going down in chuckles over the ridges of his waistcoat. Then he became preternaturally solemn.

'The centre of the whole plot,' he repeated, 'is still Miss Lesley Grant. Now a very important question. Regarding this little tale of locked rooms and hypodermic syringes – did the impostor tell this story to anybody except you two?'

'I don't know,' said Dick.

'Nor I,' admitted Middlesworth.

'While he was telling you the story, could anybody have over-heard him?'

Very vividly Dick recalled that scene last night: the rough flowered curtains not quite drawn close over the windows, and one window pushed fully open. He recalled Middlesworth suddenly getting up, in the course of the so-called Sir Harvey's recital, and putting his head out of that window. Dick related the incident now.

'*Was* there somebody out here?' he asked Middlesworth.

'Yes.'

'Could you see who it was?'

'No. Too dark.'

'There are two alternatives,' grunted Dr Fell. 'You can say, if you like, that the impostor went through all his masquerade as Sir Harvey Gilman, spun his grotesque yarn, made all his arrangements, just so that he could lock himself in here later and give himself a dose of poison.

'That may be true, gentlemen. It may be true. But unless the fellow was an escaped lunatic, which I consider unlikely, it does not sound a very feasible explanation. H'mf, no. The other alternative –'

'Murder?'

'Yes. And you see where that leads us?'

Dr Fell resumed his pacing, addressed his ghostly parliament, and finally came to a stop once more.

'The whole point, d'ye see, is this. Last night a crime was reproduced here, line for line like a fine drawing. The joke being that the original crime didn't exist! It was imagined, a piece of pure fantasy, by the impostor calling himself Sir Harvey Gilman. Yet it was reproduced. Why? Because, of course, the murderer believed he was reproducing a real crime.

'The people of Six Ashes believed – and still believe – that this fellow is Sir Harvey Gilman, the Home Office pathologist. What Sir Harvey says is gospel. What Sir Harvey mentions as a real case *is* a real case. Why should the good people doubt it?

'Either he told this prussic-acid story to somebody in private, or else somebody overheard it last night. Somebody believes, firmly believes, that Lesley Grant is a murderess who has killed three men. Somebody, with joy in the heart, suddenly thinks of a way to commit this "impossible" crime. And therefore some-body commits it, serene in the belief that Lesley Grant will be blamed.'

Dr Fell paused, drawing a wheezy breath. He added, somewhat less eloquently:

'That's the ticket, gents. You can bet your shirts on it.'

'Are you saying,' Dick demanded, 'that somebody hates Lesley enough to commit murder in order to...?'

Dr Fell looked distressed.

'My dear sir,' he protested, 'we can't say anything about motive. We don't know the identity of the dead man. Before you begin saying so-and-so had a motive, it is just as well to know whose murder you are investigating.'

'Then –?'

'All we do see with certainty is that Lesley Grant presented a convenient scapegoat. The murderer didn't doubt, probably doesn't doubt to this minute, that the dirty work will be attributed to her, since she is a real poisoner.' He blinked at Dick. 'You believed that yourself, I think, until a few minutes ago?'

'Yes. I'm afraid I did.'

'Tut, now!' rumbled Dr Fell, and again the chronic chuckle ran over him. 'There is no need for this hangdog look, and this violent inner cursing of yourself!'

'*I* think there is.'

'When, as I understand it from Middlesworth, you were prepared to shield this lady no matter what she had done? Sir, that was very reprehensible of you. It makes me cluck my tongue. It was not the act of a good citizen. But, by thunder, it was the act of a true lover!' Dr Fell struck the ferrule of his cane on the ground. 'However, with regard to the present difficulties...'

'Well?'

'You must remember, sir, that I've had only the outline of yesterday's events from Dr Middlesworth, and the barest outlines of to-day's events from Major Price via the constable. But one other thing does emerge. If the blame for this crime is intended for Miss Lesley Grant, it follows as a corollary that...'

Again he paused, sunk fathoms deep in obscure musing. Then he said:

'Who, by the way, was the gentleman here a moment ago?'

'I ought to have introduced you,' Dick apologized, 'but I was too flummoxed to think of it. That was Bill Earnshaw, the bank-manager.'

'Oh, ah. I see. Did he want anything in particular?'

'He was worried about this infernal rifle. Also, he supplied at least a partial explanation as to why a box of drawing-pins should turn up in the sitting-room.'

Dick gave a sketch of Earnshaw's information. Dr Fell gave close attention to the account of Colonel Pope's habits with drawing-pins. He gave equally close attention to the account of yesterday's garden-party and the inexplicable disappearance of the rifle under everybody's eyes. Something in this latter secondary mystery appeared to interest Dr Fell very much indeed, for the doctor eyed him with a hideous face of speculation. But, instead of saying what was really in his mind, Dr Fell went off on another tack.

'Tell me,' he mused. 'When our friend the impostor acted as fortune-teller, was he a good fortune-teller? Did he appear to have made shrewd guesses about people in general?'

'His information seems to have paralysed everybody. Including –'

Back again, sharp and quick as the jab of a needle, came the recollection that something *had* been said to Lesley about which she patently lied afterwards. Dr Fell saw this.

'May I suggest,' he said, 'that you don't plunge back into the horrors again? Archons of Athens! If he so thoroughly hypnotized you with a false story, isn't it possible he may have done the same thing with her?'

'You mean told Lesley some walloping yarn...'

'That,' Dr Fell pointed out, 'appears to have been his speciality.'

More and more was a strengthening sanity emerging, to explain away all difficulties. Dick spoke with fervour.

'As soon as the constable comes back, and I can be let off standing guard, there's just one thing I want to do. I want to go straight to Lesley and apologize.'

Dr Fell was delighted.

'Apologize,' he inquired, 'for shielding her?'

'Apologize for everything! Tell her what a swine I am! Have the whole thing out with her!'

'If you want to go now,' said Dr Fell, '*I* can stand guard. It will interest me very much to make an examination of that room. Later, if you please, I want you to tell me EVERYTHING. I have a feeling' – he groped at the air – 'that my present information is not only incomplete, but misleading. When you return, by the way, you will probably find me at Ashe Hall.'

'At Ashe Hall? Do you know Lord Ashe?'

Dr Fell pointed with his cane.

'Those, I take it, *are* the grounds of the Hall?'

'Yes. You can go through the coppice up over a field, and get to it by a short cut.'

'I am acquainted with Lord Ashe,' resumed Dr Fell, 'only through correspondence. But his antiquarian researches interest me. The first Ashe was a favourite of Queen Elizabeth. The last Ashe, before this present one, was a sizzler who upset half Europe with the most notorious bawd of her day. Between those two he plans a family history which shall be, in actual fact, a history of England for three and a half centuries. If he had enough money to…' Dr Fell woke up. 'Never mind! Shall *I* stand guard for you, sir?'

Middlesworth touched Dick's arm.

'Come along,' he said, 'and I'll give you a lift. I've got to be back myself for surgery at half-past ten.'

Utterly oblivious of them now, Dr Fell lumbered up the two stone steps into the cottage. In the last glimpse they had of him, as Middlesworth backed the car round in the lane, they could see him inside the sitting-room. They could see him first owlishly examining the shattered window on the left, and then examining the other window with its bullet-hole below and to one side of the metal catch.

Dick rode in Middlesworth's car with very different feelings from last night. While they bumped along Gallows Lane – it was no very great distance from here to the High Street, and to Lesley's house – each of them made only one remark. Dick said, 'Thanks!' and Middlesworth said, 'Not at all.' But it was as though they had shaken hands.

When Middlesworth dropped him off in front of Lesley's house, Dick stood for a time looking north along the sedate High Street. The daze of the nightmare had not quite passed, but he wanted to execute a dance, or throw a stone through the post office window, as a sheer explosion of relief. He took pleasure, physical pleasure, even in the sight of the High Street.

There were the familiar houses. There was the post office, with its temperamental postmistress and no stamp-machine. There were the shops, the public-house 'Griffin and Ash-tree', the three or four offices, the trim brick premises of the City and Provincial Bank. Beyond rose the low grey spire of the church, presided over by the Rev. Arthur Goodflower; and its clock was now striking the quarter-hour after ten.

The clock-note had a melody not noticeable to anybody except Dick Markham. He strode up the path towards Lesley's house.

Nobody answered his ring at the door-bell. He rang again, still without effect, before he noticed that the front door was not quite closed.

Pushing it open, he put his head into the cool, dusky, pleasant hall.

'Lesley!' he called.

How the devil was he going to face up to her now? How to tell her, in so many words, that he had last night suspected her of being an angelic murderess with poison, or a diary, or some unnamed horror hidden away in a wall-safe? But the only thing to do was to tell her straight out, ending this nightmare in one gust of laughter.

For the fact remained that yesterday's business with the rifle *had* been an accident after all.

Lesley, rattled by some weird story – for all Dick knew, maybe even that *he* was a murderer himself – had loosed off that rifle without meaning it. And the fraudulent Gilman had instantly and glibly used this to his own advantage.

Still no reply from the house.

'*Lesley!*' he called again.

The grandfather clock in the hall ticked with its metronome-note. Mrs Rackley, in all probability, would be out marketing at this hour. But Lesley – he was about to turn away, and close the door after him, when he caught sight of Lesley's handbag, with her front-door key beside it, lying on a small table in the hall.

Shouting her name, he wandered into the sitting-room. Then he glanced into the dining-room opposite, and investigated the kitchen behind that. One look through the back kitchen-windows told him that she was not in the garden either.

He told himself that he had no reason to feel disquiet. She might only have gone a step or two down the road. Standing in the middle of the tidy white kitchen, where a tap drizzled with hollow effect in the silence, he told himself this; but he had now reached such a state of mind that he wanted the reassurance of merely seeing her.

As a last resort he peered into the little room, hardly more than a cubicle, where Lesley was accustomed to have breakfast. Its furniture was of bright-painted blue and white wood, like nursery furniture. On the table, set for one with precise array of silver and china, the bacon and eggs had turned stone cold. The toast had withered to hardness in its rack. No coffee had been poured out into a waiting cup.

Dick hurried out of that room, returned to the hall again, and started upstairs three steps at a time.

So thoroughly were the proprieties observed in this house that he had never so much as looked inside her bedroom, though he knew which room it was. He halted outside the closed door. He knocked once without reply, hesitated, and opened the door.

The two windows of the bedroom faced the High Street. Between them showed, like a scar, an evilly significant wall-safe with its steel front swung wide open. That was not all he could see, when three strides took him forward. The inside of the safe, not much bigger than a large biscuit-barrel, was empty.

Passing the foot of the bed, Dick swung round.

Huddled on the floor near the foot of the bed, her left cheek against the carpet, lay Cynthia Drew. One knee was partly drawn up, and Cynthia's arms in the pinkish-coloured jumper were thrown wide. A purplish bruise on her right temple had split a little to let dark blood trickle and congeal down the cheekbone. She did not move.

12

A N EMPTY SAFE.
Cynthia, waxen of complexion and with her yellow hair disarranged.

Dick picked her up – Cynthia's sturdiness made her no light weight, despite the fact that she was not tall – and carried her to the bed, where she lay as limply as a doll.

There could be no question, thank God, about her being alive. She was not even, he hoped, seriously hurt. Her half-parted lips stirred to an audible if jerky breathing. But she was pale, and the devil's brush of the bruise showed ugly against the very fair skin.

Another door opposite the windows displayed a thoroughly modern, even sybaritic bathroom. Dick plunged into it, turned on the cold-water tap with a rush into the wash-basin, soaked a face-cloth, wrung it out, and rummaged in the medicine-chest for smelling-salts and iodine. In doing so he confronted his own reflexion – stubbly-bearded, not even washed, a spectre to offsight decent people – in the mirror over the wash-basin. He found neither smelling-salts nor iodine, but there was a bottle of hydrogen peroxide and a box of cotton-wool.

He went back to Cynthia, and he was just pressing the wet cloth to her forehead when he heard, from downstairs, the hollow slam of the front door.

Lesley?

But it was not Lesley. When he hurried downstairs, taking them at mountaineering jumps, it was to find Mrs Rackley: in a regrettable hat, with a market-basket over one arm and a bulging paper carrier in the other hand.

'Mr Markham!' exclaimed Mrs Rackley. Her eyes added, 'Now, then!' as plainly as any Metropolitan police-constable.

'Where's Miss Lesley?'

'She's 'ere, sir.'

'She's *not* here, Mrs Rackley!'

'I left 'er 'ere,' the other pointed out, dumping the parcels on the hall table with something of alarm.

'When did you leave her?'

'An hour ago, it might be.' Mrs Rackley's eyes moved to the clock. 'Miss Cynthia –'

'What about Miss Cynthia?'

A flustered cook-maid-housekeeper was having some trouble with the parcels in market-basket and carrier, which seemed to be developing a tendency to roll like billiard-balls.

'Well, sir, it was while Major Price was here. Miss Cynthia, she come to the back door and said, could she slip up the back stairs to Miss Lesley's room, because she had something she wanted to surprise her with? I said yes, she could, Miss Cynthia being a Nice Girl and holding no offence towards you and Miss Lesley for... I beg-pardon-I'm-sure!'

'Well? What happened then?'

'Sir, what's wrong?'

'Never mind that! Go on!'

'Then Major Price left, and Miss Lesley went upstairs too, and I heard them talking up there.'

'Yes?'

'I went upstairs myself, and tapped on the bedroom door, and said, "Miss, your breakfast's ready." And she called out and said, "I'll come down straightaway; please go out and do your marketing." Speaking up very sharp, which she's never done before. And so I marched straight out like she said.' Mrs Rackley's sense of bitter offence melted into concern as the possibility of a new enormity occurred to her. 'Don't you tell me, sir, she didn't get her breakfast?'

Dick ignored this.

'I'm afraid there's been an accident.' He hesitated. 'Miss Cynthia fell and hurt her head. If you could –'

It was unnecessary to say any more. Though a heavy woman, Mrs Rackley ascended the stairs with surprising agility, holding a hand under her heart as though to prevent it from falling out. Her treatment of Cynthia was deft and effective.

After bathing the bruise, sponging away blood, she applied restoratives of her own which she fetched from an upper floor. Cynthia, coming out of the faint, began to fight. Cynthia writhed and squirmed and muttered and kicked out; and Mrs Rackley held her shoulders patiently until she quietened.

'Now, now!' urged Mrs Rackley. 'Now, now!' Her neck craned round. 'Do you think, sir, as we ought to send for the doctor?'

'No.'

''Ow did this 'appen, sir?'

'She – she slipped and hit her head on the foot of the bed.'

'Was *you* here, sir?'

'Thank you, Mrs Rackley. That will be all. If you could let me speak to Miss Cynthia alone for a moment…'

'I don't know,' said Mrs Rackley deliberately, 'as I ought to do that.'

'What she needs,' said Dick, 'is tea.' He had no idea whether this might be the right measure, but he counted on the effect on Mrs Rackley of suggesting anything prepared in the kitchen. 'Hot black tea,' he declared with assurance, 'without any sugar or milk. If we could have some of that...'

It worked.

Then he sat down on the edge of the bed beside Cynthia, who hastily smoothed down her skirt and must have felt the pain burn through her head as she tried to get up. Cynthia breathed hard. The blue eyes, becoming less cloudy, grew fixed; she went red under the eyes, and then pale again.

'It's all right, Cynthia. What happened?'

'She hit me. It sounds a-absurd, but she hit me. With that mirror.'

'What mirror?'

Cynthia tried to struggle up in order to point; as soon as her shoulders left the coverlet she caught sight of the open safe; and she caught in manifest dizziness at Dick's arm.

'Dick! That safe!'

'What about it?'

'It's empty. What was in it?'

'Don't *you* know?'

'No! I tried to –' Abruptly Cynthia checked herself. Her face smoothed itself out to utter, pretty stolidity; without the prettiness, it would have been bovine. She attempted a light laugh. 'My dear old boy,' she added in her tennis-court voice, 'we're being rather absurd. Please let me get up.'

'Lie still, Cynthia.'

'Just as you like, of course!'

'Where did you hear that there was something, anything at all, supposed to be in that safe?'

'My dear Richard, I didn't! That safe is the mystery of the whole village. Half of Six Ashes talks about it, thank you. And, s-since we've got so many mysteries on our hands –!' Again Cynthia checked herself. 'She hit at me, Dick. I walked towards her, intending to reason with her. And she hit out at me like a snake striking. With that mirror.'

Dick glanced round.

On the dressing-table was a silver toilet-service: plain, unobtrusive, but costly and very heavy. Its hand-mirror, which would have made a murderous weapon, now lay balanced on the edge of the dressing-table as though hastily put down.

Dick Markham – he felt it himself with surprise – was no longer the mentally dazed and drugged person of yesterday. He had torn loose from evil, or so he thought; he had become again an alert, alive young man with more than his fair share of intelligence.

'Why did she do that, Cynthia?'

'I've told you! I asked her to open the safe.'

'Was she standing in front of you?'

'Yes. With her back to that dressing-table, and her hand behind her. And she lashed out with the mirror before I could lift a finger.'

'Cynthia, are you sure you're telling me the truth?'

'Why shouldn't I be telling you the truth?'

'Lesley's right-handed. If she hit out at you with the mirror while you were facing her, that bruise ought to be on your left temple. How is it that the bruise is on your right temple?'

Cynthia stared at him.

'Don't you believe me, Dick Markham?'

'I'm not saying I don't believe you, Cynthia. I'm trying to find out what happened here.'

'Of course,' Cynthia said with sudden fierce bitterness, *'you'd take her part.'* And then, disregarding appearances, this girl who was always so careful of appearances rolled over on her face and began passionately to sob.

Dick, with a hot and cold feeling of embarrassment, made the mistake of trying to touch her arm; she shook him off with a gesture of intense loathing. He got up, went to the window, and stared out blankly at the High Street.

Across the road, and to the left, loomed the entrance-gates of Ashe Hall. Nothing stirred in the High Street except a tall military-looking man – a stranger in the village, Dick vaguely noticed – who was crossing the street on this side in the direction of the post office.

Dick was fond of Cynthia, very fond, though not in the same way as his feeling for Lesley. The thought which flashed through his head was so ugly that it turned him cold: the more so as Cynthia's emotional storm spent itself immediately. With a calm and amazing change of mood, she sat up and put her feet down to the floor.

'I must look a sight,' she observed.

He whirled round.

'Cynthia, *where is Lesley?*'

'How on earth should I know?'

'She isn't here. She isn't in the house. And, as you said, that safe is empty now.'

'You don't think *I've* done anything to her, surely?'

'No, no! But –'

'But you admit,' interposed Cynthia, with careful coldness, 'that she does have something to hide. In the safe, which she's taken away now. I see!'

'For God's sake listen! The thing I'm trying to get at is this. What excuse did you have for asking her to open the safe? What made you do it?'

'If you'd heard the dreadful things that are being said about her –'

'Is that all, Cynthia? *You* weren't by any chance listening outside the windows last night?'

'What windows, Dick? What is all this?'

No: it was absurd.

The puzzled straightforwardness of her manner made him put the thought away from him. He touched the little door of the safe, which swung gently shut. He picked up from the carpet a picture which had evidently hung in front of the safe. Replacing its wire on the picture-hook, he saw that it was a black-and-white Aubrey Beardsley drawing: a sly mosaic of evil whose inner design did not become immediately apparent but, when it did become apparent, struck you in the face.

'I insist,' cried Cynthia, 'on knowing what you mean!'

Dick groped for excuses. 'I mean,' he lied, 'that you were there this morning. Near the cottage. You might have heard or seen something that would help us.'

He had meant nothing by this, he was merely flinging out words at random, but to his surprise Cynthia's voice changed.

'As a matter of fact, Dick, I did see something.'

'*What?*'

Cynthia's fingers plucked at the quilted coverlet of the bed.

'I meant to tell you earlier. But we were in such an awful flap that it completely slipped my mind. It's not important, anyway, because Sir Harvey Gilman killed himself.' Her eyes moved up. 'Didn't he?'

'Never mind! What did you see?'

'I saw somebody running,' answered Cynthia.

'When? Where?'

Cynthia reflected. 'It was a minute or so before the rifle was fired at the window.'

'*Before* the rifle was fired at the window?'

'Yes. I was coming along the lane from the east, you remember? Whereas you were coming from the west? I hadn't seen you yet, and naturally I couldn't tell there was anything wrong. But I saw somebody dodge across the lane in front of me.'

'Dodge across the lane in front of you?'

'That's right. From the fruit-orchard beside the cottage, across to the wall opposite and over the wall into the coppice.'

'Could you see who the person was?'

'No. Only a shadow. It was that queer funny light just at sunrise.'

'Any description at all?'

'No, I'm afraid not.'

'Man or woman?'

Cynthia hesitated. 'I can't say, really. And now, Mr Richard Markham, if you've quite finished your interrogation and your various suspicions of me, I think I'd better go home.'

'Yes, of course. Steady on! You're still groggy. I'll take you home.'

'You'll do nothing of the kind, Mr Richard Markham,' said Cynthia, with a cold concentration of anger which kept her voice at a steady level. 'If you think I'm going to walk along the High Street looking as though – well, as though heaven knows what! – and if you think you're going to take me home to my parents in this state, all I can say is you're very much mistaken. Please keep away from me.'

'Don't be a fool, Cynthia!'

'So now,' said Cynthia, 'I'm a fool.'

'I didn't mean that, exactly. I meant...'

'It's not as though you showed any concern about me to begin with. Oh, no. All you could think about was her. That's very proper, I'm sure; I'm not in the least blaming you for it; but when you first call me a liar and then a fool, and only think of showing any scrap of concern for me when you realize how it may look in public, then I must really ask you to excuse me.'

Dick walked forward to expostulate. He took her by the arms, with something in his mind between kindly reasoning and an impulse to shake her until her teeth rattled. Then, he could never afterwards remember how, Cynthia was in his arms, very warm and tight-holding so that he could feel the firm muscles of her body, crying against his shoulder.

And this was the exact moment when Mrs Rackley walked in with the tea-tray.

'Thanks awfully, Dick,' murmured Cynthia, disengaging herself and giving him her friendly smile. 'Thank you too, Mrs Rackley. You're not to see me home. I shall be quite all right. Good-bye.'

Then she was gone.

Though Mrs Rackley did not actually say, 'Well!' her eyebrows expressed much. She creaked over and put down the tea-tray with something of a bang on the bedside-table.

'Mrs Rackley,' said Dick, 'where has she got to?'

'May I ask, sir,' inquired Mrs Rackley, keeping her eye carefully away from him, 'who you're referring to?'

'Miss Lesley, of course.'

'If you'll excuse the liberty, sir, I was just a-wondering whether it mattered to you where she'd got to.'

'For the love of Mike, Mrs Rackley, don't get the wrong impression of anything you saw!'

'For Miss Lesley's sake, sir, I did *not* see it. That's for Miss Lesley's sake,' explained Mrs Rackley, still keeping her eye on a corner of the ceiling. 'What's past should be past, if you know what I mean; not that it's any of my business.'

'There never was anything...'

'I don't wish to 'ear,' said Mrs Rackley, 'about what is not none of my business. Isn't anybody going to drink this tea?'

'No, I'm afraid not. Miss Cynthia...'

'This tea,' said Mrs Rackley, lifting up the tray about two inches and then slamming it down on the bedside table again, 'was distinctly ordered.'

'All right! All right! *I'll* drink the damn tea!'

'Mr Markham,' said Mrs Rackley, 'I have always thought of you as a gentleman. Though it seems that men which is gentlemen and gentlemen which is others are not one and the same thing.'

Breathing a curse on all women, Dick held hard to his temper and set about pacifying her. The situation would have been grotesque if it had not been for his genuine worry about Lesley.

And he could submit that he had cause for worry. The open safe, the inexplicably empty safe, provided that. In her concern for Cynthia, Mrs Rackley had evidently not noticed that open safe when she first came in; and it was closed, with the picture again hanging before it, at her second entrance.

But it was a dangerous cavity, an ugly gap with its secret gone, when you related it to Lesley's disappearance. A dozen possibilities, most of them melodramatic but all diabolically vivid, presented themselves to Dick Markham. Of the scenes from criminal history which occurred to him – laughable, no doubt – most lifelike was that of Mrs Pearcey playing the piano in a blood-spattered parlour while the police searched for the body of Phoebe Hogg. Dick had just decided to try a round of telephone-calls when, downstairs, the telephone rang.

Disregarding Mrs Rackley's further protests, Dick got down to the phone ahead of her. His hands were not very steady when he picked it up. Over the wire, making carbon crackle, came the unmistakable voice of Dr Fell.

'Ah!' said the doctor, clearing his throat with earthquake violence to the phone. 'I rather hoped to find you there. I'm at Ashe Hall. Can you come up here straightaway?'

'Is it about Lesley?'

'Yes.'

He gripped the telephone tightly, and muttered something like a prayer before he spoke. 'She's all right, isn't she?'

'All right?' thundered Dr Fell. 'Of course she's all right! She's sitting here in the room with me now.'

'Then what –?'

'But we have, as a matter of fact,' pursued Dr Fell, 'some rather important news. We've identified the dead man.'

13

I N THE NORTHERN WING ON THE GROUND FLOOR AT ASHE HALL, along a musty dark little passage carpeted with matting, was a room which Lord Ashe used as a study. Four persons were waiting here when Dick arrived.

A green-baize door muffled this room from domestic noises. Over the small cavern of the fireplace hung a portrait now so age-darkened, even where the light splashed it, that little emerged except a spindle-shanked ghost with a curious collar. A line of narrow windows, of crinkly bottle-glass with ancient rings, looked out on a walled garden which had once been a Ladies' Retiring Garden. Against these windows, pushed so that the light would fall across the left shoulder of anyone sitting there, was a big table covered with papers.

In a creaky swivel-chair at this table sat Lord Ashe, half turning out into the room.

Across from him, bolt upright, sat Lesley Grant.

Dr Fell was enthroned in a huge wooden chair, a very emperor's chair, which gave him some resemblance to Old King Cole. And with his back to the fireplace stood a tall military-looking man – Dick had seen him in the High Street not half an hour before – with hard eyes and a hard jaw, whistling between his teeth.

Lesley jumped to her feet.

'If you don't mind,' Lesley observed, 'I shall just go out while you tell him. You can call me in afterwards. I just don't want to be here when you tell him.'

And she was smiling.

People would not, Dick was reflecting, behave as you expected them to behave.

Only a short time ago he had seen the rather unimaginative Cynthia Drew go through such an emotional tumult as you might not have believed possible. The nerve-strain of the day considered, its effect on Lesley should have been much worse. And yet this was not so.

Nerve-strain existed, certainly. But most of all you felt a lessening of tension, a radiance of relief, which touched on the borders of happiness. Lesley walked straight towards Dick.

'Hello, darling,' she said. Laughter twinkled in the brown eyes. 'You *have* been having fun and games with my career as a murderess.'

And, after ducking a mocking curtsy to Dr Fell – who responded by waving the crutch-handled cane and chuckling with an alarming violence which threatened to become a coughing-fit – Lesley slipped demurely out of the room, closing the green-baize door after her.

'Ah, well, gentlemen!' remarked Lord Ashe, and drew a deep breath.

'Admirable!' roared Dr Fell. 'Admirable!'

'Idiotic,' curtly commented the military-looking man by the fireplace. 'And damned risky too. But women are like that.'

Dick held hard to reason.

'I don't want to butt in, Dr Fell,' he said; 'but you asked me over here, and here I am. If you could manage to tell me…'

Dr Fell blinked at him.

'Eh, my boy? Tell you what?'

'Tell me what this is all about!'

'Oh, ah! Yes!' cried Dr Fell, enlightened. The Gargantuan doctor was not trying to be mystifying; he had merely slipped ahead into some obscure mental calculation, and forgotten all about what had been on his mind a few minutes before. 'By the way, let me introduce you to my friend Superintendent Hadley. Mr Markham, Superintendent Hadley.'

Dick shook hands with the military-looking man.

'Hadley, of course,' pursued Dr Fell, 'recognized the dead man as soon as he clapped eyes on him.'

'I'm rather sorry to lose Sam, in a way,' said Hadley, chopping his teeth together in a way that meant trouble for somebody. 'He had his points, Sam had. Though I sometimes wanted to kill him myself, I admit.' Then Hadley grinned. 'Steady, Mr Markham! You want to know who this fellow really was?'

'Yes!'

'He was a professional crook named Samuel De Villa,' replied Hadley. 'Probably the cleverest confidence-man in the business.'

'Imagination, Hadley,' said Dr Fell, shaking his head. 'Imagination! Oh, my eye!'

'Too much imagination,' retorted Hadley. 'It killed him.'

'*Confidence-man?*' yelled Dick Markham.

'Perhaps, my dear boy,' interposed the thoughtful voice of Lord Ashe, 'it would interest you to see this.'

Pushing back the creaky swivel-chair, he pulled open the long drawer of the table at which he was sitting. From the drawer he took out a largish square of dark-coloured velvet, folded together like a bag, and spread it out on the table.

'Gaudy, eh?' inquired Dr Fell.

'Gaudy' was a mild word. Outside a musical comedy, Dick had never seen anything like the objects which lay against that dark square of velvet. There were only four of them: a triple-tiered necklace, a bracelet, a single earring, and what looked like a collar. But they stunned the eye with their antique combination of what can only be called beauty with vulgarity.

And now Dick realized why a certain heraldic device seemed to have been haunting him. He had seen the Ashe arms, a griffin and ash-tree, often enough on the entrance-gates of the Hall. He had seen it on the small signet-ring which Lord Ashe usually wore. He had even seen it, heaven knew, on the sign of the local public-house.

But it was all over these exhibits as a convict's uniform used to be starred with broad-arrows. It decorated the clasp of the brace-let, it was woven into the design of the gold collar. It marked and stamped them as the property of the Ashe family.

Of course, Dick thought to himself, such flamboyant jewels couldn't possibly be real. The pearls of the triple-tiered necklace, opalescent and alive when light through the windows fell on them; the intense hard malignant glitter of diamond on the bracelet; the fluid red glow of ruby on that antique, curiously wrought gold collar...

Interpreting his expression, Lord Ashe glanced up.

'Oh, yes,' said Lord Ashe. 'The jewels are real enough.'

Delicately he touched first the necklace and then the bracelet.

'These,' he continued, 'are early eighteenth century. This,' he touched the earring, 'I suspect of being modern and spurious. But this,' he touched the collar, 'this is what tradition describes as a gift to George Converse, in the year fifteen seventy-six, from Gloriana herself.'

And Lord Ashe raised his eyes to the portrait above the fireplace, that black portrait through which only a shadow-image could be discerned.

There was a long silence.

Outside, in the walled garden, stood a solitary plum-tree. As in a dream Dick saw the sunlight filling that garden, pouring through the tall narrow windows on the blaze of these coloured fires. He saw the dingy room with its rows of brown books round the walls. He saw the portrait, breathing of English soil at a time when such finery as these gauds decorated arm and throat and ear as a matter of everyday wear.

But most of all he saw the face of Lord Ashe – that combination of the scholar and the outdoor man, with evasive-looking eyes – as Lord Ashe's hand hovered over the jewels. And Dick at last broke the silence.

'Yours, sir?'

The other shook his head.

'I wish I could say they were,' he answered regretfully. He looked up and smiled. 'They belong, now, to Miss Lesley Grant.'

'But that's impossible! Lesley doesn't own any jewellery!'

'I beg your pardon,' said Lord Ashe. 'She hates jewellery, yes. She never wears jewellery, yes. But this is a question of owning things in spite of herself.'

He meditated for a time, and then looked at Dr Fell.

'You don't mind, sir, if I explain matters as Miss Grant explained them to me this morning?'

'No,' said Dr Fell.

'It's a foolish story,' said Lord Ashe, 'and in many ways it's a pathetic story. It's the story of this girl's – what shall I say? – frantic search for respectability. Did you ever hear, Mr Markham, of a woman called Lily Jewell?'

'No,' said Dick.

But more than a suspicion grew in his mind nevertheless.

'Oddly enough, I mentioned her to you only this morning. It would be an understatement,' said Lord Ashe, 'to describe her as a lady of easy virtue. My elder brother Frank ruined himself and others for her just before the fourteen-eighteen war. Among other things he gave her those trinkets there. Are you beginning to follow me now?'

'Yes. I think so.'

'Lily Jewell died in obscurity a few years ago. But she died a violent death. She was an elderly woman, paying young lovers to attend her –'

'Yes.'

'She threatened one of them with a gun, for being unfaithful to her. In the scuffle and accident, she was herself shot. She was the mother, by a certain Captain Jewell, of the young lady whom you know as Lesley Grant.'

Lord Ashe paused.

Dick turned away and stared out into the walled garden. A hundred pictures returned to him. Every word, every gesture, every inflexion now took on significance out of what had hitherto been so meaningless. Dick nodded.

'I – er – live somewhat out of the world,' explained Lord Ashe, ruffling his finger-tips across his temples. 'I was hardly prepared for it when she burst in here this morning, and threw this lot of trinkets on the table, and said, "Please take the damned things, if you think you're entitled to them."'

Again Lord Ashe paused.

Dr Fell cleared his throat.

'After her mother's death,' pursued Lord Ashe, 'her one idea was to cut off from the previous life and to be as *un*like her mother as possible in every way. Do you follow that too, Mr Markham?'

'Yes. Very easily.'

'The girl, I judge, is highly strung…'

Lesley! Lesley! Lesley!

'… and it was something of a shock when she settled down here and found out what family was living just opposite.'

'She didn't know?'

'No. When she was a small girl, my brother had been known officially as "Mr Converse" or "Uncle Frank" rather than by his title. The name of Ashe meant nothing to her. It was customary in my day' – Lord Ashe spoke dryly – 'to suppress names.'

'Then by pure chance…?'

'Oh, no. A spiteful friend.'

'How do you mean?'

'A spiteful friend suggested that, if she left the Continent and settled down in England, she would probably find it pleasant to live in a village called Six Ashes. She came here. She liked the place. She saw a suitable house. She had been living here for several weeks before she properly noticed the design on the gates opposite.' Lord Ashe reached out to touch the necklace. 'And compared it,' he added.

'I see.'

'She could have left, of course. But she liked the people. She liked' – he looked at Dick – 'one in particular. And I gather that this, our humdrum little life, was what she *wanted*. Desperately wanted. And wouldn't give up.

'What really maddened her, I gather also, was a morbid sense of guilt. Guilt towards us. Guilt towards any of my family. I'm sure I can't say why. As I told her this morning, she had no concern with her mother's affairs.'

Lord Ashe hesitated.

He picked up first the collar, then the bracelet, and then the necklace, weighing each in his hand and putting it down as though his fingers loved it.

'But it's also true that there was some question, at the time, as to whether my brother had any right to give these things to Lily Jewell. Whether they were not, in fact, part of an entailed estate. This girl, in addition to her fear of what the village-ladies would say if they learned she was the daughter of Lily Jewell, even had cloudy visions of the police coming to arrest her.

'She was desperately afraid somebody would see these things and recognize the Ashe arms: as, of course, everybody would have. But she wouldn't part with them, wouldn't keep them at a bank. Hence the wall-safe. Which showed at least some sense of reality, considering how valuable the articles are.'

Superintendent Hadley threw in a question.

'How valuable?'

'My dear Superintendent!' said Lord Ashe, and again showed signs of running down like a clock. 'Their historic interest…'

'In cash, I mean?'

'I can't appraise them, I'm afraid. Very many thousands, as you can judge for yourself.'

Lord Ashe again addressed himself to Dick Markham.

'When I first set eyes on – er – Miss Grant, some six months ago, I noticed her resemblance to Lily Jewell. It puzzled me. It bothered me. But, on my word of honour, I never actually connected her with Mrs Jewell! They seemed so utterly different, so –!' Lord Ashe waved his fingers in the air. 'Well, my dear fellow! If you had ever been acquainted with Lily Jewell, you would understand what I mean.'

'But Lesley thought…?'

'She thought, I'm afraid, I might have guessed who she was. This small foolish fear, the dread of being talked about, had grown and grown. She was already in a somewhat morbid state of mind. And you well recollect the events of yesterday.'

Superintendent Hadley uttered a short, sharp laugh.

'Sam De Villa,' Hadley said.

Line by line, image by image, with colour where only shadow had lain before, Dick saw the picture take form. Each inconsistency was fitting into place now.

'De Villa, alias Sir Harvey Gilman,' he asked, 'was after that load of jewellery?'

'What else do you think he was after?' inquired a sardonic but admiring Hadley. He jingled coins in his pocket. 'And, by George, Sam never played a part better! When I first got to that cottage down there with your local P.C. – what's his name –?'

'Bert Miller?'

'Miller, yes. I gave Dr Fell a little sketch of Sam De Villa's life and achievements.'

'You did,' agreed Dr Fell very thoughtfully.

'Sam was a confidence-man. He wasn't a burglar. He could never in the world have cracked a Florida Bulldog safe, and wouldn't have tried. But he *could* coax the stuff out of that safe, as slick as a whistle. There was only one way to get at jewels which Miss Grant wouldn't even admit were there. That was to get the help of Mr Markham. And Sam did it. He was an artist.'

'He's an artist,' Dick said viciously, 'who – I hope – is burning in hell at this minute. Go on!'

Hadley lifted his shoulders.

'Simple as simple. Sam usually worked the Continent, you understand. He traced Lily Jewell's daughter to Six Ashes, and decided on the best way. First of all he carefully cased the district…'

'Cased it?' repeated Lord Ashe.

'Studied it. Got as much information as he could about everybody concerned. One of his devices was first to go about in some inconspicuous role, like a salesman…'

'Bibles!' exclaimed Lord Ashe.

They all stared at him.

'I beg your pardon, gentlemen,' said Lord Ashe, shifting in the creaky chair, 'but I told our young friend this morning that the fellow reminded me of a man who was here long ago selling Bibles. You mean this was the – er – criminal figure you call Sam?'

Hadley nodded.

'Always a good device, Bibles,' he declared. 'It gives the salesman access to the family Bible and to family history, if anybody's willing to talk.'

Dr Fell, whose several chins were propped over his collar while he stared at the floor, appeared vaguely disturbed. Internal rumblings disturbed his bandit's moustache.

'I say, Hadley,' he muttered, 'I'm rather curious to know, in fact I want very much to know, whether he visited any other house at Six Ashes except this one.'

'I imagine he had a good thorough round of it,' the Superintendent said grimly. 'It accounts for his great success as a fortune-teller. Naturally he consented to do that. Sam had what he called a sense of humour –'

'God damn his sense of humour,' said Dick Markham, with quiet sincerity.

There was an uncomfortable silence.

Hadley's voice grew quiet.

'I know, Mr Markham. I know!' Hadley smiled as though he had gone a trifle too far. 'But you've got to understand that these gentry will use *anything*, any weapon at all, when they think they can bring off a good haul. The garden-party gave him a heaven-sent opportunity to upset Miss Grant, and, consequently, upset you in preparation for his plan.'

'What did he actually say to her, by the way?'

Hadley grunted, continuing his wry friendly smile.

'Can't you guess, Mr Markham?'

'References,' said Dick, 'to the fact that he, the great fortune-teller, knew all about her past life? And her mother's past life?'

'That's it. With the practical certainty, you see, that she wouldn't tell you: at least, not yet. He was a great psychologist, Sam was.'

'A great psychologist. Yes.'

'Which,' Hadley pointed out, 'put you in the position to be upset by the hint of even more sinister secrets. Oh, yes. He couldn't know an accident would play into his hands when that rifle went off. But he used that too, with smacking good effect.

'I don't think there's much more to tell you, Mr Markham. His whole game, the story about the terrible poisoner and the diary or poison or something locked up in a safe, was to get that safe open.

And how to do that? Easy! He told you, if I've got the story straight from Dr Fell, that he wanted to be present *unseen* while you had dinner with Miss Grant? And that he was very anxious to see what was in the safe?'

'Yes.'

'And that he would give you his "final instructions" about it next morning?'

'Yes. Those were the exact words.'

Again Hadley lifted his shoulders.

'You were to get the combination of the safe for him,' the Superintendent said. 'The combination of that impregnable safe. He'd have told you that this morning – if he'd been alive.'

'Wait a minute! Do you think Lesley would have...?'

'Given you the combination? You know ruddy well she would have, if you pressed her! She meant to tell you about the whole thing, anyway, at this dinner she projected for to-night.'

(Words floated back to him, words which Lesley had spoken in his own cottage the night before: 'I want everything to be perfect to-morrow. Because I've got something to tell you. And I've got something to show you.' He saw her sitting in the lamplight, stung and brooding.)

'But would you have believed *anything* she'd told you, by that time?'

'No. I suppose not.'

(He was glad Lesley wasn't here, now.)

'You'd have got that combination during the day. And while you were at dinner, Sam would have cleaned out the safe and quietly faded away. That's all there is to it, Mr Markham. Only –'

'Only,' interposed Dr Fell, 'somebody murdered him.'

THE WORDS FELL WITH A HEAVY CHILLING WEIGHT.

And the cautious Hadley, thrusting out his jaw, made formal protest.

'Stop a bit, Fell! We can't say for certain this is murder. Not at the present stage of the game.'

'Oh, my boy! What do *you* think?'

'And I, perhaps,' interposed Lord Ashe, 'can answer one of your questions now.'

Both Hadley and Dr Fell, surprised, turned to look at him. Lord Ashe, who was again weighing the gold ruby-studded collar in his hand, made a deprecating noise as though warning them not to expect too much.

'You were asking a while ago,' he said, 'whether this fraudulent Bible-salesman visited any other house except mine. The matter is hardly very important. But I can tell you. He didn't. I made inquiries about him.'

'So!' muttered Dr Fell. 'So!'

Hadley regarded him suspiciously – the doctor's scatterbrain had been having this effect on his friend for twenty-five years – though Hadley said nothing.

'But surely, gentlemen!' protested Lord Ashe, putting down the gold collar. 'Come, now! You make use of the word "murder"?'

'*I* use it,' affirmed Dr Fell.

'For myself, I know little of such matters,' said Lord Ashe.

'Though I used to read those novels of the gentleman who wrote them over the weekend, about mysterious deaths in ancestral mansions. But surely now! As I understand it, this man De Villa died of poison in a room with the doors and windows locked up on the inside.'

'Yes,' agreed Dr Fell. 'That,' he added, 'is why I must repeat that the centre of the whole plot, apparently, is Miss Lesley Grant.'

'Wait a minute, please!' urged Dick, and appealed to Lord Ashe. 'You say, sir, that Lesley came here this morning, and threw those jewels at you, and poured out this story about her mother?'

'Yes. Rather to my discomfort.'

'Why did she do it, sir?'

Lord Ashe looked bewildered.

'Because, apparently, little Cynthia Drew had come to her and accused her of being a poisoner.'

Lesley herself slipped into the room now, closing the green-baize door softly after her. Though outwardly composed, she was clearly nerving herself to meet this interview. She stood at the corner of the windows, her back to the light, and faced them.

'You'd better let me answer that,' she said. 'Though I loathe telling it!' A little curving smile, the smile Dick Markham found so irresistible, flashed round her lips and was gone in concern. 'It's *all right*, Dick,' she added. 'I'll – I'll talk to you about it later. But it was rather dreadful for me.'

'Cynthia?'

'Yes! She turned up in my room this morning. Heaven knows how she got there, but she was trying to open the safe.'

'I've – er – heard about it.'

Lesley's arms were straight down at her sides, her breast heaving.

'Cynthia said to me, "I want to know what's in this safe. And I mean to find out before I leave here." I asked her what she was talking about. She said, "That's where you keep the poison, isn't it? The poison you used on those three men who were in love with you before?"'

'Well!' cried Lesley helplessly, and turned out her hands.

'Steady, now!'

'I'd been thinking,' she went on, 'that the whole village must be saying or at least imagining some terrible things about me. But never in my wildest dreams did I think it could be anything like *that!* Especially as she went on to say Dick knew all about it, and the police were coming for me because I'd got poison or something locked up in that safe. I – I rather lost my head.'

'Just a minute. Did you hit her?'

Lesley blinked.

'Hit her?'

'With a hand-mirror off the dressing-table.'

'Good gracious, no!' The brown eyes widened. 'Did she say I hit her?'

'What happened?'

'Cynthia ran at me, that's all. She's stronger than I am and I didn't know what to do. I dodged, and she tripped and went over like a sack of coals against the footboard of the bed.

'When I saw she was just knocked out, not badly hurt at all' – the full lips compressed, and Lesley looked elaborately out of the window – 'maybe it was callous of me, but I just let her stay there. Wouldn't *you?*'

'Go on!'

'I thought to myself, "This is too much; I can't stand any more."
So I got those things out of the safe, and rushed over here to Lord
Ashe, and told him the true story. While I was telling it, Dr – Dr Fell,
isn't it? – and Superintendent Hadley got here. So I thought I might
as well tell everybody.' Lesley moistened her lips. 'There's only one
thing I'm curious about, Dick,' she added with great intensity. 'Did
you tell Cynthia?'

'Tell her what?'

'This horrible story about the three husbands, and – and the rest
of it.' Lesley coloured. 'She kept repeating, "Till death do us part,
till death do us part," like a mad woman. That's all I care about,
that's all I'm concerned about! Did you tell Cynthia, in confidence,
something that you wouldn't tell *me?*'

'No.'

'Do you swear that's true, Dick? You were messing about out
there with her this morning. Major Price said you were.'

'On my word of honour, I never said one word to Cynthia!'

Lesley drew the back of her hand across her forehead.

'Then where did Cynthia get the story?'

'That,' observed Dr Fell, 'is something which interests all of us.'

Reaching into his hip pocket under the folds of the big cape, Dr
Fell drew out a large red bandanna handkerchief. He mopped his
forehead with such thoroughness that his big mop of grey-streaked
hair tumbled over one eye. Then, assuming an argumentative pose
which made Hadley instinctively bristle, he pointed to the chair on
the other side of Lord Ashe's desk.

'Sit down, my dear,' he said to Lesley.

Lesley obeyed.

'If you're going to lecture –!' began a very suspicious Hadley.

'I am not,' said Dr Fell with dignity, 'going to lecture. I am going to ask Miss Grant whether she has, in this village, any very deadly enemy.'

'That's impossible!' cried Lesley.

There was a silence.

'Well,' said Dr Fell, returning the handkerchief to his pocket, 'let us consider the evidence. Sam De Villa, may he rest in peace, came to Six Ashes as an outsider. He had, it would seem' – here Dr Fell hesitated slightly – 'no connexion with anybody in this village. Agreed, Hadley?'

'So far as we know at the moment, agreed.'

'Therefore Sam, *qua* Sam, ceased to become important in the scheme of murder.'

'If it was murder,' Hadley said quickly.

'If it was murder. Oh, ah. Very well. It is now inescapable, as we agreed this morning, that the whole reproduction of an imaginary crime – hypodermic syringe, prussic acid, locked entrances – was a deliberate attempt to throw the blame on Lesley Grant, whom somebody believed to be a murderess. Otherwise there is no point to it.'

'Now look here!' Hadley began.

'Otherwise,' inquired Dr Fell politely but firmly, 'do you see any point to it?'

Hadley jingled coins in his pocket. He did not reply.

'Consequently,' pursued Dr Fell, blinking across at Lesley, 'we must face the question. Is there anyone who hates you enough to want to see you charged with murder? Or, putting the matter more broadly, is there anyone who would profit by it if you were put in an extremely sticky position?'

Lesley regarded him helplessly.

'There isn't anybody,' she replied. 'Except – but that's *utterly* impossible!'

Dr Fell remained imperturbable.

'This,' he continued, 'is the conclusion to be drawn from our facts. The corollary to that conclusion…'

'Is there a corollary?' demanded Hadley.

'Oh, yes. It shines with great light.' Dr Fell peered at Dick. 'By the way, my boy. In the excitement of the moment, while we were at that cottage, I forgot to warn you about being very, very discreet. When you left me this morning to go and see Miss Grant, I gather you did meet Miss Cynthia Drew?'

'Yes.'

'Did you – harrumph – enlighten her? Did you tell her that Miss Grant was not, in fact, an evilly disposed character suspected of three murders?'

'No. She wouldn't admit she'd heard anything at all about Lesley. So I didn't say anything, naturally.'

'Did you tell anybody else?'

'No. I haven't seen anybody else.'

'What about your friend Dr Middlesworth? Is *he* likely to spill the beans that Miss Grant is not a poisoner?'

'Hugh Middlesworth,' answered Dick, 'is as close-mouthed a chap as you'll find anywhere. He'll be especially close-mouthed about this. You can bet your shirt he won't talk.'

Dr Fell mused for a moment.

'Therefore,' he went on, 'there is somewhere within reach a person who STILL believes this yarn. This person killed Sam De Villa, arranged all the trappings to suggest murder by Lesley Grant, and is now hugging himself or herself for sheer joy. Except in the unlikely event that the murderer is our friend Lord Ashe...'

'Good God!' exclaimed Lord Ashe.

Totally taken aback, he dropped on the table the pearl necklace which he had been examining. His grey eyes, with their darkish eyebrows in contrast to the iron-grey hair, wore behind the pince-nez a look of consternation. His mouth was open.

'That, sir,' growled Superintendent Hadley, 'was just an example of Dr Fell's own peculiar idea of humour.'

'Oh. A joke. I see. But...'

'Except in that unlikely event,' pursued Dr Fell, 'I repeat that the real murderer still believes this yarn. Now come on! Use your very capable intelligence, Hadley! Having provided us with a problem, it follows as a corollary that the real murderer must do what?'

'Well?'

'Why, damn it,' thundered Dr Fell, rapping the ferrule of his cane against the floor, 'he must now provide us with a *solution*.'

Wheezing, Dr Fell looked from one to the other of them.

'Sam De Villa's corpse,' he emphasized, 'is found in a room locked up on the inside. So far, so good. Lesley Grant, argues the murderer, will be blamed for doing this. But how did she do it?

'Remember, these imaginary crimes were supposed to have been unsolved. You, the police, were supposed to have been baffled. Very well: but it won't do to have you baffled this time. If the blame is to be placed on Miss Grant, we must learn how the thing was done or we still can't touch her. The murderer's whole design against her fails unless it is proved how the locked room worked. Do you follow me now?'

Dick Markham hesitated. 'Then you think...?'

'I rather think,' responded Dr Fell, 'we shall get a communication of some kind.'

Hadley's face wore a suspicious frown.

'Hold on!' the superintendent muttered. 'Was that why you asked me, a while ago, to –'

He checked himself as Dr Fell gave him a warning glance of portentous entreaty. To Dick Markham it seemed that this was a little too obvious a warning glance, a little too portentous; and Dick had an uncomfortable sense of a battle of wits being fought, somehow, under the surface.

'I mean,' amplified Dr Fell, 'that we shall get a communication from A Friend or a Well-Wisher that will hint at, if not ruddy well indicate in detail, how the locked-room trick was worked. The police were supposed to have been duffers once. It won't do to risk their being duffers again.'

'A communication – how?' asked Dick.

'Why not by telephone?'

After a pause during which Dr Fell again addressed his ghostly parliament, the doctor scowled at Dick.

'You had a telephone-call early this morning,' he said, 'which interests me very much. The local policeman gave me a summary of your evidence. But I should like to question you rather closely about it, because... Archons of Athens! Wow, wow, wow!'

The latter dog-like noises, made by a scholar of international reputation, caused Lord Ashe to survey him in perplexity.

Lesley bit at her under-lip.

'I don't understand any of this,' she burst out. 'But I don't believe it, because it's more hateful than anything else yet. You don't mean, you can't possibly mean' – all Lesley's appeal went into her voice – 'that anybody on earth would do a thing like this *just* to throw the blame on me?'

'It does take a bit of believing, doesn't it?' asked Dr Fell, with his eye on vacancy. 'Yes, it does take a bit of believing.'

'Then, please, what *are* you getting at?'

'Exactly,' snapped an exasperated Hadley, 'what I want to know myself.'

'I must confess,' said Lord Ashe, 'that this kind of thing is a little beyond me too.' He looked at his wrist-watch and added hopefully: 'You'll all stay to lunch, of course?'

Lesley jumped to her feet.

'Thanks, but I won't,' she said. 'Considering my new status in the community, as the daughter of Lily Jewell –'

'My dear girl,' said Lord Ashe gently, 'don't be a fool.'

Setting the four glittering trinkets together in the middle of the dark-velvet cloth, he folded it together like a bag and held it out to her.

'Take them,' he said.

'I *won't* take them!' retorted Lesley, as though she were about to stamp her foot. The tears rose to her eyes again. 'I never want to see them again! They're yours, aren't they? Or, at least, your family always said so. Then take them, take all of them, and please for heaven's sake let me have a little peace!'

'My dear Miss Grant,' said Lord Ashe, insistently shaking the bag at her, 'we mustn't stay here arguing over who will or won't take anything as valuable as this. You might tempt me too much. Or, if you'd rather my wife didn't see them until after lunch –'

'Do you think I could ever face Lady Ashe again?'

'Frankly,' replied the husband of the lady in question, 'I do.'

'Or anyone else here in the village, for that matter? I'm glad it's all over. I'm free, and relieved, and a human being again. But, as for facing people again...!'

Dick went over and took her by the arm.

'You're coming with me,' he said, 'for a walk in the Dutch Garden before lunch.'

'An excellent idea,' approved Lord Ashe. Opening the table-drawer, he dropped the velvet cloth with its contents inside. As an afterthought, he selected a small key off a much-crowded key-ring and locked the drawer. 'We can settle afterwards the vexed question of – er – taking your own property. In the meantime, if country air is to do you any good at all, you must get rid of these morbid ideas.'

Lesley whirled round.

'Are they morbid ideas, Dick? Are they?'

'They're morbid nonsense, my dear.'

'Does it matter to you *who* I am?'

Dick laughed so uproariously that he saw her self-distrust shaken.

'What did Cynthia say to you?' Lesley persisted. 'And how is she? And how did it happen she was with you early in the morning?'

'Will you please FORGET it, Lesley?'

'Exactly,' said Lord Ashe. 'But one thing does seem to be evident, Mr Markham.' His face hardened a little, with an expression about the eyes Dick could not read. 'Miss Grant has more than one very spiteful friend.'

'How do you mean?' cried Lesley.

'One of them,' Lord Ashe pointed out, 'sends you here to live at Six Ashes. Another, if we can credit what we've just heard, is trying to get you hanged for murder.'

'Don't you see,' urged Lesley, holding tightly to Dick's arm, 'that's just what I can't face? And won't face? The idea that somebody, anybody, could hate you as much as that is the most terrifying thing of all. I don't even want to hear about it!'

Lord Ashe reflected.

'Of course, if Dr Fell has by any chance some notion of how and why this extraordinary locked-room crime was committed –?'

'Oh, yes,' said Dr Fell apologetically. 'I think I might manage that, if I hear one or two answers I expect.'

A sense of new danger, hidden danger, darted along Dick Markham's nerves.

Turning round half a second before, he surprised between Dr Fell and Superintendent Hadley a kind of pantomime communication. It was only a raising of eyebrows, a sketched motion of lips; yet it vanished instantly, and he had no idea of its meaning. Hitherto he had regarded both Dr Fell and Hadley as allies, as helpers, here to tear away phantom dangers. No doubt they still were allies. At the same time...

Dr Fell frowned.

'You understand, don't you,' he asked, 'the most important consideration in this case?'

15

I T WAS LATE IN THE AFTERNOON, OUTSIDE THE EVIL-LOOKING cottage in Gallows Lane, when Dr Fell asked that same question again.

After lunch at Ashe Hall, Dr Fell and Hadley and Dick Markham made a little tour of the village. Dick had wanted to go home with Lesley, but Dr Fell would not hear of this. He seemed interested in meeting as many persons as possible.

No word had as yet slipped out that the dead man was not Sir Harvey Gilman, or that the police had any reason to suspect anything but suicide. You could almost feel the lure of the trap, the invitation of the deadfall, the whistling summons to a murderer. Faces of bursting curiosity were directed towards them, though only the averted eye asked a question. Dick had never felt more uncomfortable in his life.

And they met many people.

An attempt to interview Cynthia Drew was frustrated by Cynthia's mother, a sad little woman who pointedly refrained from speaking to Dick Markham. Cynthia, she explained, had sustained a bad fall on some stone steps, bruising her temple. She was in no condition to see anyone; nor should anyone *expect* – raising of eyebrows here – to see her.

But they encountered Major Price coming out of his office. They were introduced to Earnshaw making some purchases at the post office. Dr Fell bought chocolate cigars as well as real ones at

the sweet-and-tobacconist's; he exchanged views on church archi-
tecture with the Rev. Mr Goodflower; he visited the saloon-bar of
the 'Griffin and Ash-Tree' in order to lower several pints before
closing-time.

The low, yellow-blazing sun lay behind the village before they
turned back again towards Gallows Lane. Passing Lesley's house,
Dick remembered her last words to him. 'You *will* come to dinner
to-night, just as we planned?' and his agreement with some fervency.
He looked for her face at a window, and didn't see it. Instead he
presently saw, looming ahead beside a darkling orchard, the low-
pitched black-and-white cottage with the defaced windows.

The body of Sam De Villa, alias Sir Harvey Gilman, had long
ago been removed to the mortuary at Hawkstone. Bert Miller the
constable now patiently stood guard in the front garden. Hadley
addressed him as soon as they were within hailing distance.

'Any post-mortem report?'

'No, sir. They've promised to phone when there is one.'

'Any luck with tracing that telephone-call?'

Bert Miller required to have things explained. His large face was
impassive under its imposing helmet.

'Which telephone-call, sir?'

Hadley looked at him.

'An anonymous telephone-call,' he said, 'was put through to
Mr Markham at his cottage very early this morning, asking him to
come here in a hurry. You remember that?'

'Yes, sir.'

'Have they traced that call?'

'Yes, sir. It was put through from this cottage.'

'From this cottage, eh?' repeated Hadley, and glanced at Dr Fell.

'From the phone in there,' explained Miller, nodding towards the open hall door behind him, 'at two minutes past five in the morning. Exchange said so.'

Again Hadley glanced at Dr Fell.

'I suppose you're going to say,' he remarked dryly, 'you anticipated that?'

'Dash it all, Hadley!' Dr Fell complained querulously. 'I am not trying to stand here like a high-priest of hocus-pocus, making mesmeric passes over a crystal as Sam De Villa did. But certain things do emerge because they can't help emerging. You understand, don't you, the most important consideration in this case?'

Hadley remained discreetly silent.

'Look here, sir,' said Dick. 'You asked that question once before. Then, when we tried to answer you, you never supplied your own answer at all. What is it?'

'The most important consideration, in my humble opinion,' said Dr Fell, 'is how Sam De Villa spent the last six hours of his life.'

Dick, who had been expecting something else altogether, stared at him.

'You took leave of him here,' pursued Dr Fell, 'at about eleven o'clock last night. Good! You found him dead – very recently dead – at about twenty minutes past five this morning. Good! How did he spend the interval, then? Let us see.'

Dr Fell lumbered up the two stone steps into the little front hall. But he did not go into the sitting-room, for the moment at least. He stood turning round and round in the hall, with majestic slowness suggesting a battleship at manoeuvres, while his vacant eye wandered.

'Sitting-room on the left.' He pointed. 'Dining-room across the passage on the right.' He pointed. 'Back-kitchen and scullery at the

rear.' He pointed again. 'I had a look at all of 'em while I was waiting here this morning. Including, by the way, a look at the electric
meter in the scullery.' Dr Fell brushed at his moustache, and then
addressed Dick again. 'When you left him at eleven o'clock, De
Villa said he intended to go to bed?'

'Yes.'

'And presumably he did go to bed,' argued Dr Fell, 'since Lord
Ashe called here shortly afterwards to see how the wounded man
was getting on, and found the place all dark. Lord Ashe told you
that, didn't he?'

'Yes.'

'I didn't go upstairs this morning. But it's worth a try now.'

The staircase was a narrow affair with heavy balustrades and a
sharp right-angled turn. It led them into the low-ceilinged upper
floor. Here, where a shingled roof pressed down with a thick blanket
of heat, they found two good-sized front bedrooms as well as a tiny
back bedroom and a bathroom. It was the front bedroom just over
the sitting-room which showed signs of occupancy.

Dr Fell pushed open a close-fitting door with a latch, which
creaked and scraped along the bare floor. Two windows, in the
sloping wall facing the lane, admitted late afternoon light to
which the shade of the birch-coppice opposite gave a muddy
reddish tinge.

The room's furnishings were as austere as its white-plaster walls.
A single bed, a chest-of-drawers with mirror, an oak wardrobe, a
straight chair, and one or two small rugs on the floor. The room
smelt fusty in spite of its open windows; it spoke of haste and
untidiness. The bed had been slept in, its bedclothes now thrown
back as though the occupant had got up hastily.

So much they noticed in the litter of personal belongings – loose collars, toilet-articles, books, a plaited dressing-gown-cord – which overflowed from two big suit-cases not yet quite unpacked.

'He was only camping here, you see,' observed Dr Fell, and pointed with the cane. 'Ready to cut and run as soon as he got the dibs. A perfect scheme nobly executed. And instead of that... Stop a bit!'

On the floor beside the bed was an ashtray with two or three cigar-stubs. Beside it stood a tumbler partly full of stale, beaded water, and a tiny bottle. Following the doctor's inquiring glance, Hadley picked up the bottle. It contained a few small white pills, and he carried it to the window to read the label.

'Luminal,' said the superintendent. 'Quarter-grain tablets.'

'That's all right,' interposed Dick. 'It was mentioned last night that he'd brought some luminal with him. Middlesworth told him he could take a quarter-grain if his back got very painful.'

Dr Fell reflected.

'A quarter-grain? No more?'

'That's what Middlesworth said, anyway.'

'And I rather imagine his wound *was* paining him?'

'Like the devil. He wasn't faking about that much, I'll swear.'

'No!' rumbled Dr Fell, shaking his head violently and making a very dismal face. 'No, no, no, no, no! Look here, Hadley. It's not in human nature for De Villa to have been as moderate as that!'

'How do you mean?'

'Well, suppose you were in that position? Suppose you're a strung-up, imaginative chap, facing a long night with a painful bullet-wound? And you've got plenty of luminal handy. Would you stop short with a modest quarter-grain? Wouldn't you give yourself a thorough-good dose and make sure you went off heavily to sleep?'

'Yes,' admitted Hadley, 'I suppose I would. But –'

'We are trying,' roared Dr Fell, taking a few lumbering strides to and from the door, 'to reconstruct the prelude to this crime. And what have we got?'

'Not a hell of a lot, if you want my candid opinion.'

'All the same, follow De Villa's movements. His guests leave him at eleven. He's already in his pyjamas, dressing-gown, and slippers, so he doesn't have to undress. He comes upstairs to this room.'

Here Dr Fell's wandering glance encountered the plaited dressing-gown-cord, which protruded from the suit-case. He stared at it, pulling at his under-lip.

'I say, Hadley. De Villa's body was found this morning in pyjamas and dressing-gown. I didn't notice myself; but do you happen to remember whether the dressing-gown-cord was attached to the dressing-gown?' He looked at Dick. 'What about you, my boy?'

'I don't remember,' Dick confessed.

'Neither do I,' said Hadley. 'But the stuff is at the Hawkstone mortuary now. We can easily ring up and inquire.'

Dr Fell's gesture dismissed the subject.

'Anyway, follow our reconstruction of the dark hours before the murder. De Villa comes up here to bed. He fetches a glass of water. He takes a thorough-good dose of luminal, and sits up in bed to finish a cigar – *vide* ashtray – while the drug takes effect. And then…'

Hadley snorted derisively.

'And then,' said Hadley, 'he gets up and goes downstairs at five o'clock in the morning?'

'Apparently, yes.'

'But why?'

'That,' Dr Fell said abruptly, 'is what I hope Mr Markham can tell us here and now. Come downstairs.'

The sitting-room below looked far less repulsive when no motionless figure sat at the writing-table. The Hawkstone technical men had already covered the room for photographs and finger-prints. And the hypodermic syringe had been removed, though the .22 rifle still stood propped up by the fireplace and the box of spilled drawing-pins lay on the floor beside the easy-chair.

Hadley, who had already said some powerful, realistic words to Dick on the subject of touching exhibits and interfering with evidence, did not comment except by a significant look. And Dr Fell did not comment at all. Folding his arms, the doctor set his back to the wall between the two windows. On one side of him was the bullet-hole in the lower pane, on the other side an empty window-frame with shattered glass lying strewn beneath. Outside the windows loomed the helmet of Bert Miller, endlessly passing and repassing as the constable paced.

'Mr Markham,' began Dr Fell, with such fiery earnestness that Dick felt a few qualms, 'if ever in your life you concentrated, I want you to concentrate now.'

'On what?'

'On what you saw this morning.'

It required no effort of concentration. Dick wondered if that infernal odour of bitter almonds would ever fade, even weeks afterwards, so that images did not pop up from corners of the sitting-room.

'Listen, sir! Let's get one thing straight first. Do you think I'm lying to you?'

'Why should I think that?'

'Because everybody, from Miller out there to Superintendent Hadley and Lord Ashe, seems to think I must have been lying or else dreaming. I tell you, those windows *were* locked on the inside! And the door *was* locked and bolted on the inside. Do you doubt that?'

'Oh, no,' said Dr Fell. 'I don't doubt it.'

'Yet the murderer did get – what's the word I want? – did get his physical body in and out of this room in order to kill De Villa? In spite of the locked door and windows?'

'Yes,' said Dr Fell.

Across the line of the windows passed Miller's figure, like a shadow of the law.

Superintendent Hadley, hitching up the easy-chair to the writing-table, sat down where the dead man had sat, and got out his note-book. Dr Fell added:

'I mean that, Hadley. I mean quite literally that.'

'Go on!' said Hadley.

'Let's begin,' growled Dr Fell, holding his folded arms more tightly, 'with this mysterious telephone-call at two minutes past five. You've heard, now, that the call came from this house?'

'Yes.'

'It couldn't, for instance, have been De Villa's voice speaking?'

'It might have been, yes. I can't say whose voice it was. It whispered.'

'Yet it did convey' – Dr Fell tilted up his chin, squaring himself – 'an impression of urgency?'

'Of very great urgency. Yes.'

'Right. You ran out of your cottage, and along the lane. When you were still some distance from this house, you saw a light switched on in this sitting-room.'

Dr Fell paused, with cross-eyed concentration behind his eye-glasses. 'How far were you away when you saw that light?'

Dick considered.

'A little over a hundred yards, I should say.'

'So you couldn't actually see *into* this room at that time?'

'Lord, no! Nothing like that! I was too far away. I just saw the light shine out when the sky was still pretty dark.'

Without a word Superintendent Hadley got to his feet. The only light in the room was the bright tan-shaded hanging lamp over the writing-table. Its switch was in the wall beside the door to the hall. Hadley walked over to this; he clicked the switch down, and then up again, so that the lamp flashed on and off; afterwards, still without a word, he returned to his notebook at the writing-table.

Dr Fell cleared his throat.

'You then,' he resumed, 'walked more slowly along the lane? Yes! A little later, I understand, you saw this .22 rifle poked over the wall? Yes. How far were you away when you saw that?'

Again Dick reflected.

'Well… say thirty yards. Perhaps less.'

'So you *still* couldn't see into this room here?'

'No. Naturally not.'

'But you distinctly saw the rifle?'

'Yes.'

'You even' – Dr Fell reached out with his right hand and tapped the window-glass – 'you even made out the bullet-hole when, to use your expressive phrase to the constable, it "jumped up in the window-pane"?'

Dick gestured helplessly.

'That's a literary way of putting it, I'm afraid. I was thinking of the fortune-teller's tent. But that's exactly what it amounts to. I was watching the rifle; I saw it fired; and even at that distance I could make out the bullet-hole.'

'You've got long eyesight, I take it?'

'Very long eyesight. Yesterday, for instance, when I was target-shooting at Major Price's range, I could tell exactly where my hits were scored without having the target drawn in to the counter.'

Superintendent Hadley intervened.

'If you're thinking there's any flummery about that bullet-hole,' he said, 'you can wash it out. Purvis's people have verified every-thing: angle of fire, force of projectile, damage to window. And,' he nodded towards the shattered picture over the fireplace, 'checked the bullet they dug out of the wall. It *was* fired from that .22 rifle, and no other rifle.'

Dr Fell slowly turned a red face.

'My God, Hadley,' he said, with a sudden and far-from-characteristic burst of anger which startled Hadley almost as much as it startled Dick, 'will you please allow me to handle this witness in my own way?'

His face grew even more fiery.

'You, sir, are a superintendent of Metropolitan Police. I am very much at your service. I am merely your consultant on the *outré*, or, to put it in a less high-falutin way, the old guy whom you drag in during peculiar, not so loony, cases of this kind. You have done me the honour of consulting me now in a case which we both believe to be murder. May I ask my own questions, sir, or may I not?'

Outside the windows, the moving helmet of Bert Miller stopped for a fraction of a second before Miller resumed his pacing. Not for nothing had Dick, when he related the story to Miller that morning, insisted on suicide with such a wealth of detail that the constable dreamed of no other contingency. This was the first time Miller had heard mention of the word murder from his superior officers.

But Dick hardly noticed this now; it was swept away by the extraordinary violence of Dr Fell's outburst.

'Sorry if I've stepped on your toes,' Hadley said mildly. 'Carry on.'

'Harrumph! Ha! Very well.' Dr Fell adjusted his eyeglasses, drawing the air through his nostrils with a long challenging sound. 'On hearing the shot, Mr Markham, you ran forward again?'

'Yes.'

'And met Miss Cynthia Drew in the lane?'

'That's right.'

'How was it, with your long eyesight, that you hadn't seen *her* before?'

'Because,' answered Dick, 'the sun was smack in my eyes. Straight down the lane, and she was coming from the east. I could see things on either side, but not in the lane itself.'

'H'm, yes. That accounts for it. What explanation did Miss Drew give for her presence in the lane at that hour?'

'Look here, sir! You don't think –?'

'What explanation,' Dr Fell repeated gently, 'did Miss Drew give for her presence in the lane at that hour?'

Outside, in the hall, the telephone began to ring shrilly.

It made each of these three men, each with his own separate thoughts, start a little to hear that clamouring bell. Was this, Dick wondered, the communication Dr Fell expected? Was the murderer – behind a bland friendly countenance of all the bland friendly countenances at Six Ashes – ringing up to whisper more hatred against Lesley Grant? Hadley hurried out to the phone; they heard him speaking in a low voice. When he returned his face was very grave.

'Well?' prompted Dr Fell.

'No,' said the superintendent quickly, 'it's not what you're think-ing. That telephone-communication idea of yours is rubbish, and you know it. Nobody would take such a fool's risk as that. But your other idea, I admit –'

'*Who was it, Hadley?*'

'It was the police-surgeon at Hawkstone. He's just done the post-mortem. And it's upset the apple-cart again.'

Dr Fell, with his big bulk propped against the wall, straightened up. His mouth fell open under the bandit's moustache.

'Look here, Hadley! You're not going to tell me Sam De Villa wasn't killed by prussic acid after all?'

'Oh, yes. He was killed with prussic acid, right enough. About three grains of anhydrous prussic acid, administered in a hypoder-mic by somebody unskilled in the use of it. But...'

'But what?'

'It's the stomach-contents,' said Hadley.

'Go on, man!'

'About six hours before death,' replied Hadley, 'Sam swallowed what must have amounted to three or four grains of luminal.'

Again Hadley sat down at his desk, and opened his notebook.

'Don't you understand?' he went on. 'If Sam took that much luminal before going to bed at some time past eleven, it's practi-cally impossible that he could have come downstairs under his own steam at five o'clock the following morning.'

16

'MIND!' ADDED THE CAUTIOUS SUPERINTENDENT. 'WE CAN'T say it is impossible.' He picked up a pencil and examined its point. 'There are people capable of resistance to the strongest drugs, and people who shake off their effects very quickly. All we can say is that it's very unlikely. But according to the evidence at least, Sam did come downstairs this morning?'

'Apparently, yes.'

'And, unless we call Mr Markham a liar, a light did go on in this room when he says it did?'

'Undoubtedly.'

'But you think that doesn't upset the apple-cart in any way?'

'No,' answered Dr Fell, pushing himself back against the wall so that the front of his shovel-hat rose up as though tilted by an invisible hand, 'no, my lad, I can't say it does. This may become clearer,' he screwed up his face hideously, 'if you let me get on with a few relevant matters. What explanation (may I repeat) did Miss Cynthia Drew give for her presence in the lane at that hour?'

Dick looked away.

'She couldn't sleep. She'd been out for a walk.'

'A walk. Oh, ah. And is Gallows Lane the fashionable place for an early morning walk hereabouts?'

'It could be. Why not?'

Dr Fell frowned. 'The lane, Lord Ashe informed me, ends only a few hundred yards east of here: where, in the eighteenth century, a gallows actually stood.'

'Technically it ends, yes. But there's a hard path across open fields towards Goblin Wood, where everybody goes for a walk. Miller the constable lives near there, as a matter of fact.'

'Really, my boy,' said Dr Fell with exceptional mildness, 'you needn't yell. I quite understand. The point is that Miss Drew was also smack on the scene of the crime, or very nearly so. Did *she* see or hear anything that would help us?'

'No. Cynthia… Wait a minute, yes she did!' exclaimed Dick, catching himself up and obsessed with new, torturing puzzles. 'I didn't mention this in my evidence early this morning, because Cynthia hadn't told me then. She only told me afterwards, when I saw her at Lesley's house.'

'Well?'

'A minute or so before the rifle was fired,' explained Dick, 'Cynthia saw somebody run across the lane from the orchard on this side to the coppice on the other.'

He related the incident.

And the effect of this on Dr Fell was electric.

'Got it!' said the doctor thunderously, and snapped his fingers in the air. 'Archons of Athens, but this is almost too good to be true! Got it!'

Hadley, who knew his obese friend of old, pushed back the easy-chair from the writing-table and got up in a hurry. The movement of the chair – whose rollers slid creakily on the worn brown carpet, past the spilled box of drawing-pins – disclosed something else.

On the floor, open and face down as though it had been shoved under the chair to get it out of sight, lay a cloth-bound book. Hadley, despite his momentary distraction of attention, stooped down to pick up the book.

'I say, Hadley,' remonstrated Dr Fell, with his eye on one drawing-pin which had evidently rolled wide of the others. 'I wish you'd be careful not to step on those drawing-pins. Well? What is it?'

Hadley held out the book. It was a well-thumbed copy of Hazlitt's essays in the Everyman edition, with the name *Samuel R. De Villa* on the fly-leaf and many annotations in the same neat handwriting. Dr Fell inspected it curiously before throwing it on the table.

'Hadn't Sam,' he grunted, 'rather a sophisticated taste in reading-matter?'

'Will you get the idea out of your amateur head,' snapped Hadley, 'that the professional confidence-man is always a flashy hanger-on at fashionable hotels and bars?'

'All right, all right!'

'Sam's donnish manner, as I kept telling you this morning, was worth five thousand a year to him. His father was a West Country clergyman; he took honours at Bristol University; he really did study medicine, and he's played pathologist before without too many slips. Once, in the south of France, he hooked a hard-headed English lawyer out of a thumping sum just because...' Hadley paused, himself picking up and throwing down the book. 'Never mind that, for the moment! What's this brain-wave of yours?'

'Cynthia Drew,' said Dr Fell.

'What about her?'

'What she saw, or claims to have seen, tends to put the lid on it. Somebody has made a bad howler. Now *you*, my lad' – he blinked at Dick – 'saw no sign of this mysterious prowler in the lane?'

'I tell you, the sun was in my eyes!'

'The sun,' returned Dr Fell, 'has been in everybody's eyes. Look there!'

With a sense of impending disaster, with a sense that the whole affair was now running downhill towards a smash, Dick followed the doctor's nod towards the window. A shiny but conservative black two-seater car, which he recognized as belonging to Bill Earnshaw, rattled along the lane and came to a stop. Cynthia Drew sat with Earnshaw in the front seat.

'We haven't met the lady,' observed Dr Fell, 'but I think I can guess who that is. Would you like to bet, Hadley, that she's heard Miss Grant is not an evil poisoner after all? And is coming along here in something like horror to find out the truth from us?'

Hadley whacked his hand down on the table.

'She can't have discovered anything, I tell you!' the superintendent declared. 'Nobody knows but ourselves and Miss Grant and Lord Ashe. Lord Ashe swore he wouldn't say a word. She can't have discovered anything.'

'Oh, yes, she can,' said Dick Markham. 'Earnshaw!'

Hadley looked puzzled.

'Earnshaw?'

'The bank-manager! That fellow who's getting out of the car with her now! He was here this morning, and he stayed long enough to hear Dr Fell say, "That's not Sir Harvey Gilman!" – Don't you remember, Dr Fell?'

There was a silence, while they clearly heard the swishing noise of footsteps in grass as Cynthia and Earnshaw approached the cottage.

Dr Fell swore under his breath.

'Hadley,' he said, in a thunderous whisper like the wind along an Underground-railway tunnel, 'I am an ass. Archons of Athens, what an outstanding ASS am I! I completely forgot the fellow, in spite of the fact that we met him in the post office this afternoon.'

Here Dr Fell smote his fist against his pink forehead.

'I should keep a secretary,' he roared, 'merely to remind me of what I was thinking about two minutes before. Of course! That erect back! That Anthony Eden hat! That polished hair and dental smile! When we met him at the post office, you know, I *had* a vague feeling I'd seen the blighter somewhere before. Absence of mind, my good Hadley…!'

'Well,' said Hadley unsympathetically, 'don't blame me. But, speaking of post offices, doesn't this dish your other scheme?'

'No, not necessarily. At the same time, I would rather have had it work out in a different way.'

The meaning of this reference to the post office – with its temperamental proprietress Miss Laura Feathers, who shouted lectures at you from behind her wire-guarded counter for the smallest postal infringement – was far from clear to Dick.

But every other consideration went out of his mind, was swept away, in his concern for Cynthia Drew.

'Miller!' called Superintendent Hadley.

Outside the window, Bert Miller wheeled round. He looked as though about to say something on his own account, but altered his mind.

'Sir?'

'You can admit both Miss Drew and Mr Earnshaw,' Hadley told

him. 'But *I*' – here he directed a very significant glance at Dr Fell '– I, my friend, will do the questioning of this witness.'

Cynthia, with Earnshaw just behind her, hurried into the room from the hall and stopped dead. The weight of emotional tensity, while Hadley stood looking politely at Cynthia, could be felt like the warmth of that sitting-room. Cynthia had almost managed to disguise, with powder, the darkish bruise on her right temple. Other things she could not disguise.

'Miss Cynthia Drew?' Hadley said without inflexion.

'Yes, yes. I –'

Hadley introduced himself, and presented Dr Fell. He did this with deliberation, with smoothness, and with what was, to Dick Markham, a horrible sense of imminent danger.

'You wanted to see us about something, Miss Drew?'

'My mother told me,' returned Cynthia, with a steady hardness and shine about her blue eyes, 'that you came to see *me*.' Cynthia made a slight gesture. 'She didn't tell me at the time you were there, I'm afraid. She thought she was keeping me from unpleasantness. It wasn't until Mr Earnshaw dropped in –'

'Ah, yes,' Hadley said pleasantly. 'Mr Earnshaw!'

'– dropped in, and mentioned one thing or another,' said Cynthia, fighting to control her breathing but keeping her eyes steadily fixed on Hadley's, 'that I learned you *had* been there. Did you want to see me about anything, Mr Hadley?'

'As a matter of fact, Miss Drew, I did. Will you sit down?'

And he indicated the heavy easy-chair in which the dead man had been sitting.

If it was meant as a gesture of studied callousness, it had its effect. Yet Cynthia never flinched or took her eyes from his.

'In that chair, Mr Hadley?'

'In another chair, by all means. If you've got any objection to that one.'

Cynthia went over and plumped down in the easy-chair.

Earnshaw, hesitating and smiling in the doorway, cleared his throat.

'I just happened to tell Cynthia –' he began. But his voice rose with shattering loudness, and then fell away to nothing, because of the silence and the battery of looks directed at him by both Hadley and Dr Fell. Hadley faced Cynthia across the writing-table, leaning his hands on the edge of it.

'Your mother told us, Miss Drew, that you got that bruise on your temple from slipping and falling on some stone steps.'

'I'm afraid,' answered Cynthia, 'that was just a polite fiction for the benefit of the neighbours.'

Hadley nodded.

'Actually, I'm told, you got the bruise when Miss Lesley Grant hit out at you with a hand-mirror?'

'Yes. I'm afraid that's true.'

'Would it interest you to hear, Miss Drew, that Miss Grant denies hitting you with a mirror or with anything else?'

Cynthia raised her head. She put the palms of her hands flat along the arms of the chair. Her blue eyes opened in amazement.

'But that's simply not true!'

'It's not true, Miss Drew, that you fell and struck the side of your head against the footboard of a bed?'

'I... no, of course not!' After a speculative silence, while they again heard distantly the voice of the church-clock, Cynthia added: 'Let's come straight out with this, shall we? I hate beating about the bush. I hate – crooked things! And I'm pretty sure you know why I've come here to see you. Mr Earnshaw has been telling me…'

Earnshaw intervened before anybody could stop him.

'If you don't mind,' he said with polite sharpness, 'I'd rather be kept out of this.'

'So?' inquired Dr Fell.

'I came here early to-day,' Earnshaw continued, smiling away unconsciously even as he registered a protest, 'to ask about a rifle. That rifle there by the fireplace. While I was here, I gave Dick Markham a theory about this affair. I also gave him some information.'

'Concerning,' said Dr Fell, 'drawing-pins?'

'Yes!' Earnshaw now poured with volubility. 'Colonel Pope always used to use drawing-pins for his gauze screens, as you can see for yourself if you examine the marks on any window-frame in this house. Though what a box of them should be doing on the floor now I can't say. Never mind!'

Here Earnshaw raised his hand.

'While I was here,' he went on to Dr Fell, 'I heard a certain thing. About – Sir Harvey Gilman. You said it, Dr Fell. I wasn't sworn to secrecy, if you remember. Nobody asked me not to mention it. All the same, I decided not to mention it. Because of my position; because I didn't understand it; because discretion is discretion.'

Nobody now tried to stop Earnshaw. It was as though he spoke into a void, as though he spoke to Dr Fell round a corner, utterly ignoring the tableau presented by Hadley and Cynthia in the middle of the room. The silent struggle between the eyes of Hadley and the eyes of Cynthia was emphasized and heightened to fever-pitch by Earnshaw's words.

'On my way home from the bank to-day…'

(Cynthia made a short, slight movement.)

'On my way home from the bank to-day,' said Earnshaw, 'I stopped at Cynthia's house to give her a message from my wife. She saw me. She broke down a little. She told me an absolutely ghastly story' – here Earnshaw uttered a loud laugh – 'about Lesley Grant.'

'A true story,' said Cynthia, with her eyes on Hadley.

'A ghastly story,' repeated Earnshaw. 'I felt bound to warn her, you know. Discretion or no discretion. I said, "Look here, where did you hear that?"'

'A very interesting question,' said Hadley.

'I said, "Because I'm bound to warn you that Dr Gideon Fell says this Sir Harvey Gilman wasn't Sir Harvey Gilman at all. And Middlesworth claims he was an impostor too."'

'Is the story true? The story about Lesley?' demanded Cynthia.

'*Is* it true?' asked Earnshaw, who was white to the forehead.

Superintendent Hadley remained for a second or two supporting his weight with both hands on the writing-table; his face betraying nothing.

'Suppose I told you, Miss Drew – and you too, Mr Earnshaw – that the story about Miss Lesley Grant is perfectly true?'

'Oh, my God,' murmured Earnshaw in a flat voice.

Cynthia dropped her eyes at last. She seemed to gasp at the air, as though she had been holding her breath for a full minute.

'Officially, mind,' the superintendent spoke in a warning tone, 'I have no information to give you. I merely say "suppose" that. And I think, Mr Earnshaw, I'd rather excuse you while I have a further word with Miss Drew. If you wouldn't mind waiting out in the car?'

'No, no, no,' Earnshaw assured him. Earnshaw glanced at Dick, and looked away with perplexed embarrassment. 'Lesley Grant a poisoner with – Never mind! Discretion. It's incredible! Excuse me.'

He closed the door firmly after him. They heard his footsteps in the hall, and their tempo seemed to quicken in the grass outside.

For the first time Cynthia addressed herself to Dick Markham.

'I *couldn't* tell you about it this morning, Dick,' she said in a low, steady voice. There was pity in her gaze: if this were acting, it struck him with honest horror. 'I couldn't bring myself to hurt you that much! When it came to the test, I'm afraid I simply failed it.'

'Yes,' said Dick. His throat felt thick; he did not look back at her.

'I've been wondering all afternoon,' Cynthia went on in a conscience-stricken voice, 'whether I might be doing her an injustice. Honestly, if there had been any mistake about this, I should have gone down on my knees to beg her pardon!'

'Yes. Of course. I see.'

'When Bill Earnshaw told me what he did, I wondered for half a second...! But there it is!'

'Just one moment, Miss Drew.' Hadley did not speak loudly. 'You couldn't bring yourself to hurt Mr Markham by telling him about this, though you believed he knew it already?' He paused. 'You told Miss Grant, didn't you, that Mr Markham already knew all about it?'

Cynthia uttered a small harsh laugh.

'I'm a rotten bad hand at expressing myself,' she replied. 'Yes. I knew he'd heard it. But *I* didn't want to be the one who threw it in his teeth and reminded him of it. Can't you understand that?'

'By the way, Miss Drew, where did you hear the story?'

'Oh, does that matter now? If the story is true?'

Hadley reached over and picked up his notebook.

'It might not matter,' he conceded in an even voice, 'if the story were true. But it's not true at all, Miss Drew. It was a pack of lies invented by a crook who called himself Sir Harvey Gilman.'

Cynthia stared at him.

'You said –!'

'Oh, no. I carefully said "suppose" that, as any of these gentlemen can testify.' Hadley poised his pencil over the notebook. 'Where did you hear the story?'

Incredulity, defiance, still a straightforward virtuousness all mingled in Cynthia's expression, despite the pallor of her face and the rigidity of her body.

'Don't be silly!' she burst out. And then: 'If this isn't true, why should anybody say it was?'

'Certain people might not like Miss Grant very much. Can't you understand that?'

'No. I like Lesley, or *thought* I liked her, very much.'

'Yet you attacked her?'

'I didn't attack her,' replied Cynthia, raising her chin with pale calm.

'She attacked you, then? You still maintain you got that bruise on your temple from being hit with a hand-mirror?'

'Yes.'

'Where did you hear this story, Miss Drew?'

Cynthia still disregarded this.

'It's utterly absurd,' she declared, 'that anybody should give all those details unless there was some truth in it. *Some* truth, don't you see?' She spread out her hands. 'What *do* you know about Lesley? How many times *has* she been married? What does she keep in that safe?'

'Listen, Miss Drew.' Hadley put down notebook and pencil. Again he balanced his hands on the edge of the table, with powerful patience, as though he were going to push the table towards her. 'I keep telling you there's NO truth in the whole thing.'

'But...!'

'Miss Grant isn't a criminal. She has never been married. What she kept in the safe was perfectly innocent. She was nowhere near this cottage last night or this morning. Let me carry that further. The house here remained dark from eleven o'clock last night until some minutes past five this morning, when a light was turned on in...'

'Sir!' interposed a new voice.

For some minutes Dick had been aware of what might be called a background difference. The helmet of Police-Constable Miller still passed and repassed outside the windows. But it had been moving a little more rapidly.

And it was Miller's large face which appeared now, poked through the frame of the shattered window: sideways, almost comic-looking if it had not been for Miller's heavy urgency.

'Sir,' he addressed the superintendent huskily, 'can *I* say something?'

Hadley turned in exasperation.

'Later! We're –'

'But it's important, sir. It's about,' he thrust a big arm through the window to point, 'it's about *this*.'

'Come in,' said Hadley; and not a person in that room moved until Miller had clumped round outside, entered by the hall door, and stood at attention.

'I could 'a' told you before, sir.' A mole beside Bert's nose looked defiantly reproachful. 'Only nobody said nothing to me about what you might call murder.'

'Well?'

'I live over near Goblin Wood, sir.'

'All right! Well!'

'I was out very late last night, sir. Because a drunken man was making trouble at Newton Farm. I always cycle home through this lane, and over the path to Goblin Wood. And,' added Miller, 'I passed these cottages 'ere, on my bike, about three o'clock this morning.'

Silence.

'Well?' prompted Hadley.

'Mr Markham's house, sir,' Miller nodded towards Dick, 'was all bright-lighted in one room. I could see it plain.'

'That's all right,' said Dick. 'I went to sleep on the sofa in the study, and left the lights burning.'

'But,' continued Miller with emphasis, 'this cottage 'ere was much more than that. It was all lighted up like a Christmas tree.'

Hadley took one step round the side of the writing-table. '*What's that you're saying?*'

Miller remained emphatic and dogged.

'Sir, it's true what I'm telling you. All the curtains was drawn on the windows, yes. But you could just see lights inside. And practically every room in this cottage – at least, what I could see when I rode past on my bike – had a light burning inside it.'

The open bewilderment of Cynthia Drew, who had craned round from the easy-chair; the more suave perplexity of Superintendent Hadley at this vision of a house lighted in loneliness with a drugged man inside it: both these were lost to Dick's notice in the over-whelming satisfaction which radiated from Dr Gideon Fell. Dr Fell's 'Aha!' – breathed across the room with a melodramatic gusto springing from sheer sincerity – indicated that he was very sure of himself now.

Miller cleared his throat.

'I thinks to myself, "That's all right." Because I'd heard the gentleman had been hurt, and I thinks to myself about nurses and doctors and people. And I thinks to myself, "Shall I go in and inquire!" But I thinks to myself it's too late, and it can wait.

'But, sir,' continued Miller, raising his voice as though fearful of being interrupted, 'I did see somebody standing by the front door. It was a bit dark, I know. But it was the white blouse or sweater or whatever you call it that made me notice; and I'm pretty sure...'

Hadley stood rigid.

'White blouse?' he repeated.

'Sir, it was Miss Lesley Grant.'

17

W AS CYNTHIA LYING? OR WAS LESLEY?
Let's face it.

Walking home through the twilight of Gallows Lane, an eerie whispering twilight where the birds bickered before going to sleep, Dick Markham tried to face it out.

It was past eight o'clock. Even if he bathed and shaved in a hurry, he would still be late for his dinner-engagement with Lesley. This seemed a minor treachery, since Lesley put such a romantic store by it. But, in the matter of a little thing like a murder, was Cynthia lying or was Lesley?

The whole damned business was too close! Too personal! Too entwined with emotion! It seemed to resolve itself into a balance of what you believed between Lesley Grant on the one hand and Cynthia Drew on the other. And the balance-weights wouldn't stay still.

One of these girls, reading the matter like that, was clear-eyed and honest, telling the truth with sincere purpose. The other hid many ugly thoughts behind a pretty face, which might wear a very different expression if you caught it off guard.

Both of these girls you know well. Both you have recently held in your arms – though Cynthia only for the purpose of consoling her, of course – and to think of such matters in connexion with either seems fantastic foolery. Yet the hypodermic needle jabbed like a cobra, fanged with poison; and somebody's hand held it, and somebody laughed.

Not that he wavered in his loyalty to Lesley. He was in love with Lesley.

But suppose, just suppose after all...?

Nonsense! She couldn't have had any motive!

Couldn't she?

Yet, in Cynthia's case, it was almost as bad. He himself had written a good deal of learned balderdash about repressions, very useful if you wanted motives for a play or a book. But if this turned up on the doorstep, if the repressions exploded in your face, you were like a man who dabbles pleasantly in diabolism and then finds the devil really following you.

And, in either event, how had the thing been done in that locked and bolted room?

Dr Fell evidently knew, though he would say nothing. Dr Fell and Hadley, in fact, had adjourned to a private conference at the back of the cottage: from which emerged much shouting and banging of fists on tables but no audible explanation. Dick had not been present. He and Cynthia had even been kept in separate rooms, eyed by the watchful Miller. But now...?

Tramping disconsolately down the lane, Dick turned in at the gate of his own cottage. It loomed up dark ahead of him, the diamond-paned windows dusted with twilight.

Curse it all, he'd got to *hurry!* Lesley would be waiting. He was badly in need of a shave, he must change his rumpled clothes...

Dick closed the front door on a dusky hall. In dimness he barged through the passage into the study, where the outlines of books and melodramatic playbills were not quite lost in shadow. He touched the light-switch by the door. He clicked it, and clicked it back again, before realizing that the switch was already down but that the lights failed to work.

That infernal shilling-in-the-slot meter again!

Mrs Bewford, the woman who "did" for him, was usually kept well supplied with shillings to feed this monster. But Dick himself had kept the lights burning all night before; the supply was exhausted, and the lights had gone out.

Groping his way across the study, Dick penetrated through the kitchen and then into the scullery: whose windows were on the east side like those of his study. By rare good luck – this seldom happens – he did manage to find a shilling among the coins in his pocket. Feeling his way blindly under the sink, he found the meter, twisted the catch as he pushed the coin through, and heard it fall inside.

And the light went on in his study.

The light went on in his study.

He was standing by the scullery-sink, raising himself from the meter and staring out through the scullery-window, when he noticed it. He saw a bright glow spring up in his own side garden, just as many hours before he had seen the glow spring up through the windows of that other sitting-room...

The light was not switched on; but it went on. Dick Markham gripped the edges of the sink.

'Wow!' he said aloud.

He went back to the study, surveyed it, and addressed the typewriter.

'Do you want to know, old son,' he said to the typewriter, 'how to create the illusion that a light is switched on inside a locked and bolted room?'

Dick stopped abruptly.

For Major Horace Price, his sandy eyebrows raised in astonishment, was standing by the door to the front hall.

Major Price's round speckled face, with its cropped sandy moustache and light-blue eyes, assumed a tolerant look. His hearty manner conveyed that he rather expected to find a writer of sensational plays talking to his typewriter as to a friend; and that, though it mightn't be his own way, he quite understood.

'What did you say, my dear chap?' asked the major.

'Do *you* want to know, Major Price,' demanded Dick, 'how to create the illusion that a light is switched on inside a locked and bolted room?'

He was not now concerned with keeping secrets. He wanted to blurt out with emphasis this particular secret.

Real interest appeared in Major Price's rather prominent eyes. After a hasty glance over his shoulder to make sure nobody was listening, the major came in and closed the study door. Dick remained engrossed and enwrapped.

'I was thinking last night,' Dick swept on, 'that all three cottages in this lane have shilling-in-the-slot meters. By God, *that's* why he did it! That's why the lights down there were turned on and left burning half the night!'

Major Price looked fussed.

'You'd better stop a bit, my dear chap! That's why who did what?'

'Bert Miller,' said Dick, 'rode past on his bike last night and saw that all the lights down there were burning behind closed curtains.'

'Did he, my dear chap? Well?'

'Somebody,' said Dick, 'switched on all the lights and left them like that until the current was used up.'

'I say! If you wouldn't mind...?'

"The lights went out. Then somebody turned off all the switches *except* the switch in the sitting-room, which was left pressed down. At the proper time in the morning, somebody had only to drop a shilling into the electric meter in the scullery. And a light went on, as though switched on, in the sitting-room.'

Major Price gave a puzzled little chuckle.

Peering round at the playbills on the walls – *Poisoner's Mistake*, *Panic in the Family*, and *I Never Suspected*, which always afforded the major quiet amusement though he had seen them so often before – he went over and sat down in tweedy untidiness on the sofa.

'Mind telling me about it?' he suggested. 'I'm afraid I haven't got the slightest idea what you're getting at.'

Then Dick saw the flaw.

This business about the light was true. Dr Fell knew it was true, since the doctor had made special and curious reference to that electric meter in the other cottage.

But it still didn't explain the problem.

'It doesn't explain,' Dick declared aloud, 'how the murderer got his physical body out of a locked room, leaving Sam De Villa there! And the room is still locked. And Sam, I'll take my oath, had been dead only a very few minutes when I arrived.'

Just as before. The puzzle remained unchanged.

In a leisurely way Major Price got out pipe and tobacco-pouch. His cropped sandy head, like a Prussian's, was inclined forward; his eyes grew keen with interest.

'Who,' he asked in a sharper tone, 'is Sam De Villa?'

And Dick woke up.

'Look here, Major: you've got to excuse me! I was so jarred by something that's just happened that I've been babbling away aloud. And the fact is, you know, I've got no right to be talking. If you understood why…'

'My dear chap! None of my business! Unless –'

'Unless?'

'Unless it concerns one of my clients, of course.' Major Price punched tobacco into the pipe-bowl with a large thumb. 'Village opinion now seems about divided between suicide and murder. I – er – can't say.'

'It was just a brain-wave of mine,' Dick explained. 'But I'm afraid it doesn't amount to anything. No, confound it! The only person who's made an intelligent suggestion so far is Bill Earnshaw.'

Major Price's whale-like back grew rigid.

'Earnshaw,' he said, 'made an intelligent suggestion?'

'Yes! And I wonder why Dr Fell hasn't looked into it! Earnshaw said –'

'My dear chap,' the major interposed stiffly, 'I really don't think I care to hear about it. All that surprises me is that Earnshaw made what you call an intelligent suggestion.'

'Look here, Major! Are you and Bill still at loggerheads?'

The sandy eyebrows went up.

'Loggerheads? I don't understand that. But it does seem a pity, after all, if a chap who prides himself on his sense of humour can't take a harmless joke without wanting to make a personal issue of it.'

'Was this the joke you played on Earnshaw at the shooting-range yesterday? What was the joke, by the way?'

'Doesn't matter! Doesn't matter at all!' The pipe was filled to Major Price's satisfaction, but a red bar showed across his amiable forehead. He still held himself stiffly as he sat on the sofa. 'I didn't come here to talk about that. I did come here – if you'll excuse me –'

'I'm afraid, Major, you'll have to excuse *me*. I'm overdue at Lesley's for dinner, and I haven't even got dressed yet.'

'Exactly,' said Major Price, and consulted the pipe. Then he looked up. 'Do you know what time it is now?'

Dick glanced at a useless wrist-watch.

'It's twenty minutes to nine,' Major Price told him. 'And I think you were due at the gal's place, for cocktails, at half-past seven?'

'Now stop a bit!' urged the major, lifting his hand as Dick began to make a beeline to get upstairs. 'It's all very well to start hurrying now. All very well! But the question is, my dear chap: will you find her at home when you do get there?'

Dick stopped dead.

'Meaning what?'

With a shake of his head Major Price devoted close attention to the top of the pipe.

'I speak,' he said, 'as a man old enough to be the father of both of you. And as a friend. No offence meant. But, dash it all, you know, I wish to blazes you'd do the thing right one way or the other! Is it true, or isn't it, that Mrs Rackley saw you and Cynthia Drew up to no good in Lesley's blasted bedroom to-day?'

It was the very grotesqueness of this, at a time like the present, which took Dick aback.

'I tell you,' he said, 'there was absolutely no…!'

'Of course not, my dear chap! I quite understand! At the same time –'

'Mrs Rackley told Lesley about it?'

'Yes. Especially when you didn't turn up at half-past seven, or at eight, or even at half-past eight. And another thing.' Major Price put the pipe in his mouth. 'Has Cynthia been down there,' he nodded his head towards the other cottage, 'down there with you all this time?'

'Cynthia left, with Bill Earnshaw, an hour ago.'

'If you'd only telephoned, my dear chap!'

'Listen, Major Price. There have been some very serious developments in this business, which threaten to turn the whole case upside down again. I can't tell you any more than that, except that Hadley may be descending on Lesley at any minute' – he saw Major Price's thick-set figure stiffen – 'to ask her some questions.'

'Really? You don't tell me!'

'I only got away myself because Hadley and Dr Fell are in the middle of an argument, and...'

'Argument about what?'

'For one thing, about distillation of prussic acid. And how easy it is from non-poisonous ingredients you can buy at any chemist's. But most of it wasn't either audible or clear. Anyway, I can easily explain to Lesley!'

Major Price spun the wheel of a lighter and lit his pipe.

'My dear chap,' he said, 'all I can tell you is that the girl is very upset and rather hysterical. She must have been through a lot to-day, though she won't' – his forehead darkened '– she won't even confide in her legal adviser. If you want to do her a good service, you'll cut along there straightaway.'

'Looking like this?'

The major was emphatic.

'Yes. Looking like that. It's a bit diplomatically late, you know, to use the phone now.'

Dick went.

As he turned out into the lane again and headed west towards the village, he could faintly hear a murmur of voices approaching behind him. They were the voices of Dr Fell and Superintendent Hadley, still arguing.

If these two were on their way to Lesley's themselves at this minute, with further questions for a girl whom Major Price described as already very upset and rather hysterical, then Dick meant to get there first. And then – what?

He didn't know. No doubt there was some innocent explanation of why Bert Miller swore he saw Lesley beside the cottage in the middle of the night; Dick shut up his mind and refused to think about this, because he told himself he would not go through the same anguish, only to have it naturally explained, twice in one day. But he quickened his step nevertheless.

Three or four minutes brought him to the High Street. Lesley's house was very close now.

A wraith of pink sunset lingered behind these roof-tops, making a slate gleam here or silhouetting chimney-stacks there. But dusk filled the High Street, which lay entirely deserted. Those inhabitants of Six Ashes not to be found at the 'Griffin and Ash-tree' would be at home, getting ready to switch on the nine o'clock news.

Dick turned to the right out of Gallows Lane, crossed the road, and walked at long strides along the brick-paved path which served as a pavement for the High Street.

Here was Lesley's house, set back behind its chestnut trees, with a good stretch of grass on each side as well. No lights showed now behind its thick, drawn curtains except upstairs in the bedroom; but a tiny porch-light shone out over the front door. Dick halted at the front gate, looking left and right.

The only dwelling nearby (if it could be called a dwelling at all) was the post office next door. Dick, looking towards his right, saw this weather-boarded little building in all its lack of dignity.

Two dingy plate-glass windows, with a door between and slots for letters and parcels under one window, faced the High Street. In the front premises, Miss Laura Feathers combined her postal duties with a sketchy drapery-business which never seemed to sell anything. In the straggling back-premises, Miss Laura Feathers made her home. The post office always closed at six – malcontents said before six – and it was closed now, dark blinds drawn down on door and windows, with an air of defying customers as a fort would defy attackers.

Dick looked at it without curiosity in the mild summer dusk.

From somewhere not far away, a late lawn-mower was whirring drowsily. Dick put Miss Laura Feathers out of his mind. He opened the front gate. He started up the path to see Lesley.

And then, inside the post office, somebody fired a shot.

There is somewhere a nightmare story of two lovers for ever condemned to push through the revolving doors of the same hotel. Something of the same quality, a sense of doors revolving only to shut him in again with the same nightmare scene, welled up in Dick Markham's heart and soul.

It had been a firearm, right enough. A pistol or maybe even a rifle. And he knew where the noise had come from.

Dick wanted to run away, to run blindly, to get away from what eternally pursued him. But he knew with equal clarity that he couldn't do it. He must go where it led him, if only because of Lesley. He turned back, and raced along the brick pavement to the post office. The noise of his own footsteps on brick made flat clamour; it was the only sound in the High Street.

Close at hand, you could see a faint pale edge of electric light behind the close-drawn blinds of windows and door.

'Hello!' he called. 'Hello there!'

He expected no reply, but in a sense he received one. Behind that closed door, footsteps on bare boards moved away: quick footsteps, tiptoe and stealthy, retreating towards the living-premises behind.

Dick took hold of the door-handle. Though this door never opened after six – except when Henry Garrett the postman came at nine for the evening mail-collection which Miss Feathers put ready for him in a canvas bag – still the door was unlocked now.

An image of Miss Feathers, who would talk of nothing but her gastritis and the enormities of her customers, rose in Dick's mind now. He flung the door open, and smelled burnt powder-smoke.

Inside the little dingy premises of the post office, a dusty electric bulb shone down on the wire-grilled postal counter along the right, and the drapery counter with its shelves along the left. Its floor-boards, worn smooth and black after so many years, reflected that light. At the rear Dick saw an open door leading to the living-premises, from which he could hear the singing and knocking of a boiling tea-kettle.

But he did not look at that, first of all.

The inside of the letter-and-parcels box was under the window on the same side as the drapery counter. Its little wooden door stood wide open. You dropped letters through those slots facing the street, and they fell into the box on this side; but few of them remained in the box now.

The floor on that side, in fact, was scattered with trampled envelopes of all sizes, as though they had been blown wide by a gust of wind. A tightly rolled magazine in its wrapper still bumped along the uneven floor, its blue stamp turning over and over until it lodged against the counter opposite.

And behind the drapery counter, swaying on her feet, stood Miss Laura Feathers herself.

Her dark eyes, though they were glazing and could have seen little, nevertheless had an electric wildness. Incredibly ugly, incredibly dingy she looked, with the greyish hair drawn up in a knot from her ravaged face, and the shapeless dark dress. Shot through the body at close range, she kept the fingers of her right hand, bloodied fingers, pressed hard under her left breast. She must have had some dim comprehension of a newcomer. For with her left hand, which seemed to clutch a fragment of paper, she kept shaking and pointing with frantic vitality towards the door at the rear.

For a second more she kept gaspingly pointing and shaking that hand, trying to speak before she fell over in a heap behind the counter.

Then there was silence, except for the singing and knocking of the tea-kettle in the back room.

18

I N HIS DREAMS, FOR LONG AFTERWARDS, DICK MARKHAM REMEM-bered those eyes fixed on him. They had a pathos, a sick realization of her plight, an appeal which Miss Feathers had never exercised in life.

For she was dead now.

Dick found her lying behind the counter, the eyes wide open. She lay on a drift of scattered envelopes, her left hand still pointing forward. But the fingers had relaxed a little before they tightened, suddenly, in the pinching grip of death. The piece of paper she had been holding, slightly bloodstained along the edges, lay beside her hand.

Dick picked it up mechanically, when Miss Feather's body jerked like a fish and then lay still. He could not have told why he picked it up. Yet, subconsciously, something had caught his eye.

The piece of paper was a narrow fragment of the top of an envelope, torn lengthwise and upwards, just missing the stamp. Inside it stuck an even smaller fragment of a sheet of notepaper which had been inside the missing envelope. Typewritten words, a few words which had been left behind of the original note, struck up at him. The torn strip said: *why be such fools? If you want to know how Lesley Grant did it*

No more. And nothing on the opposite side. But Dick stared at the words as though they were enlarging before his eyes.

For they had been written on his own typewriter.

No mistaking that cranky 'y', which always gave him so much trouble, or the black 'w', which he could never get properly clear. Dick lived for and at and with typewriters; he would have known his own Underwood anywhere. For seconds he stood looking at this nightmare fragment before something else made him jerk up his head.

Somewhere in the living-premises at the rear, stealthy footsteps again began to run.

He never knew until afterwards how near he came to getting a revolver-bullet through his own heart. For he acted mechanically, without thinking of consequences. Still tightly holding the shred of note and envelope, he vaulted over the counter and ran for the door at the rear.

Three straggling rooms, one behind the other in a straight line, ran out ahead of him. In the first, a sitting-room-kitchen of greasy wallpaper, the table was set for supper and the banging kettle on the hob sent up a cloud of steam. The room was empty. Beyond, another door led to a bedroom – and across this, as he plunged in, he saw an opposite door to the scullery sharply close.

He was chasing the murderer, no doubt of that. The bedroom was dark. Somebody, on the other side of the door in the scullery, was frantically fumbling to turn the key on that side; frantically fumbling to lock the door against him.

And the key wouldn't turn.

Dick, racing for that door, fell at full length over a clothes-horse of underwear set straight in his path. He came down with a jar that bit needles into the palms of his hands, and struck his wits as though with a blow across the brain. But he was up again like an india-rubber cat, kicking the clattering clothes-horse out of his way.

The scullery was empty too.

Smelling of stale water and soap-suds, it was not quite so dark as the bedroom. Its back door, glass-panelled, still quivered against the wall where somebody had flung it open after running out only a few seconds before.

Got away?

No! But...

Grey light outlined against black the oblongs of the scullery windows. Dick emerged from the back door into a sweet-scented dusk rustling with the leaves of chestnut trees, and realized with a start where he had come.

The length of this narrow post office building carried him over fifty feet back from the High Street. Beyond a waist-high stone wall which surrounded the grounds, he could see across from him the side and part of the back of Lesley Grant's house.

The running shadow of the murderer, a shadow blurred to shapelessness, streaked across the lawn. It melted into the outline of a tree, hesitated, and moved softly towards the back door of Lesley's house. No light showed from the kitchen there; no light illuminated a face. Dick was just able to see the edge of the back door open and close, soundlessly, as the figure melted inside.

Into Lesley's house. That meant...

Hold on!

Panting, Dick climbed over the low wall into the grounds. As his eyes grew accustomed to the dimness, other figures swam towards him. For some seconds he had been conscious of a bumping, rattly sound, the noise of a lawn-mower upended and rolled through grass.

He could now identify the lawn-mower he had heard a while ago. It had been pushed by McIntyre, Lesley's gardener, whose tall gaunt figure now appeared near the back door. Glancing to the left, towards the front of the house, Dick saw the vast, the unmistakable figure of Dr Gideon Fell, in cape and shovel-hat, advancing along the path towards the front door.

Dr Fell and Hadley had been walking not far behind him. They must have heard that gunshot too.

But this was not what caused the rush of elation which flooded through Dick's nerves as his intelligence began to work again. He held up the torn shreds of notepaper and envelope in his hand. His mind suddenly fitted together a number of isolated facts. And he breathed for joy and relief at what he had to tell himself. *The murder of Laura Feathers was the final, convincing proof of Lesley Grant's innocence.*

He could demonstrate it.

Yet it brought the shock of new dangers. The real murderer, bolting out at the rear of the post office, had unexpectedly been penned in on three sides. McIntyre was approaching from one direction. Dr Fell from another direction, and Dick from still a third. The murderer had taken refuge in Lesley's house. Since Lesley was there alone, with only Mrs Rackley to attend her...

It was an unnerving thought. Dick ran hard across the lawn to the back door.

'Stand in front of this door!' he shouted to an astounded McIntyre. 'Don't let anybody get out! Do you understand?'

'Yes, sir. But –'

He did not stop to inquire into McIntyre's astonishment. Opening the back door, he entered a dark kitchen heavy with the

smell of cooking, saw a line of light shining under the swing-door
to the dining-room, and hurried through.

Lesley, in a light-green dinner-dress frilled at the shoulders, got
up hastily from the other side of the table. The chandelier lights
shone down on the polished mahogany of that table: on the round
lace mats, on the china and cutlery for a meal which had not been
served, on the silver candlesticks with tall white candles which had
not been lighted.

Lesley herself, after the start she could not help giving, stood
with her arms straight down at her side. He saw the sleekness of
the brown hair, the soft line of chin and neck, the brown eyes suddenly turned away.

'Your dinner's out there,' she said, and nodded towards the
kitchen without looking at him. 'It's cold. I – I told Mrs Rackley
to go. When you came to face it, couldn't you bear to eat with the
daughter of Lily Jewell?'

Yet, even in the midst of the morbid thoughts which he guessed
must have been torturing her, she could not help noticing his
expression.

'Lesley,' he said, 'who came into this house just now?'

Her hand tightened on the back of a chair. She looked away
for a second, as though to clear her head of angry and half-tearful
confusion, before turning back to him in perplexity.

'Into this house? Nobody!'

'Through the back door. Not half a minute ago.'

'Nobody came in except you. I've been here all the time! I ought
to know!'

'There's that breakfast-room,' said Dick. 'He, or she' – a fleeting
glimpse of Cynthia Drew's face appeared to his imagination – 'or

whoever it is, could have gone through there into the front hall without your knowing it.'

'Dick, what on earth *is* all this?'

He didn't want to alarm her, but it had to be told.

'Listen, my dear. Laura Feathers has been killed. Somebody got into the post office and shot her only a few minutes ago.' He saw Lesley's slim fingers tighten on the back of the chair; she swayed, her head thrown back under this final bedevilment. 'What's more, the murderer is the same person who killed Sam De Villa. And I'm afraid he's in the house now.'

The shrill pealing of the front door-bell, whose buzzer was in this room, made them both jump like the whirr of a rattlesnake.

Lesley stared at him.

'It's all right!' Dick assured her. 'That's Dr Fell. He was coming up the front path; I saw him. You say Mrs Rackley isn't here?'

'No. I sent her away because...'

'Then come along with me,' said Dick, taking firm hold of her wrist. 'There probably isn't any danger, but I don't want you out of my sight while I answer that door.'

A voice in his mind said: You're a liar, my lad. There's a very great deal of danger when a person who hates Lesley Grant as the devil hates holy-water is trapped and cornered with a loaded gun in the same girl's house. Every corner of a familiar house, every curtain and stair-landing, was fanged and poisoned with danger. Dick held even more tightly to Lesley's wrist, despite her struggles to get away.

'I'd really rather you didn't touch me,' Lesley said breathlessly. 'When you and Cynthia –'

'Don't mention Cynthia!'

'Why not?'

Half dragging her into the front hall, Dick opened the door; and saw, as he had hoped, the reassuring immensity of Dr Fell outside.

'Laura Feathers –' Dick began.

'I know,' said Dr Fell. His waistcoat rose and fell wheezily; his voice was subdued. 'We heard the shot and saw you run in. Hadley's there now. May I ask, sir, just what devil's wasp-nest you've over-turned *now?*'

'That,' said Dick, 'is exactly what you can call it. In the first place, I can prove Lesley had no hand in any funny business at all. In the second place, I don't have to prove it, because if you give a shout for whatever policemen you've got at hand, we can nail the murderer in this house.'

In three sentences he outlined the story. Its effect on Dr Fell was rather curious. The Gargantuan doctor stood motionless on the doorstep, his shovel-hat still on his head and his hands folded over his cane, breathing noisily. He kept his eyes fixed on the two tiny scraps of paper Dick held out to him.

This phlegmatic attitude, when Dick Markham half expected somebody to fire a bullet from the direction of the stairs, drove Dick into a frenzy.

'Don't you understand, sir?' he repeated, with a sort of wild patience. '*In the house!*'

'Oh, ah,' said Dr Fell. His eyes moved over the hall behind. 'In the house. Can he get out the back way?'

'I hope not. Anyway, Joe McIntyre the gardener is there.'

'And he can't get out the front way,' said Dr Fell, moving his bulk to peer round behind him, 'because Bert Miller is there, and a man who's just come down from the Criminal Records Department at Scotland. Harrumph, yes. Excuse me for just one moment.'

He lumbered off into the gloom, where they saw him conferring with two shadows in the path. One of these shadows slipped away towards the back of the house; the other remained where it was; and Dr Fell returned.

'Look here, sir!' protested Dick. 'Aren't we going to search the place?'

'At the moment,' answered Dr Fell, 'no. With your permission, I should much prefer to come in and talk for a little.'

'Then for God's sake let me get Lesley away from here while...'

'It would be better, I assure you, if Miss Grant remained.'

'Even with the murderer in the house?'

'Even,' replied Dr Fell gravely, 'with the murderer in the house.'

And he stepped into the hall, sweeping off his shovel-hat and thrusting his cane under his arm.

The brightly lighted dining-room attracted his attention. Ponderously gesturing Lesley and Dick to precede him, he followed them into the dining-room. He blinked round him with abstracted interest. He murmured some excuse about the heat. Rather clumsily emphasizing this excuse – it *was* warm in the room – Dr Fell threw open the thick curtains of the opened windows.

Under these two front windows stood a heavy Florentine oak chest. Dr Fell sat down on it, again propping his hands over his cane.

'Sir,' he began, 'those two shreds of paper, as you very properly remark, must go to Hadley. But I gather from your recital you believe you have discovered the meaning of what happened at the post office? Of that murder, in short?'

'Yes. I think I have.'

'Very well,' said Dr Fell. 'Suppose you tell me what it is?'

'Hang it, Doctor! At a time like this...!'

'Yes, by thunder!' said Dr Fell. 'At a time like this!'

Lesley, though plainly she understood not one word of this, was trembling. Dick put his arm round her shoulders. The whole house seemed full of unaccountable creaks and cracks, as though it were poised; and the metronome-clock ticked in the hall.

'Just as you like,' said Dick. 'When I met Superintendent Hadley at Ashe Hall this morning, that wasn't the first time I'd seen him.'

'Aha! Well?'

'The first time I saw him, I was standing at the window of Lesley's bedroom upstairs,' Dick pointed to the ceiling, 'and I saw him cross the road towards the post office.'

'Go on,' said Dr Fell.

'Then,' continued Dick, 'we had that conference in Lord Ashe's study at the Hall. You explained how this whole murder-scheme was an attempt to frame Lesley for the job –'

Dr Fell intervened.

'One moment,' he said. 'What I did, if you recall, was to challenge anyone to say what *else* it could be. But continue.'

'You said the real murderer had provided us a problem. Now he'd got to provide a solution, a solution for the locked room, or the police couldn't touch Lesley. You suggested there would be a "communication".'

'I did.'

'When you told us that,' Dick went on, 'Superintendent Hadley looked up all of a sudden and said, "Was that why you asked me, a while ago, to –?" And you shut up very quickly. You suggested it might be a telephone-call.

'But Hadley never for a second believed in that "telephone-call". He mentioned it later, at the dead man's cottage. He pointed out

it would be too risky, and added "But your other idea, I admit –"
Whereupon you cut him off again. Not long afterwards, up cropped
still another reference to your other scheme, and this time in flat-out
connexion with the post office.

'I'm a cloth-headed goop,' Dick concluded bitterly, 'for not guessing it long ago. Of course it's the old poison-pen trick.'

Lesley peered up at him in bewilderment.

'Poison-pen trick?' she repeated.

'Yes. If the real murderer wanted to get in touch with the police,
then the obvious and safest anonymous way would be to write.
And there's no stamp-machine at the post office, if you remember?'

'Stop a bit!' cried Lesley. 'I think I *do* begin to…'

'Anybody who wants stamps must buy 'em from Laura over the
counter. Dr Fell,' said Dick, 'believed this morning that one person,
or maybe one of a small group of persons, would drop a line to
explain how you committed the murder.'

'You mean –?'

'So he asked Hadley to do what the police often do when
there's a plague of poison-pen letters. With the co-operation of
whoever's in charge of the post office, every stamp sold to a suspected person or persons has a private mark on it. Then, when
the anonymous letter arrives, the police can infallibly prove who
wrote it.

'Would Laura Feathers have enjoyed helping in a trick like that?
She'd have cackled and loved it! Dr Fell had a shot at the same trick
for trapping this murderer. And it very nearly worked.

'The real murderer did write a note, all right. I've got the proof
here in my hand. The real murderer slipped into my cottage and
wrote the blasted thing on my typewriter…'

Lesley drew away from him. She could not seem to believe her ears, and she dashed her hand out as though trying to push something away.

'*On your typewriter?*' she exclaimed.

'Yes. But that's no clue, I'm afraid. I haven't been at my place all day. Anyway, half the neighbourhood walks in and out of there without bothering to knock. Cynthia Drew, Major Price –'

'And myself,' smiled Lesley.

'Don't joke about this!' Dick said sharply. 'The murderer wrote this note accusing Lesley of being a famous poisoner, and probably showing how De Villa had been killed. The murderer posted it. Then somehow he, or she, tumbled to it that a trap had been set. He, or she, tried to get the letter back by waiting until Laura Feathers cleared the box, and then begging it on some excuse. But Laura was a wily old bird; she knew, and let the murderer know she knew. And so…'

Dick made the motion of one who pulls a trigger. He turned to Dr Fell.

'Is this true, sir, or isn't it?'

Dr Fell's face was very serious.

Blinking, he removed his eyeglasses, stared at them reflectively, and pinched at the deep red mark they made across the bridge of his nose before putting them on again.

'Oh, yes,' he admitted. 'It's true enough.'

The tension went out of Dick's muscles, and his lungs relaxed in a long breath of relief.

'That *was* your game with the post office, sir?'

'Yes.' Dr Fell brooded. 'It was a long shot, of course.'

'How so?'

'Well, dash it all!' complained Dr Fell. 'It's simple enough to use that trick on a poison-pen writer, who writes numbers of letters and therefore requires numbers of stamps. But suppose your quarry has a casual stamp in his pocket or at home, and doesn't have to buy one? Still, it was worth trying. And it worked. Archons of Athens' – a curious violent look overspread his face – 'Archons of Athens, how it worked!'

'I don't follow that, sir.'

'Almost too soon, don't you think? Almost' – Dr Fell snapped his fingers – 'like that. All the same, I agree, it did work. And it cost a human life.'

'You couldn't have helped that!'

'I wonder,' said Dr Fell.

'Anyway, however that game worked out, there's one thing these two bits of paper and the whole evening's events definitely do prove. I hope you'll at least agree with that?'

'With what?'

'The original theory! You said this might happen, and it has happened! You said Lesley might be accused by an anonymous communication, and she's been accused! You said the real murderer might take this line, and he has taken this line! What more can we want? I submit that this proves the murder of Sam De Villa was a deliberate attempt to fasten the blame on Lesley Grant! Don't you agree?'

Dr Fell blinked at the floor. His hands, clasped over his cane, seemed to draw his whole huge frame closer together. Then he rolled up his head.

'Well, no,' he answered reluctantly. 'I can't say I do agree.'

19

'What's that?'

'I don't agree,' Dr Fell explained mildly, 'that the explanation you've just given is the only possible one.'

'But your own theory –!'

'I beg your pardon.' Dr Fell spoke very sharply. 'If you think back far enough, I imagine you'll agree it was not my theory at all.'

'But you distinctly said –'

'I said,' Dr Fell raised his big voice, 'I said we must consider the evidence. I said that, if we did consider the evidence, this was the conclusion to which we must come. I challenged Hadley to cite any other conclusion from the facts as presented to us.'

'Well? What's the difference? That's the same thing, isn't it?'

'But I also said, if you remember,' Dr Fell observed gently, 'that it took a bit of believing.'

The whole weird, unnatural situation had begun to turn Dick Markham's nerves.

'What *is* all this?' he demanded. 'What are you leading up to?'

'I asked him,' said Lesley, 'I asked him the same thing this morning!'

'Laura Feathers is shot,' said Dick. 'You ring the door-bell. I tell you there's a murderer in the house – I tell you I've seen the murderer run in here – and I expect at least you'll want to do something about it. Instead you say you'd rather sit down and talk a bit. May I repeat that there's a murderer in the house?'

'Is there?' asked Dr Fell.

And now Dick noticed something which made the roots of his scalp stir. Dr Fell, in the doctor's own heavy way, was no less strung-up, no less poised and tense, than he was himself. Dick had a nervous sensation that something moved, something lurked in ambush: that, any moment now, the whole case might turn upside down again with the most appalling crash yet.

'At risk of perhaps deserved assault and battery' – Dr Fell's voice seemed to come from far away – 'I should like to try your patience a little further.'

'Why should you do that?'

'Because I'm waiting for something.'

'You're waiting for what?'

Dr Fell ignored the question.

'A moment ago,' he continued, 'you made some precise and accurate deductions from the post office trap and its ugly sequel. Have you made any other deductions?'

Dick's throat felt dry.

'I think I've found out how an electric light can be made to go on in a room when the room's locked up on the inside.' He related the incident at his own cottage. 'Is that true too, Doctor?'

'Oh, yes,' returned Dr Fell, blinking at him with refreshed interest. 'Whang in the gold once more. But, come now!' He rapped the ferrule of his cane on the floor. 'If you get that far, isn't it possible to spur just a little farther and see the truth – the whole truth – about the murder of Sam De Villa?'

'No!'

'Why not?'

'Because the room remains locked up on the inside, whoever puts a shilling in the electric meter outside it!'

'True, of course. And yet...' Dr Fell's manner became vague. He puffed out his cheeks. 'What,' he asked in an off-handed way, 'did you make of the row yesterday between Mr Earnshaw and Major Price?'

'Does that business matter, sir?'

'As evidence, no. As an interesting lead, yes. I think it does.'

Dick shook his head.

'I've heard that there *was* a row between Bill and Major Price at the shooting-range, because the major played a joke on Bill. But I haven't even heard what it was about.'

'*I* have,' said Dr Fell. 'From Lord Ashe. I heard some very interesting things from Lord Ashe. Mr Earnshaw, I believe, rather fancies himself as a crack shot?'

'Yes, that's right.'

'He arrived at the shooting-range early yesterday afternoon, to show off his prowess before Mrs Earnshaw and a group of other ladies.' Dr Fell scratched the side of his nose. 'Major Price, with a very grave face, handed him a rifle loaded with blank cartridges. Mr Earnshaw blazed away six times at the target without scoring a hit on any part of it.'

Dr Fell eyed the floor as he went on:

'Major Price said, "Bad luck, my dear chap; you're off your form to-day." It was several minutes before Mr Earnshaw tumbled to the joke. And he didn't like it a bit. It was some time afterwards, you recall, that Mr Earnshaw accused Major Price of stealing the Winchester 61 rifle from the range – whereas the major intimated that the thief must have been Mr Earnshaw. Don't you find something rather suggestive in all that?'

'No. I can't say I do. It's the sort of joke Major Price is always playing.'

'So!' said Dr Fell.

'But, if you're on the subject of Bill Earnshaw, it seems to me he made the most intelligent suggestion so far with regard to the locked room. I tried to sketch it out to you this morning, but you didn't seem to pay much attention to it.'

'Forgive my scatterbrain,' apologized Dr Fell. 'What was the suggestion?'

Dick waved his fists in the air.

'*Who fired that damned rifle at Sam De Villa, at very nearly the same time Sam was poisoned?*' he demanded. 'Bill suggested – and I agree with him – that, aside from the actual murderer, the person who fired the rifle is the most important figure in the case. Don't you agree?'

'In a way. Yes.'

'The marksman,' persisted Dick, 'could see into that room. He had a clear view of what went on in that sitting-room. All right! But you haven't tried to find out who he was, you haven't asked a question about him, you don't even seem to have any curiosity concerning him!'

Dr Fell raised a hand and called for silence.

'Now there,' he pointed with satisfaction, 'we have the crux of the whole matter. There we see the point at which the light went out, figuratively speaking. There we have the place at which a cloud of obfuscation (pray excuse me if I sound like a leading article in *The Times*), a cloud of obfuscation misted the wits of all detectives, and sent them hareing off in the wrong direction.'

He pointed at Dick with his cane.

'You say to me, "This is gross negligence. Why don't you try to find that marksman with the rifle, as well as trying to find the murderer?" Very good! Yes! But I can reply, with my hand on my heart, that this would be a waste of effort.'

Dick stared at him.

'A waste of effort? Why?'

'Because the marksman with the rifle, and the poisoner who killed De Villa with prussic acid, are one and the same person.'

Again the summons of the front door-bell shrilled out strongly, from the buzzer over their heads.

Dick's own head was spinning. Dr Fell's words seemed quite literally to make no sense. He had a mad vision – derived from the cheaper thrillers, where anything is possible – of the murderer firing at Sam De Villa some fantastic bullet containing a hypodermic injection of prussic acid to pierce the victim's arm.

Again the door-bell shrilled. Lesley hastened to answer it; and, though Dick had meant to seize her arm and restrain her, she got away from him. From the corner of his eye he saw, as Lesley opened the front door, that the visitor was only Superintendent Hadley, and he could relax his vigilance. For he was blindly obsessed now, concentrated on Dr Fell, trying to grope closer to an explanation which he sensed as *there* yet always eluding him.

'Let's get this quite straight!' Dick pleaded. 'You say that the murderer…'

Dr Fell spoke with toiling patience.

'The murderer,' he said, 'killed Sam De Villa by injecting a hypodermic of prussic acid into his arm.'

'In the sitting-room?'

'Yes. In the sitting-room.'

'And then?'

'Then the murderer slipped out of the sitting-room…'

'Leaving the room all locked up behind him?'

'Yes. Leaving the room all locked up.'

'But *how*?'

'We're coming to that,' said Dr Fell imperturbably. 'I ask you merely to follow this elusive person's movements. The murderer injected the prussic acid, which would render De Villa unconscious almost at once but would take two minutes or more to render life extinct. The murderer then left the room –'

(Windows locked. Door locked and bolted.)

'– and put through a phone call to you, summoning you there, from the telephone outside in the hall. The murderer waited until you were on your way, and dropped a shilling into the electric meter: thus turning on the light in the sitting-room.

'Having now a good light to see by, the murderer ran across the lane, hid behind the wall, and with the stolen Winchester 61 fired in the direction of the window.'

'At a dead man?'

'At a dead or dying man, yes.'

'Even though the room was already locked up on the inside?'

'Yes.'

'But why?'

'Because the whole scheme could never have succeeded otherwise,' replied Dr Fell.

'*Hoy!*' interposed the bellow of an angry voice, which for some seconds had been trying to attract their attention. Dick was only now conscious of it.

Superintendent Hadley came into the dining-room. Over his shoulder they heard him say, 'Stand by,' before he closed the door after him. Hadley's countenance was grim and hard under the bowler hat, even with a suggestion of pallor which scared Dick still more. Hadley put his big hands together and cracked the knuckle-joints.

'Fell,' he said harshly, 'are you insane?'

Dr Fell, who had been keeping on Dick Markham eyes almost as hypnotic as those of the bogus Sir Harvey Gilman last night, did not reply.

'I've been expecting you,' Hadley went on, 'to come over to the place where that woman was murdered. I came over here to find out what the devil was the matter with you. And it's a good thing I did.' It was not pallor in Hadley's face so much as an evil greyish tinge. 'Because I discover –'

'Not yet, Hadley,' said Dr Fell, turning his head round briefly. 'For God's sake not yet!'

'What do you mean, not yet? Miller tells me...'

Dr Fell got to his feet, with the imploring gestures of one who urges calm and serenity. He seemed trying to ignore Hadley, to shoo the superintendent away, to pretend that Hadley did not even exist. And still he addressed Dick Markham.

'When I first came in here,' he said, 'I remarked – er – that it was a trifle warm. Harrumph. Yes. So it was. I drew back the curtains on these windows. But that, I am afraid, was not the main reason why I drew back the curtains from the windows, which, you notice, are open. Please observe the windows!'

Yet, as the big voice grew more rapid. Dick had an eerie conviction that Dr Fell was not in the least interested in the windows as such. He was talking at them, talking out of them, making his voice carry; any topic of conversation, it seemed, would do.

'You observe,' he insisted, 'the windows?'

'Look here!' roared Hadley.

'What about the windows?' demanded Dick Markham.

The three speeches seemed to rattle on top of each other.

'They are, as you see, ordinary sash-windows. Such as you or Hadley or I might have in our own homes. This one here is raised. But I pull it down… so.'

The window closed with a soft thud.

'When the window is unlocked, as it is now, you note that the fastening of the metal catch lies flat back: parallel with the window glass and the joining of the sashes, turned to the right. But suppose, my dear boy, I wish to lock the window?'

This was the point at which Dick noticed for the first time that Lesley Grant was not in the room.

She had not returned; she had not come with Hadley. And the Superintendent, with his hard face grim under its greyish complexion, stood like a man who intends trying a wrestling-bout with the devil. A sudden suspicion, which he thought he had fought successfully away from him, flowed back into Dick's mind…

'Dr Fell,' he said, 'where is Lesley?'

Dr Fell pretended not to have heard. Perhaps he did not hear.

'Suppose, my dear boy, I wish to lock the window? I take hold of the thumb-grip of this metal catch. I pull it towards me and turn it towards my left. Like this! The catch swings round into its socket; it now projects straight out towards me, at right angles to the sash; and the window is locked.'

'Dr Fell, where is Lesley?'

'You observe, my dear boy, that the catch projects straight out towards me? And, therefore –'

He paused, having now no need to go on. For the last time in this case, but with a shattering distinctness which made the whole house shake, they heard the explosion of a gunshot.

Dr Fell, his big red face reflected with nightmare quality in the black shining glass of the window, did not turn round. They stood there for a second or two like three men paralysed. Then Dick slowly raised his eyes to the ceiling.

He knew where the explosion of that shot had come from. It had come from Lesley's bedroom, just overhead.

'You bloody idiot!' shouted Hadley. He stared at Dr Fell, and more than suspicion dawned in his eyes. 'You let this happen!'

Dr Fell's voice sounded muffled against the glass of the window.

'I let it happen. God help me, yes.'

'Suicide?'

'I rather think so. There was no other way out, you see.'

'No!' cried Dick Markham. '*No!*'

He was not sure whether he could move, for his legs seemed turned to water and he could not even trust his eyesight. The image of Lesley, of Lesley's brown eyes; the thought of Lesley, and how much he loved her, and would continue to love her until – the iron phrase rang again – until death did them part; these things caught at him and maddened him and spun his nerves into a whirlpool that would not let go.

Then he found himself running for the door.

Hadley was running too; they crashed into each other in the doorway as Hadley got the door open, but the events took place in such a void that Dick could not even hear what the superintendent was saying.

Bright lights shone in the hall. Bert Miller, moving rapidly for so heavy a man, was already on his way up the staircase at the rear. Bert's footsteps made no noise on the staircase carpet, or perhaps Dick Markham could not hear it.

In the same dreamlike state, amid a blur of colour and light, he raced after Hadley up the stairs. They found Bert Miller, his mouth open, standing before the closed door of Lesley's bedroom. Neither Miller nor Hadley spoke loudly.

'This door's locked, sir.'

'Then break it in!'

'I don't know, sir, as we ought to do...'

'Break it in, I tell you!'

It was a thin door. Miller stood back, opening his large shoulders. Then he studied the door, and had a better idea. As he assumed the position for a football kick-off, Dick Markham turned away. When the sole of Miller's number eleven boot struck that door just under the knob, Dick did not even hear it.

For Dr Fell was lumbering up the stairs, slowly and heavily, wheezing as he set his weight on the crutch-handled cane. And ahead of him, running lightly, came Lesley Grant.

Lesley stopped abruptly, her hand on the post at the top of the stairs. Her eyes widened.

'Dick!' she cried. 'What on earth is the matter with you?'

Crash! went the sole of Miller's boot, for the second time against that door.

'What's the *matter* with you, Dick? Why are you looking at me like that?'

Crash! went the sole of Miller's boot.

It was Dr Fell, painfully heaving himself up the last few steps and pausing to get his breath, who got the first inkling of what Dick might have been thinking. Dr Fell's vacant gaze sharpened into focus as he looked from Lesley to Dick Markham, and back again. His mouth fell open under the bandit's moustache, and his head drew back so far that another chin appeared.

'Great Scott, my dear fellow!' he said in a tone of Gargantuan distress. 'You weren't under the impression… it hadn't occurred to you…?'

Crash! went Miller's boot for the last time. The lock ripped out; the thin door, buckling, flew open and rebounded with such violence that it tore loose the lower hinge.

Dick did not answer Dr Fell. He put his arms around Lesley, and gripped her so tightly that she cried out for breath.

They heard the creaking of Dr Fell's shoes as he walked slowly down the hall and joined Hadley at the shattered door. Hadley, Miller, and Dr Fell looked into the bedroom. The lights inside showed a faint tinge and mist of powder-smoke which drifted out past those three watching faces. Dr Fell lumbered round, and creaked back again.

'I suppose you'd better go and have a look,' he said. 'Lying in there, almost in the same spot where Cynthia Drew must have been lying when you found her knocked out…'

Dick found his voice.

'Cynthia? Then it *was* Cynthia after all?'

'Good God, no!' said Dr Fell.

After a look of genuine surprise that such a notion should occur, Dr Fell fastened his hand on Dick's shoulder. He walked him down to the doorway where the bright light poured out, and Hadley and Miller made way for them.

Dr Fell motioned Dick to enter.

Swept and garnished was the bedroom, the curtains on its front windows drawn fully back to the summer night, and neat except for the sprawled figure near the foot of the bed, neat except for the .38 calibre automatic pistol lying beside it, neat except for the spreading blotch on the chest of a human being whose lungs still whistled thinly to draw breath. Dr Fell's voice spoke at Dick's ear.

It said:

'There's the only person who could have committed both murders – Dr Hugh Middlesworth.'

20

T HAT HAPPENED ON THE NIGHT OF FRIDAY, JUNE 11TH. IT WAS
the afternoon of Sunday the 13th that a little group composed
of Dr Fell, Hadley, Lesley Grant, and Dick Markham drove out to
a certain ill-omened cottage in a police-car. Hadley was writing his
final report; the details had to be checked; and so they heard the
whole story.

Neither Lesley nor Dick made any comment until they entered
the sitting-room. The face of Dr Middlesworth – harassed, patient,
thin-haired on top, very intelligent but cold now in death – remained
always before them.

When they entered the sitting-room, where Dr Fell occupied the
sofa and Hadley the big chair at the writing-table with his notebook,
two voices spoke at last.

'Dr Middlesworth!' exclaimed Dick. 'But *how* he did it…!'

'Dr Middlesworth!' breathed Lesley. 'And *why* he did it, trying
to throw the blame on me…!'

Dr Fell, who had lighted a cigar with great concentration, shook
out the match sharply.

'No, no, no!' he protested.

'What do you mean by that?'

'The thing we must grasp,' said Dr Fell, in the same toiling
way, 'is that there was never the slightest intention of throwing the blame on Miss Grant. That's what we were expected to
believe; that's what we were meant to fall for. We were meant to

assume that De Villa's murder was carried out by someone who thoroughly believed in "Sir Harvey Gilman", who accepted him as the original Home Office pathologist, and who believed Lesley Grant to be a poisoner. Therefore – do you see? – therefore the one person we could not possibly suspect was the man who doubted "Sir Harvey" from the first, and, in fact, brought me in to prove him an impostor!

'Therein lies the whole ingenuity of this crime.'

Dr Fell's cigar was not drawing to his liking. He struck another match and lit it more carefully.

'H'mf. Yes. So. Let me tell you about this, step for step, just as the evidence presented itself to me.

'At an unearthly hour on Friday morning, a mild-mannered man of intelligent aspect and harassed ways came rushing over to Hastings in his car. He routed me out of bed, and introduced himself as Dr Hugh Middlesworth, G.P., of Six Ashes. He poured out the story of the night, saying he had reason to suspect "Sir Harvey" of being an impostor.

'Was I acquainted with the real Sir Harvey Gilman? Yes, I was. Was the real Sir Harvey a little thin man of fifty-odd, with a bald head? No, certainly not. And that was that.

'"Well," said Middlesworth to me, "this impostor has been scaring a friend of mine named Markham with a damnable pack of lies about his *fiancée*. Will you come over to Six Ashes with me – now – and expose the blighter?"'

Dr Fell made a hideous face.

'Naturally I agreed. Oh, ah! My chivalry was stirred. I rose and roared to the relief of a lady in distress and a young man racked by horrors. So we bowled back into the High Street of Six Ashes:

only to be greeted by Major Price with the news that Sir Harvey Gilman had been found dead in exactly the same circumstances as his own imaginary cases.

'Wow, ladies and gentlemen! I repeat: wow!

'Middlesworth seemed dumbfounded. So was I.'

Here Dr Fell, assuming a look of powerful earnestness, pointed the end of the cigar at Dick and leaned forward on the sofa.

'Please note,' he said, 'that first-off this original theory – Miss Grant to be made scapegoat by somebody who had swallowed "Sir Harvey's" yarn – came from *Middlesworth*. He and I drove out here to this cottage at shortly past nine o'clock, where we met you and Mr Earnshaw. And I distinctly recall announcing that the suggestion came from Middlesworth. Do you remember?'

Dick nodded.

'Yes. I remember.'

'I accepted that theory,' said Dr Fell, spreading out his hands. 'I took it unto myself. At first glance it seemed the only possible explanation. Only one small thing about it bothered me; and I started to mention this before thinking it more prudent to hold my tongue.

'Now, Mr Markham, "Sir Harvey's" tale of a notorious female poisoner was hand-tailored for *you*. It was scaled for you. It was directed solely at you. It was spun for somebody who would be… would be…'

'Go on,' Dick interrupted bitterly. 'Say it. Gullible.'

Dr Fell considered this.

'Not gullible, no. But emotionally concerned, emotionally strung-up, and imaginatively receptive to just such a horror-tale as you heard. Very well! That's fair enough! But why is the impostor so casual about telling all this nonsense in front of the local G.P., who isn't emotionally concerned or receptive, and who might upset his apple-cart?

'His attitude towards Middlesworth was rather curious, even by Middlesworth's own showing. He didn't try to hypnotize Middlesworth as he tried to hypnotize you. He didn't try to impress Middlesworth. He didn't seem to care about Middlesworth. He didn't even seem to *notice* Middlesworth.'

Dick sat up.

'That's true!' Dick declared, remembering the scene in this same room on Thursday night. 'De Villa treated the fellow as a piece of furniture. He got annoyed when Middlesworth spoke, and tried to – what do I want to say? – brush him off.'

Dr Fell smoked reflectively.

'Thus it occurred to my low suspicious mind,' he said, 'briefly to wonder whether Middlesworth might not know a good deal more than he pretended. Whether he might not be, in short, a kind of accomplice.'

'Accomplice?' cried Lesley.

Dr Fell waved her to silence.

'At this time, of course, I couldn't guess what the impostor's game was. But this wonder about Middlesworth was strengthened only a few minutes later, when you' – he looked at Dick – 'prompted by Earnshaw's worries about the rifle, told me the *full* story of the garden-party the day before.

'Two things emerged from that recital. The first was the impostor's phenomenal success as a fortune-teller. And, mind you, he didn't say to his clients such vague things as, "You are good-natured but strong-willed; beware of a business venture during Lent." No, by thunder! He had real *information*, facts in plenty about everybody! Where did the impostor get all that information, unless we presupposed someone also in on the secret? In short, an accomplice.

'The second thing to emerge from the account of the garden-party was rather damning. I mean the mystery of the vanishing rifle.'

Dick took Lesley's hand.

'But the rifle did vanish, confound it!' he protested. 'I suppose you're going to say the person who stole it was Middlesworth?'

'Oh, yes.'

'But how? The only people who came anywhere near that shooting-range were Major Price and Bill Earnshaw and Dr Middlesworth and Lesley and myself. And we're all willing to swear none of us could have taken the rifle. As for Middlesworth, he helped carry De Villa to the motor-car in plain sight of everybody when he went away from there! How did he manage to pinch the rifle? As I said to Bill Earnshaw, you can't stick a rifle in your pocket or shove it under your coat.'

'No,' agreed Dr Fell. 'But you can shove it into a bag of golf-clubs, and carry it away absolutely unnoticed. And Middlesworth, you informed me, was carrying a bag of golf-clubs.'

There was a long silence. Superintendent Hadley, writing away methodically at the table, lifted his head to smile slightly. Dick, remembering only too well Dr Middlesworth, tramping back from the golf-hazard with that heavy bag slung over his shoulder – the conspicuous, unnoticed golf-bag! – Dick Markham swore with some comprehensiveness.

'The old blighter,' observed Hadley, indicating Dr Fell, 'does get an idea or two sometimes. That's why I let him rampage on.'

'Thank'ee,' said Dr Fell, with absent-minded dignity. He squinted in cross-eyed fashion at his cigar, and turned back to Dick.

'Middlesworth, even at that early hour, already appeared in very curious and fishy colours. He was the only one who could have stolen the rifle. And then…

'You and Middlesworth drove back to the village in his car, he to his surgery and you to see Miss Grant. I went into this cottage here' – he swept his hand round – 'to look my first on the scene of the crime. Here I discovered something which spiritually raised my hat to human ingenuity; for I discerned a way in which the locked-room trick might have been worked.'

'Well?' asked Lesley. 'How?'

Dr Fell did not immediately answer this.

'While I was tinkering with various things in this room,' he continued, 'Hadley arrived. Hadley took one look at the corpse and said, "My God, it's Sam De Villa!" He then went on, as you afterwards heard, to give me a sketch of De Villa's career. And he told me something which made me certain the person we were after was Middlesworth. For, do you see, *Sam De Villa really had studied medicine.*'

'Came within six months,' Hadley amplified, 'of getting his degree.'

Again Dr Fell pointed the cigar at Dick.

'Think back,' he requested. 'I asked Middlesworth, very early in the morning, and you yourself asked him in my hearing, what was the first thing which made him suspicious that "Sir Harvey Gilman" was an impostor. Remember?'

'Yes.'

'Middlesworth's reply went something like this. He said he had questioned the supposed Sir Harvey about one of the latter's famous cases. And "Sir Harvey," Middlesworth informed us, "made some grandiose reference to the two chambers of the heart. That brought me up a bit," Middlesworth declared, "because any medical student knows the heart has four chambers."

'Now that just wasn't possible. Sam De Villa, impersonating Sir Harvey Gilman in earnest, never would and never could have made such a medical howler as that. It wasn't in character; it wasn't in sense!

'Therefore Middlesworth himself was lying.'

'But why?'

Here Dr Fell glanced across at Hadley, whose pencil continued to travel across the pages of the notebook.

'Have you got Middlesworth's confession there, Hadley?'

From beside the chair Hadley picked up a brief-case and opened it. He took out a flimsy typewritten sheet, enclosed in a blue folder and signed at the bottom with a blurred wavering scrawl. He carried this across to Dr Fell, who weighed it in his hand.

Against the bright sunshine which poured into the room through two windows, one shattered and the other with a bullet-hole, Dr Fell's countenance was heavy and depressed and lowering.

'Middlesworth dictated this,' he explained, 'just before he died on Friday night. It's an ugly story, if you like. But it's an understandable and sincere and horribly human story.'

'Damn it all,' Dick Markham burst out, 'that's the trouble. I *liked* Hugh Middlesworth!'

'So did I,' said Dr Fell. 'And in a way you were very right to like him. Anyone who rids the world of slugs like Sam De Villa deserves no small degree of gratitude. If he hadn't lost his head and shot that inoffensive post-mistress –'

'You'd have covered up for him, I suppose?' inquired Hadley with sardonic dryness. 'As it was, you let him commit suicide?'

Dr Fell ignored this.

'Middlesworth's story,' he said, 'is a very simple one. Do you recall Hadley saying that gentry like Sam De Villa will use any weapon, *anything,* including blackmail, when they think they can bring off a big haul?'

'You mean it was blackmail in this case?' asked Lesley.

Dr Fell weighed the typewritten sheet in his hand.

'Hugh Middlesworth was in a position of painful respectability. But he *liked* respectability. He liked it almost as much as –' Dr Fell looked at Lesley, coughed, and looked away again. 'He had a "county" wife, a good-sized family, and many obligations.

'But he hadn't got to that state without pain. Nine years ago, when he was hard up and desperate, before Six Ashes and respectability, he took a certain job. It was a job in a rather squalid London nursing-home specializing in illegal operations. Middlesworth was the doctor who performed those operations. Sam De Villa knew that, and could prove it.

'Sam, with designs on Miss Grant's jewellery, came here and tackled Middlesworth. Middlesworth hadn't the ghost of a notion that Sam was really a medical man like himself. He knew Sam merely as a crook, and a smooth one.

'"Look here," said Sam. "I'm coming to Six Ashes impersonating somebody or other; I'm going to get that jewellery; and you're going to help me." The already-harassed Middlesworth was rather desperate. "I'm not going to sponsor you," said Middlesworth. "When you disappear with the jewellery they'll know I was implicated; I'd just as soon you blew the gaff about the other thing. So I'm ruddy well not going to sponsor you."

'"Maybe not," says Sam coolly. "But you're going to help me, and first of all you're going to tell me *everything* about this district and its people." So the background unrolled itself to this clever, pouncing Mr De Villa. Richard Markham, wildly in love with Lesley Grant. Engagement imminent! Engagement certain! Young man a writer of sensational imaginative plays dealing with the minds of murderers, especially poisoners...

'Sam constructed his scheme with slickness and ease. He took this cottage. And with dazzling cheek he introduced himself, under terms of the deepest secrecy, to the Chief Constable of the county as Sir Harvey Gilman.

'Then came the garden-party. News of the engagement of Lesley Grant to Richard Markham was winging through the place: even, assisted by Mrs Rackley, news of the invitation to dinner for Friday night. At the garden-party where he played fortune-teller, Sam decided it was time to act.

'What the self-confident Sam didn't realize was that in Hugh Middlesworth he was dealing with a man every bit as intelligent as himself. And Middlesworth was sick and desperate. He'd thought the past was forgotten: but De Villa turned up out of it. Here was this albatross round his neck, likely to continue there. Always threatening! Always disturbing his sleep! Always a nightmare, absent or present, always threatening respectability...'

Again Dr Fell, in some discomfort, coughed loudly as he glanced away from Lesley.

'Can't *you* understand that feeling, Miss Grant?'

'Yes,' said Lesley. And she shivered.

'Middlesworth decided,' Dr Fell said simply, 'that De Villa was going to die. And Middlesworth very nearly got the opportunity to kill him just after the garden-party on Thursday afternoon. Now watch the events take form!'

Adjusting his eyeglasses, spilling much cigar-ash, Dr Fell took the typewritten confession and ran his fingers down its lines. His lips moved growlingly as he searched for the proper place. Then he read aloud from it.

'... De Villa so upset Miss Grant in the fortune-teller's tent that she screamed and pulled the trigger of the rifle when Major Price happened to joggle her arm. I'm sure it was an accident.'

'It *was* an accident!' cried Lesley.

'... I saw at once De Villa had only got a flesh-wound. But he fainted from shock, and everybody thought he was dying. I saw how I could kill the swine then, if only I could get him alone. That's why I sneaked the rifle into my golf-bag and kept the bag slung over my shoulder when Major Price and I carried him to the car. I meant to take him home, put him under an anaesthetic, extract the real bullet, and fire one from the same rifle which *should* kill him. People would think it was the same bullet, the result of an accident...'

'And they ruddy well would have!' said Dick Markham.

'... but it was no good, it wouldn't work, because I couldn't get rid of Major Price no matter what I said. So I had to think of something else.'

Dr Fell weighed the confession in his hand, and then put it down beside him on the sofa.

'And,' Dr Fell commented, 'he did think of something else. The real scheme was handed to him – handed to him on a plate – while he and Dick Markham and Sam De Villa sat here in this very room on Thursday night. Sam was telling the terrible story of the notorious poisoner, and laying plans to snaffle that safe full of jewels. Middlesworth sat quietly by. But someone suggested how he could kill De Villa and get away with it.'

'Who suggested it to him?' asked Dick.

'Sam De Villa himself.'

'*Sam De Villa?*'

'So Middlesworth says. Will you cast your mind back to that scene?'

It was very easy to recreate: De Villa in the easy-chair, with the light of the tan-shaded lamp shining down. Middlesworth silent and thoughtful in the basket-chair drawing at an empty pipe. The summer night outside the windows, rustling, with the rough flowered curtains not quite drawn close. And the very thoughtfulness of Middlesworth's face returned with ugly clarity now.

'You were violently discussing the mystery of locked, sealed rooms,' pursued Dr Fell. 'De Villa remarked, *à propos* the bullet fired at him through the tent, that you couldn't have such a thing as a locked room when a bullet-hole appeared in the wall. Is that correct?'

'Yes!'

'Shortly afterwards Middlesworth heard a noise outside. He got up, went to the window, threw back the curtains, and looked out. Then he drew his head back – and stood staring at that window, with his back to you, as though something had just occurred to him. Is that correct too?'

'Yes.'

'Well?' prompted Dr Fell gently. 'When Middlesworth looked at the window, what did he see?'

With some effort Dr Fell hoisted himself to his feet. He lumbered across to the window, still locked, where the clean-drilled bullet-hole showed in the lower pane below and to one side of the metal catch.

Dr Fell pointed to it.

'Colonel Pope, as we know, always used to fasten gauze screens to these windows – sometimes the upper, sometimes the lower part – using drawing-pins to fasten the screens there. Consequently, what do we find? We find, as Earnshaw has been so fond of pointing out, innumerable tiny little holes made by the points of drawing-pins. We find those little pin-pricks peppered all over the wooden frame of the window. Is that clear?'

'Naturally! But…'

'You could push another drawing-pin into the frame anywhere, couldn't you? And, when it was plucked out again, the mark it left would never be noticed?'

'Of course not. But…'

'Middlesworth,' said Dr Fell, 'had a double inspiration. I will now tell you exactly what he did.

'He could be morally certain Sam De Villa would take a large dose of luminal before going to bed. So he left this cottage and drove you home in his car, showing alarm only when you mentioned whisky, and asking you for God's sake not to get drunk...'

'Why?'

'Because he vitally needed you in his plan. Middlesworth then drove home himself, and made certain preparations. Who would be the likeliest person to have a hypodermic syringe at hand? A medical man. We discovered in the Sodbury Cross poisoning case that prussic acid can be distilled from separately non-poisonous elements; but who would be the likeliest person to have the acid ready at hand? A medical man. These particular preparations, however, did not concern him at the moment. He had other things to attend to first.

'At shortly past midnight, when Six Ashes was asleep,' Dr Fell picked up the confession, and put it down again, 'he walked slowly out to this cottage once more.

'The house was dark. He had no trouble getting in: the place was not locked, and a window would always have served if it had been. He found Sam De Villa, as he expected, in a drugged sleep upstairs in the bedroom. So far, excellent!

'He came into this sitting-room, where he switched on the light. He set about arranging the room – notably that big easy-chair where Hadley is sitting now – exactly as he wanted it for the events that were to happen at daybreak next morning. He closed both windows, but drew back the curtains widely from both.

'You see, of course, what his next move was? Middlesworth, carrying that Winchester 61 rifle, walked across the lane, climbed over the stone wall opposite, worked out his position carefully, and *then* – time still shortly past midnight – he fired a bullet through this window into a lighted, empty room.

'*That* was when the real shot was fired. *That* was when a bullet drilled through this window, smashed the battle-of-Waterloo picture over the fireplace there, and buried itself in the wall.

'This is the loneliest of neighbourhoods after midnight. He didn't think it likely that anybody would hear the shot. Sam De Villa, in a drugged sleep upstairs, certainly wouldn't. As a matter of fact, Lord Ashe up at the Hall did happen to hear the shot in the middle of the night, because he tells me he mentioned it to you...'

Again Dr Fell looked at Dick.

'... when he saw you early next day. But Lord Ashe confused it in his mind with another shot he heard at shortly after five o'clock in the morning. As for Middlesworth, the first part of his game was now secure. He closed the curtains on all the windows in this cottage, switched on all the lights so they would be certain to burn out before morning, and then went quietly home.

'No harm had been done. Not yet.

'Chance might have wrecked Middlesworth, because he got a sick-call in the small hours of the morning. But the sick-call was to Ashe Hall, where one of the maids was taken ill; and it was admirable for his purpose. He could keep an eye on things.

'He left Ashe Hall at twenty minutes to five in the morning – speaking rather wildly to Lord Ashe about his intention of driving straight to Hastings – and drove his car to the High Street. There he abandoned the car for the moment, and walked once more into Gallows Lane. I can imagine him coming along here through the first ghostly grey of morning; and I can imagine that his heart was as cold as his hands.

'Long ago, of course, he had glanced in through a lighted wall of windows at Mr Markham's, and seen Mr Markham asleep on the sofa with a full, untouched whisky-bottle and syphon on the desk.

I fancy he glanced in once again, to make sure. Then he went on to this cottage here.

'The electricity here had burned itself out long before. The place was dark; it was chilly; it was almost the hour of the murder and the illusion. Middlesworth found De Villa still in a drug-sleep upstairs. If the victim had been awake, Middlesworth was ready to tie him with a soft dressing-gown-cord which would leave no marks, and gag him with a handkerchief and sticking-plaster.

'But it wasn't necessary. He carried De Villa downstairs – De Villa was a little chap, and Middlesworth a big man – and propped him up in that easy-chair, so that the course taken by the already-fired bullet passed just across the top of De Villa's head.

'And then, just as the first eerie glow of dawn was lighting up this room, he rolled back the sleeve of De Villa's dressing gown and with gloved hands emptied the hypodermic of prussic acid into his victim's left arm.'

Dr Fell paused.

Despite that warm afternoon, Dick Markham was cold to the heart. He seemed to see shadows moving at dawn, evil shadows in this room: the gloved physician, the corpse that jerked once, the stir of birds outside in the trees.

'He next,' said Dr Fell, 'locked up the room. He could do this, don't you see, *because there was now a bullet-hole in the window*. We kept talking about this room being "sealed". But, by thunder, it wasn't sealed! That's the whole point! De Villa had spoken truly when he remarked that you can't have a sealed room when there's a bullet-hole in the wall.

'Middlesworth took a box of drawing-pins, and spilled it artistically on the floor at the dying man's left hand. He locked and bolted the door on the inside. Finally, he… will you oblige, Hadley?'

Superintendent Hadley nodded with more than a little grimness. He got up and went out of the room.

'I burbled away on Friday night,' continued Dr Fell, 'with a little discourse on windows. Please observe this particular window and this particular bullet-hole. The bullet-hole – as I face it now – is below the line of the joined sashes, some three inches below and to the left of the metal catch. Very well!

'I take an ordinary drawing-pin, like this one in my hand now. I stick this drawing-pin into the frame of the window – the horizontal frame facing me, marking the line of the joined sashes – above the bullet-hole and a little farther to the left.

'I then take a piece of very heavy black thread, a long piece like this one' – it appeared in conjuring fashion from Dr Fell's capacious side pocket – 'and this I prepare for my trick.'

The figure of Superintendent Hadley appeared outside the window. The lower sill of the window, as Dick had been able to notice before, was not much above the level of a man's waist.

Dr Fell unlocked the window by pushing its metal catch to the right, so that it lay flat back. Folding the long pieces of thread, he fastened its loop round the thumb-grip of the catch. He ran the ends of the thread along to the left and over the drawing-pin, as though over a pulley. Then he ran the ends downwards, threading them both through the opening of the bullet-hole so that they now hung outside the window.

'Since I am of somewhat more than modest dimensions myself,' Dr Fell said apologetically, 'you will excuse me if I don't execute the movement myself. But I raise the window. Like this!'

He pushed up the window, the long loop of thread running with it but its position remaining undisturbed.

'Imagine, now, that I climb out as Middlesworth did. I climb out, I close the window after me' – down it came with a soft bang – 'and I am all ready. I have only to take those ends of the thread which now hang outside the window, and pull them downwards as Hadley is doing.

'Pressure on that loop of thread, run over the drawing-pin to act as a pulley, pulls the thumb-catch of the window *outwards*, towards me, moving slowly outwards until it is at right angles; and the window is now locked.

'Once this is done, a very strong downwards jerk on my drawing-pin-pulley dislodges the drawing-pin from the frame; it falls inwards and bounces somewhere on the floor of the room. I pull one of the ends of my loop of thread, so that I draw the thread outside the window like a snake, and have it outside the window in my hand. No trace now remains. The drawing-pin will be found in the room, of course. But it will not be noticed if I have already spilled a box of drawing-pins on the floor. All right, Hadley!'

The window-catch, pulled over by that thread, had slid into the locked position. Hadley, outside the window, gave now a sharp downwards yank. The drawing-pin, pulled loose, fell upon the inside sill, and flew out into the room. It landed on the carpet…

'Not far, you observe,' said Dr Fell, pointing, 'from another drawing-pin which *seemed* to have rolled wide from the spilled box we found here Friday morning. You perhaps recall I had my eye on it while we were here during the afternoon? Hadley almost stepped on it.'

Hadley, pulling at one end of the thread, was now drawing it outside the window into his hand.

'That's all there was to Middlesworth's dodge,' said Dr Fell. 'It takes a few minutes in the telling; but in execution it can be done in thirty seconds. The room was sealed. Middlesworth was now ready for the last, most important thing – to convince *you*, Mr Markham, that there was no bullet-hole in the window until you arrived.

'He went to the telephone in the hall, and sent that frantic whispering message. It was certain to draw you, and it did. He imagined how long it would take you to leave the house. He dropped a shilling into the electric meter, having left the switch turned on in this room; and a light came on here. He dodged across the lane – some distance eastwards, from the orchard to the coppice, where Miss Drew saw him – and all was ready.

'When you got well in sight, he made a conspicuous clatter with the rifle by rattling it against the wall. He drew your attention to it. As you shouted out to that marksman, he aimed at the window and fired…?'

'A blank cartridge,' supplied Dick.

'A blank cartridge,' agreed Dr Fell. 'Inspired by Earnshaw's adventure when Major Price played the famous joke, Middlesworth used it to very good advantage.

'Now you yourself, Mr Markham, were utterly convinced you had seen that bullet-hole, as you put it "jump up" in the window. That was what I had to break down when I questioned you on Friday afternoon. I was perhaps – hurrum! – a little on edge when I questioned you; and, when Hadley interrupted at a critical point, I fear I mentally consigned him to hopeless spiritual ruin.

'But actually you never saw anything of the kind. This became obvious from your own account of the matter. Your actual words to me were, when I pressed you: *"I was watching the rifle; I saw it fired; and even at that distance I could make out the bullet-hole in the window."*

'"Make out," yes. But that's a different thing. Naturally you had your eyes on the rifle! You saw it fired. Good! But to say that you also saw the bullet-hole appear in the window presupposes a turn of the head from left to right faster than the velocity of a rifle-bullet. This was an evident impossibility.

'I breathed, sir, with much relief. When, shortly afterwards, I was presented with Miss Cynthia Drew's story of the man – or figure – she saw running across the road, I seemed to see the case complete. But for Hadley's interruption at a difficult time...'

Superintendent Hadley, who had come back into the room, stopped short in wrath.

'My interruption?' he repeated.

'Yes.'

'If it had occurred to you,' said Hadley, 'to tell me just what the devil was the line you were working on before that time, things might have gone a little more smoothly. And aren't you running far ahead of your story?'

Dr Fell's cigar had gone out. He blinked at it, and lumbered back to the sofa, where he sat down.

'There is very little more to tell. If I may be allowed to turn back the clock again, to ten o'clock and onwards on Friday morning, I think we shall finish sweeping up any loose pieces. I was – er – inclined to think, on my first examination of this room just before Hadley's arrival, that I could fathom the lines of the locked room. Hadley arrived, as I told you a while ago, with his information about the identity of the dead man; and my attention was already on Dr Middlesworth.

'Just before I started up for Ashe Hall –'

'Why did you want so much to go up there?' inquired Dick.

'The household,' said Dr Fell, 'had been up most of the night with a sick maid. Somebody might have heard something interesting. Lord Ashe, as I told you, *had* heard that shot at past midnight. While I went on there, I asked Hadley to see whoever was in charge of the village post-office…'

'And,' snarled Hadley, 'put different marks on any stamps bought by four or five people! I didn't know until late in the afternoon you were definitely after Middlesworth. You might have been after Miss Drew, who was my choice; or Major Price or Mr Earnshaw or even…'

'Me?' asked Lesley quietly.

'Or even Lord Ashe himself,' said Hadley, smiling at her. 'This trick of laying a trap for the whole ruddy crowd –!'

'Well, I might have been wrong,' said Dr Fell, unabashed. 'But everything henceforward told me with roaring certainty that I was right. I even heard from Lord Ashe, in your presence, that the "Bible-salesman", Sam De Villa, visited *only* Ashe Hall. I daresay he was scouting by feeling out the nature of his reception: by making an estimate of the leading light in this district. But, by the Lord Harry, he could never have got all that information about village-people just from a talk with Lord Ashe. It confirmed belief in an accomplice.

'I've already given you the various indications which led to the certainty, after my interview with Mr Markham late in the afternoon, that we had the thing taped. From Middlesworth's confession we know that he tumbled to the trick about the stamps because he bought a book of stamps; and poor Laura marked them rather clumsily.

'He'd already sent a letter to *me*, of all people, accusing Miss Grant of being a noted poisoner and dropping hints – not saying anything definite, but dropping hints – about how the murder might have been committed. Don't you see he *had* to provide basis for his fictional plot? He *had* to show there was an enemy of Lesley Grant who still believed in "Sir Harvey Gilman", and was trying to frame her. That was the only way he could do it, and the surest way – in his own estimation – of turning suspicion away from himself.

'He wrote the letter. Then, in horror, he tried to get the letter back. And Laura Feathers died.'

'But his letter,' said Dick, 'didn't actually hint broadly at the real way of committing the murder?'

'Oh, no. That was too dangerous. And also unnecessary. All he had to do was plug, and plug, and plug away, at the idea of someone trying to frame Miss Grant. But he tumbled to the marked book of stamps; he got away; he took refuge in Miss Grant's house because three persons were closing in on him from different sides.

'You see,' Dr Fell hesitated, 'I was rather sure I caught a glimpse of him up in that bedroom when I was coming up the path. Mr Markham's story confirmed it. So I had the house covered. He couldn't get away. But… I talked to him, I let him hear me, and I let him die. I think that explains everything.'

There was a long silence, while the sun lay drowsy in the room.

'Not everything,' said Dick. 'It *was* Cynthia, I suppose, who listened outside these windows on Thursday night? And overheard De Villa's tale about Lesley?'

'Oh, yes. Miss Drew is a good girl. But she's a little – erratic.'

'And Lesley didn't actually wallop her with a mirror up in that bedroom when they were having the argument?'

'Of course I didn't!' cried Lesley.

They were sitting in chairs not far away from each other. Dick worked up his courage to face a last question.

'Are you thinking,' asked Lesley, 'what I've heard about since? That I was out of the house, and somebody saw me here in the front garden, at three o'clock in the morning? And you got this horrible idea that I might be the guilty one after all.'

'Well... not exactly the guilty one. But –'

'You did! Don't deny it!'

'All right, darling. I did.'

'And I don't blame you,' said Lesley. 'It's rather sad that the explanation should be so very foolish. But I can't *help* it! It worries me; it's always worried me. I've been to a number of doctors, but they say not to worry. They say it often happens to people like me: overstrung, tending to brood, making much of a trifle.

'But I did think I'd killed that man, don't you see? I mean I thought I'd killed "Sir Harvey Gilman" when the rifle went off accidentally! And I dreamed about it! I couldn't help dreaming about it! I had an awful night, and woke up very tired. So I knew it must have happened again, though I had only a hazy idea of what had happened or where I'd been. When I saw a different frock across the chair – that is, when I woke up in the morning and saw it –!'

'Look here,' said Dick. 'Are you telling us...?'

'It was just another devilment added to the rest,' said Lesley. 'Nothing more or less than sleep-walking. I *must* have come out here, maybe with an idea of finding out what was wrong or how badly he'd been hurt; but I don't remember it. The horrible thing is that I might even have run into the murderer. But I shouldn't have known it if I had. I'm not much good to you, am I? Lily Jewell's daughter, nervous tantrums, and being afflicted with sleep-walking because…'

Dick put his hand over hers.

'Your nervous state,' he said, 'is yours and I like it. But one thing I can promise you: as Dr Fell would say, with my hand on my heart. You will not be troubled with sleep-walking again.'

'Why?'

'I,' said Dick Markham, 'will see to that.'

ALSO AVAILABLE
IN THE BRITISH LIBRARY
CRIME CLASSICS SERIES

Many of our titles are also available
in eBook, large print and audio editions